THE GLASS FIELD

First published 2026 by Jaro Press, London
ISBN 978-1-9194403-0-9

Cover design by Guy Burt.

Set in Crimson Pro 11pt.

THE GLASS FIELD

GUY BURT

JARO PRESS

For my mother, Heather, who gave me stories
and my father, Roger, who showed me the heath

Sov-Blok Supreme Judge Josef Bulgarin:

> You have our terms: unconditional surrender – or the apocalypse!

– Judge Dredd, *The Apocalypse War*
January 2nd to July 26th, 1982

Question:

> By 1988 the Soviets will deploy an anti-missile shield based on beam weapons, and I am asking you what advice will you have for the United States when the Soviets act from behind their defensive shield to demand the unconditional surrender of the US and the rest of the free world.

Prime Minister:

> But you are actually talking about strategic defence, are you not?

– Press question to Margaret Thatcher
Andrews Air Force Base, USA
December 22nd 1984

1

You wake suddenly.

Everything is dark.

There is a constant, deafening roaring sound. It seems to press down and crush you.

The air is thick with dust. You can't breathe. You strain and tear your way through rubble until something gives way and you feel hot air on your face. The roaring is much louder, buffeting your eardrums, painful, incessant. You are hurt and damaged. You have no idea what has happened.

The roaring air tugs and staggers you. There is grit in your eyes and between your teeth. It's hard to see anything. It's hard to stand up.

You rub your eyes. Tears swim into a dull red glow.

You see: a cluster of mushroom clouds lifting above the burning city.

What do you want to do now?

. . .

Scott blinks. Time has slipped by without him noticing. It's nearly nine o'clock and he has to be at the Centre at ten.

He pushes the chair back; stands up. Stretches. He's been awake for maybe four hours. When he got up, dawn was just creeping over the pine trees. Now, the sky outside the attic window is a vast, cloudless blue and the air smells of resin and tarmac. It's going to be hot again.

He gathers his clothes and gets dressed: jeans and a faded grey T-shirt that's getting too small for him so he might as well use it for work. The jeans still have grass stains on the knees from yesterday, even though he's washed them and hung them on a chair to dry overnight. What are you supposed to do about grass stains? He's tried all the settings on the machine. There must be some kind of trick. His mum would have got them out.

He pads quietly downstairs, across the dark landing, down again. In the kitchen he makes orange squash and toast and butter and eats it at the table, with *The Moon Is a Harsh Mistress* propped up in front of him. He has the back door open. Framed by the doorway, the garden is half dazzling sunlight, half dense slabs of shadow, and if he stares a while the shapes burn in so that when he looks back to the novel they float there, black and red, spanning the pages.

It's not that the grass stains are a big deal. It's just that he'd like to know. It feels like it's important to know stuff like this. He's fifteen after all.

When he's finished breakfast, he washes the empty glass and the plate and puts them back in the cupboard. There's a coffee mug in the sink – his dad is up, then – and he washes that too. He allows his own bedroom to be the same familiar clutter of books and comics and sketches, game disks, tubes of paint, as always; but everywhere else he tidies after himself as he goes, methodically, almost as if it's a test of some kind. As if his mission is to leave no trace, no imprint, on the strangely resonant house.

He makes two sandwiches and wraps them in kitchen foil. His trainers are resting against the skirting behind the back door, under where the coats hang. Yesterday, Colin had him cutting the reeds at the edge of the swampy pond that's something to do with the Centre's water treatment system. The mud on the trainers is bone-dry and brittle now. Scott is about to take them outside when he falters; stops.

From along the hallway, from the door of his father's study, he can hear the sound of music, quietly discernible in the stillness. The C major recorder concerto.

Scott stands motionless, listening. Except for Capital Radio on the little Aiwa in his bedroom, it's the first music he's heard in the house since December. Eight months ago.

It could be just an accident. His dad turning a switch without thinking.

Frowning slightly, he takes his trainers out onto the lawn and thumps them together until they're clean; then sits on the step to pull them on.

Faintly, distantly, the steady, looping thread of the Telemann can still be heard, like the air itself is singing.

If this was a game, he thinks, you'd quit. Quit and start again. Start afresh.

It's nearly half past now and he's going to be late, but he can't stop himself: he goes back into the house and along to his dad's study, the old floorboards in the hall creaking a little under his feet. The door's standing slightly open and Scott pushes it wider and the music swells up around him.

Dad? he says.

His father looks up from the papers on his desk. His narrow, serious, professorial face seems for a moment utterly disconcerted, as if he has no idea what this room is, who this boy is; and then the look is gone, his eyes seem to see Scott properly, and he smiles a little smile of greeting.

Good morning, he says. You're up.

Yeah, Scott says. For a while now.

Would you like some breakfast? There are eggs, I think.

I'm okay. I had toast. I ought to be off now anyway.

Off?

The Centre, Scott says. The holiday job?

On a Saturday? his father says, sounding surprised. It's Saturday today, isn't it?

Scott shrugs. Yeah, he says. We do Saturdays too.

Goodness. Well, I hope they pay you overtime.

I don't think so, Scott says. I just – I heard the music?

A faint, unsettled look crosses his father's face. It's not bothering you, is it? he says.

No, Scott says. No, not at all, it's nice. I was just – it's nice.

It's Telemann. The recorder concerto.

Yeah, Scott says. I know.

I can turn it down, if you...

No, Dad, it's fine, Scott says again. I was going anyway. I, uh. I hope the paper's going okay.

His father blinks: nods. Yes indeed, he says. It's coming

along. Steady progress. Steady as she goes. I'm actually marking essays today, though.

Oh, right, Scott says. Okay. Well. I'll see you later.

His father smiles again: a gentle, uncertain smile. His eyes drift towards the bookcase and then to his desk, the papers. Scott closes the study door softly behind him.

He walks briskly away from the house, his footsteps crunching on the driveway. The gravel has thick drifts of greyish-brown pine needles meandering across it, and is punctured by weeds, some of them standing as tall as Scott's knees. The garden was always his mum's thing.

Their house is right at the end of the dense tangle of unadopted roads that makes up the Heights. Out of the driveway, if you turn to your right, there's a metal barrier blocking the way; and then just rough sandy track up through the pine woods until the trees thin out. After that it's open heath and the Army training range: scrubland and heather and warning notices saying not to touch suspicious objects and to keep to the paths.

Scott turns left, heading away from the barrier and down through the houses. The land here is uneven and the gravel roads sometimes cut deeply, flanked by rising earth and yew hedges. Behind the hedges are big, serious houses, some of them Victorian like Scott's house, others built in the 20s and 30s. You can get lost if you don't know your way.

There are a lot of Army families, because Sandhurst is just down the road.

And, more recently, some people from the Centre.

Unadopted means rough gravel and improvised patches of tarmac, no street lamps, no pavements. *Unadopted* also means private. He remembers once his dad said something about *the local community*, and his mum said *you mean enclave*.

Right now the tarmac patches are shiny with the heat, and every fifty yards or so the thick resinous smell of pine sap gets shot through with swimming-pool chlorine. Scott keeps up his brisk pace, winding through the Heights, skirting the sticky patches of tar. Nothing is moving and the air seems to be thickening around him. He hears a splash, a girl's voice shrieking, from far off. He can feel himself sweating now through the T-shirt.

He follows the road until it forks. One leg wanders down towards town, but he ignores that, keeping left, uphill again, deeper into the Heights; aiming for the narrow short-cut path that will loop him round to the rear gate of the Centre, near the groundsmen's block.

The pine trees that cloak the stretch of land out beyond the houses are so densely packed that nothing else grows. The spongy carpet of their needles smothers the acidic sandy soil and their feathery branches cut the sun down to a gloomy twilight all year round. Nothing much lives in the pine woods except ants: big, heavy-bodied wood ants which gather the fallen pine needles and assemble huge nests out of them, three or four feet tall, thousands upon thousands of inhabitants. Whole towering cities like irregular brown pyramids, their surfaces crawlingly alive.

Scott walks faster still, his breath quick now in his throat, his arms swinging.

If this was a game.

. . .

At the rear gate, Scott presses the button, holds up the plastic card they gave him on his first day, and waits, looking steadily at the unwinking lens in the metal box. There's a long pause; and then the lock buzzes loudly and clicks open. Scott opens the gate and steps through.

The main entrance to the Centre is down on the main road. But this is faster.

He walks the five yards across the stretch of no-man's land to the second fence and the second gate, where he has to repeat the whole process. This part, when he's trapped between two sets of chain-link and razor-wire, is always a little scary. The first time he did it he realised he could feel his heart thumping. Because what if they didn't open the inner gate? What if they decided he wasn't allowed after all, or there was a fault in the system, and the gates wouldn't unlock? What if the dogs came?

Scary, but – be honest – also kind of cool.

The inner gate buzzes open, and Scott steps through onto the grass.

The groundsmen's block is tucked into a low scoop of land, hunched down quite close to the fence-line. It's a low rectangular structure with bays for the vehicles, partly screened off from the main buildings by a curling line of saplings. Colin is on the forecourt, sharpening the blade on the tractor mower.

What time do you call this, then? Colin says, giving him a narrow look.

Sorry, Scott says.

Well, at least you're here now. You can make it up at the end. We need to get them banks done. Think you're up to it?

Scott nods. Yeah, he says.

Up until Scott's about ten or so, the Centre is just a pharmaceutical company's headquarters: a cluster of low concrete buildings beside a car park, set in some grounds. The windows are deep-set in the concrete, with rounded corners and brown glass that sometimes gleams gold if the sun catches them. There's a big corporate sign on the main road with the company's name and logo in white on a blue background.

Then one day the pharmaceutical company leaves and bulldozers and work crews come in. New buildings get put up: again low, again concrete, matching in neatly with the originals except they have fewer windows. The grounds expand outward and become more carefully manicured. The first security fence goes up early on, while they're doing the construction work; then, later, the second gets added, inside it. There are shifts of security staff in neat grey uniforms, patrolling in pairs. Some of them have dogs with them. In a couple of years it's all done. Now there's no big sign on the main road, just a small, bland plaque that says *Visitors please report to gatehouse.*

Even though they've put up more buildings, the car park is much smaller now, and far fewer people come and go. And the lights in the complex stay on all night long.

Ward becomes obsessed with the Centre: with finding out what goes on in there, what it's for, what secrets it harbours. He and Scott spend free afternoons peering at the blank grey buildings through the chain-link. Ward is the nearest Scott has to a best friend, even though they don't really get along very well.

It's Army, right? Ward keeps saying. It has to be.

My dad says so, Scott says. He says it's record-keeping and, you know, documents and all that stuff. For Sandhurst. He says they're doing it all on computers now and that's where they keep them.

Computers, Ward says in a tone of deep disgust. That's such bollocks. Your dad must be fucking retarded to believe that.

Scott shrugs slightly. He feels lazy and content and he can't be bothered to fight today. He says, It doesn't look like Army. It looks like a hospital.

Exactly. Or a science laboratory. So why would the Army need a hospital science laboratory?

Genetic infantry maybe, Scott says. Like *Rogue Trooper*.

After a moment, Ward nods to himself. Could be, he says slowly. Could be. That's it. It has to be. We should gather evidence.

But the evidence they gather never really amounts to anything. And now of course Ward has gone back to South Africa.

It would almost be worth getting in touch, just to tell him, Scott thinks as he carefully pours petrol into the Flymo. He can't help grinning to himself.

Hey, Ward, guess where I'm working this summer?

Although in fact he still doesn't know exactly what goes on inside the pale concrete buildings: only that if they let fifteen-year-old kids help out with the estate gardening, it probably isn't augmented soldiers or anything actually cool.

Probably it's just what his dad told him: filing systems keeping track of where to send crates of uniform and who to bill for supplies of combat boots and stuff like that, and windowless rooms full of big computers.

Still. You can pretend.

He hefts the Flymo out of the shed into the sunshine.

The steep grass banks that buttress the Centre are tricky to do unless you know how. Colin has shown him. The thing is to tie the Flymo to a length of rope, and then walk along the top of the bank, swinging it like a pendulum and slowly hauling it in. Then move a little further, drop it back down, and do it again.

Since they built on to it, the building is no longer a simple rectangle; now it's some kind of complicated interlocking series of boxy shapes and there are lots of corners and interior angles as well as longer straight stretches. Scott works his way round steadily. To start with he keeps missing little strips and segments. But slowly he finds the rhythm to it, learns how to swing the pendulum wide and let its own momentum take it where it needs to go. The Flymo buzzes back and forth, trailing fumes. By noon his hands are red and stinging from the rope and his back and shoulders are sore from the strain of hauling the heavy mower up and dropping it back down. He's sweating hard, the sun full on his face and arms and the thick concrete walls behind him banging out heat like an oven. But he's got it now. Neat arcs of mown grass follow, one overlapping the next, a sequence of pale green fans like radar traces. Then trail the mower along the bottom to finish it with a straight edge.

He's working his way into an angle where the building is casting a narrow wedge of shade across the grass. He glances towards it and decides to stop here: he's done plenty, and he can sit to eat lunch without the sun on him.

He reels the mower in, shuts off the frantically chattering engine, and leans it against the wall; blinks sweat out of his eyes; ducks to wipe his face on the arm of his T-shirt. For a moment he stares back critically along the bank he's just finished, looking for mistakes. But it's good; he's done a good neat job; and he feels a little pleasant bloom of satisfaction, like he used to get when he was small and he did well colouring inside the lines.

He steps into the shade, into the small oasis of silence and suddenly cooler air. He's right beside one of the strange smoothed-off windows. Recessed in the concrete, and in shadow, the smoked glass looks like a pool of dark water. His reflection wavers in it: a lanky boy with blondish hair, dirty jeans, his T-shirt patchy with sweat.

And then, with a start, he realises he's being watched: that from within the room beyond the window a boy he doesn't recognise is staring back at him. Short dark hair and a look of sceptical amusement on his sharp little face.

Scott blinks. He has the strong sense the kid has been watching him for a while; that the wry look – almost contemptuous – is at Scott's expense. Still, reflexively, he raises a hand in greeting: *hi.*

The boy doesn't wave back. Instead he tilts his head quizzically, as if to say, *what the fuck?* And right then Scott realises, with real surprise, that it's not a boy at all: it's Jodie Armitage. The Armitage girl.

The one everyone calls the freak.

The suspicion that he's being laughed at – that he's a source of amusement – hardens into certainty. He takes a faltering step closer. Her eyes don't move from his. He says, What? What's funny?

She doesn't reply: doesn't even move, except that her eyebrows go up a bit.

Scott can feel his throat tighten. He feels caught out somehow. He wonders how long she's been there. He says, a little too loudly, Why are you watching me?

She doesn't move.

Scott says, Come on. Say something.

She twists her face into a swift, imbecile grimace that clearly says *moron.* Gestures to the window between them. Scott realises it's soundproof and she can't hear what he's saying.

He can feel himself flushing. He takes another step towards the glass but even as he does so, the girl gets up from where she's been sitting; slips a pair of Walkman headphones over her ears; and wanders away into the room without looking back. The darkness of the window seems to swallow her and she's gone.

Scott stands there blankly, staring at his reflection.

Jodie Armitage.

Everyone in the Heights knows she tried to kill herself or cut herself or something, razor blades in the bathtub Ward said, except her parents hushed it up.

And when Susan Lewis cornered her and asked what it

felt like being a self-harming freakshow, she bit the soft part of Susan's finger right through until her teeth met and said, *Like that*. And now she has to see a shrink.

At the time he kind of felt Susan Lewis deserved it; but now all he can feel is a confused, dull resentment turning and turning, low down inside him. Maybe because he had thought he was alone: concentrating on the work, his shoulders aching, his mind empty. Almost like being happy. And now that's gone.

Well, she's gone too.

What's the Armitage kid doing inside the Centre anyway?

In his head, immediately, Ward's voice: *Bet they're doing experiments on her.*

Scott frowns. He feels fleetingly unsure of himself. Because something about the way she held herself – tense, twitchy almost – did make him think of an animal, a trapped animal, rather than a girl.

Still, he wishes he'd said something: something to show her he wasn't embarrassed, that he was fine with being seen, fine with being almost happy.

Except of course she wouldn't have heard him, because of the window.

Shaking his head slightly, he leaves the mower standing against the wall and goes to get his sandwiches from the shed.

By four o'clock he's made his way around the whole Centre, but the easy rhythm he'd attained earlier in the day has slipped out of reach and he can't get it back. The mower moves choppily and he has to go back over some parts twice or even three times.

He keeps glancing at the windows, checking them; and it throws him off his pace.

Still, in the end, it's finished. He shuts off the engine for the last time and drags the mower behind him across a wide span of lawn towards the line of saplings. Little tan grasshoppers flit through the air ahead of his feet.

Back at the sheds he stows the machine. Colin looks over from the hedge trimmer he's cleaning.

You got it all done, then?

Scott nods.

Good work. Bit slow, but then it's fucking hot pardon my French. Your pay's on the bench there. Wipe that mower down before you go.

Ten in the morning till four in the afternoon. Two pounds an hour. Twelve pounds cash in a little manila wallet. Scott says, Thanks.

See you Monday, then.

Yeah, see you.

When he comes out the back gate, the track is half in shadow: the sun's starting to slip down towards the pine trees. Scott, sore and aching, lets the gate clang shut behind him and starts to trudge home. He can feel the back of his neck where the sun's caught it. His arms too.

The air is very still. He can hear sounds of traffic from the main road, and somewhere far off some little kids shouting gleefully; and the gritty sounds of his own footsteps on the dry track; and his breathing. He reaches the junction.

Out of nowhere a voice says, So what was it?

Scott whips round. The Armitage girl is sitting right there on the ragged bank under the yew hedge, in a patch of sunlight. She's staring at him: she has the same wry, sceptical look on her face as before.

Black jeans, black long-sleeved top despite the heat, short dark hair, a tatty canvas bag slung to one side, scuffing one foot in the dirt. Headphones slung round her neck.

He says, What was what?

Whatever you were trying to tell me. Whatever it was that was *so important*.

Scott shakes his head. Says, Nothing.

Must've been something. You were all –

She breaks off speaking and does a little mime, pretending to be Scott outside the window: looking pissed off, flailing her hands jerkily with mock rage.

Scott can feel his earlier irritation starting to come back again but he holds it down. He says, evenly, I was just asking why you were looking at me. Is that something you do? Watch people when they don't know? Cos that's kind of creepy actually.

She gives him a considering look and says, I know you.

Yeah? I know you, too.

Her face twitches once and her gaze dips away from his. She digs in the canvas bag by her side and takes out a Walkman; starts to fiddle with it. She says, I bet you do.

Scott says, What does that mean?

She ignores him; pulls the headphones over her ears. Scott hears the tinny pulse of the music start up. She squints her eyes against the sun for a moment, then looks away down the track towards town; like he's not even there any more.

She must be his age but she looks about twelve. She has black makeup round her eyes, too much of it, like she's trying to be a punk; black eyebrows. Everything about her is kind of scrawny. Sitting at the side of the track she's just a nervous scrawl of black in the afternoon sunlight.

Just for a moment he can't stop himself imagining it: the parting resistance, the sudden mouthful of blood. Susan Lewis screaming, presumably.

Then he turns away and heads home.

The house, when Scott gets there, is silent. There's no music playing any more, and no sign of his father. The door to the study is closed.

Sometimes he's working. Sometimes he goes in to the university for things, even though he's on sabbatical.

Sometimes he's just gone.

Scott's hair is thick with sweat and dust and he has streaks of oil and grass stains up his arms from cleaning the mower. He puts his work clothes to wash, goes upstairs and has a shower, running the water dead cold and getting straight under: a gasping chill at first and then – as he becomes used to it – an increasingly luxurious sense of delight, of numb coolth, of the heat and weariness draining away; goosebumps on his arms, his balls shrinking up tight, as he forces himself to wait and get properly cold.

Then clean jeans and T-shirt and in the kitchen he finds bread, cheese, some sliced ham from the supermarket. He turns the little kitchen TV on and eats at the table, reading an old *2000 AD* in bare feet.

The news comes on. Ronald Reagan at a podium, talking. Gorbachev. Something about increased tension. He stops looking.

The way she said *I know you* was weird. Like she meant something more than just *I recognise you* or *I know your name.* More like a judgement: *I know about you.*

But they've never even talked, so she doesn't know anything: not really.

So the weirdness was probably just her. Just her weirdness.

If Ward had been there he would have pissed himself laughing. *The freak speaks!*

Jodie Armitage. She used to be more visible: you used to see her skulking around the Heights, never really part of anything, just hanging around on the edges. He remembers a barbecue at the Sutcliffes' house that his parents made him go to when he was maybe eleven; groups of adults talking on the patio with plastic cups of white wine and the kids splashing about in the pool. Ward doing cannonballs, aiming for the girls. And Jodie Armitage, in the shadow of one of the big redwoods in the corner of the garden, watching them all. Just watching.

Scott seems to remember her being new that summer: that her family had just moved here or something. Sometimes when people move in to the area they make a big effort, go round and say hello, invite other kids the same age as their kids to come over to play; all of that stuff. But not always. And not the Armitages.

Still: she used to be around.

And then she just faded out.

I know you, she says, squinting at him.

Yeah, right.

What was she even doing there, at the junction?

Was she waiting for him?

Standing in his memory in the shadow of the redwood, she doesn't look unhappy. Alone, perhaps, but more like she's chosen not to join in than she's been forced out; not like she might one day try to kill herself or hurt herself or whatever it is that comes later.

He goes back upstairs. The house is silent: his father is still nowhere to be seen.

In his room he switches on the Amstrad; waits for it to boot up; and loads *Dispersal.*

He clambers from the rubble; heads south. Finds the highway. This time, instead of following it towards the big cloverleaf in the distance, he crosses it, edging between the lines of stalled vehicles. He scrambles down the embankment and starts to trek determinedly south-west, away from the road, away from the blast site, into the desert.

He dies from dehydration before the radiation sickness can finish him. He quits the game. Starts again.

He clambers from the rubble.

Outside, the sun slowly falls out of the sky and the pine trees become dark. For the first time there's a breath of a breeze through the windows.

I know you.

He dies four or five more times before he gives up and switches the computer off. It's late and he ought to be exhausted but in fact he feels restless and edgy and messed up.

He takes his clothes off, brushes his teeth at the little sink in the corner of his room, and turns out the lights. The attic is dark and still. He lies on his bed, resting his eyes on the slope of the ceiling. There's just enough light coming in to make a ghost-space around him: a faint grey echo of his room. After a while he starts to masturbate, without thinking of anything much; almost unconsciously. But once he's come, he feels calmer; and in the end he does fall asleep.

He wakes.

The kitchen is dark. There's a red glow from the numerals on the microwave and a faint backwash of sodium light from some low clouds outside. The house is totally silent.

He is naked, and holding the handle of the back door.

He stands for a long moment, still gripping the handle, until the sense of everything falling fades out and the world is solid again.

The house is still silent, the kitchen is still dark, he's still standing here in bare feet.

Moving soundlessly, he climbs the stairs back to his room. With a heavy sense of futility he gets under the sheet; and lies, unable to sleep, with a muddle of thoughts tumbling around inside him, a confused incoherent static. Reagan and Gorbachev on the TV news. Which one will fire first. ICBMs ploughing lines across a clear sky and radioactive flame enfolding whole cities.

He thinks of dying. What it would feel like. If it would hurt. Whether you'd even know.

The doctor who talked to them at the hospital said it would have been over at once. That there was nothing anyone could have done.

But surely they say that to everyone. Even if she had been alive when they got there, alive and trapped in torn metal, and took time to die, they'd say it was over at once, wouldn't they?

Everyone seems to take it for granted that dying is better if it's fast. Better for the family because they don't have to think of you suffering. Better for you, because you don't have time to realise you're dying, that you're about to die, that this is it.

Like dying is a dirty secret that has to be kept hidden, even from the person doing it.

Like you wouldn't want time to think; time to recognise what was happening. Like you wouldn't want to know.

Perhaps it was true this time.

2

Every week at ten o'clock on a Monday morning, they test the Broadmoor siren. It has to be tested in case they need it for real: in case one of the mental patients escapes. For one minute, there's the two-tone alarm in the far distance, and then a pause, and then the all-clear wails up to pitch and hangs there steady.

She's learned to stay indoors. If she's out, someone will spot her, and she'll hear them shrieking with delight: Hey bitch! They're playing your *soooong!*

She gets her first computer when she's eleven. It's a reward and a consolation prize in one. The reward is for school: for being top of every maths test, every science test, every exam, all year; and for winning the Achievement Cup.

(She is exceptional; everybody says so.)

The Achievement Cup is a little silver cup on a black

plastic base. It's not hers to keep; you give it back at the end of the year for someone else to win. Her father says, I think we can do better than that, don't you?

She knows it's not just for being exceptional. It's also because they're moving house, moving school. Her dad has a new job now and Camwell Heights is going to be their new home and Jodie's going to be leaving all her friends behind when they go.

(She doesn't have friends. She is exceptional but people don't like her. She has tried, but they just don't. It's strange to realise that her parents are unaware of this; that they think moving school will be difficult for her, will be something she'll have to overcome, something that requires consolation.)

Anyway, so: computer.

Her father gets it through his work. It's brand new. This is the most advanced home computer on the planet, he tells her in a serious voice.

When she switches it on, it's like a door has opened.

The computer has an operating system called DOS and a programming language called BASIC. She reads the manual to learn how the language works. There are disks with programs already on them – a spreadsheet; a word processor; some games – but she ignores them. She is going to write her own.

Hours go by. On the softly-glowing screen, instructions unspool from her fingers and cautiously begin to take shape, to become connected to each other. The computer is like a small child, or a simple, willing alien; it will do what you want, but you have to talk to it clearly, in a way it will understand. If you want it to draw a circle, you can't just say that. You need to start from scratch: teach it what a circle actually is.

She makes mistakes. But not many. And never twice. She's good at this, just like she knew she would be.

There's wetness between her legs. For a moment she's baffled: has she been so lost in talking to the computer that she's forgotten to pee, has wet herself? But then she realises her period has started.

It's the first time, but she knows what to do. They had a talk in PE a year ago, and right afterwards she went to Boots in town and bought a box of pads which has been sitting in her dresser drawer ever since, ready. She changes her pants and settles the crisp white pad in place; and puts on new trousers; and goes back to programming.

The program starts to work.

Later on, when she thinks about this, it seems pretty symbolic that she got the computer and got her period on the same day. Or maybe not symbolic so much as just comical: *a door has opened but also the floodgates of puberty*. She can't really decide. But it's something, that's for sure.

She remembers the boy from when they first moved here. There was a pool party at someone's house. He was just a little kid then. Like her.

(Except not like her of course. Not exceptional. Not a freak either. Just a kid.)

She remembers him though. And more clearly than the others. It's as if the other faces – laughing, screaming, eyes and mouths wide like wolves – have become part of the same smeared jeering mass; but his face stands out.

Today, framed in the window of her dad's office, with the afternoon sun on him, seen through smoked glass, he is smooth and unaware and untroubled, working away in the sunlight. He looks happy.

A kind of desperation floods her.

Fuck you, she thinks as she looks at him. *Fuck you.*

She gets the modem three years later, for her fourteenth birthday. By this time the computer has changed (to a newer model with more memory and a better processor) and she has changed (from a good little scholar to whatever she is now; no-one knows; she doesn't know). She wants the modem because she wants access to bulletin boards. She drops hints for a while but it's tough. The therapist they have been making her see (ever since *the incident*) has said she should try to be less insular, more outward-facing; and this feels like a step in the opposite direction.

(Which it is.)

She concocts a carefully-reasoned, slightly emotional lie about this being a different way to connect: about feeling safe when there's the screen as a mediator of interaction: of this being perhaps one of the baby-steps she needs, in order to make progress in the right direction. Inside, she's cracking up because this is all bollocks and they're buying it.

Then later, she's not so sure. Maybe the lie is credible because it's not entirely a lie. The thought makes her feel furious and slightly sick, like she's been seen naked.

Like she's *let* herself be seen.

But she gets the modem. So long as she only uses the phone line after nine in the evening, she can go on bulletin boards and newsgroups.

There's a newsgroup for everything. For programming; for academia; for *Star Trek* and Tolkien and Asimov; for recipes and short stories and phobias and politics and bonsai and metal detectors. For esoteric jokes that rely on a comprehensive understanding of particle physics, or Aristotelian philosophy, or obscure classic cars. For rude limericks. And of course there's every computer game ever. You can download them, play them, share them around.

And in the crevices, strange stuff. People who like being hurt. People who want to fuck kids. Rape. Suicide. Death.

She reads everything. Avidly; relentlessly. Searching.

Somewhere out there is a girl-shaped, girl-sized hole in the world into which she would fit perfectly. Snug and neat. *Click.* If she can find it, things will start to make sense again.

She reads and reads. It is just around the corner; it has to be.

Some of the boards are local enough that the modem doesn't even need an area code. Others are transatlantic, or in Europe somewhere. She's not allowed to make long-distance calls but before long she has half a dozen ways around that. A man in Ohio uploads convoluted proofs of ancient Mayan prophecies. A guy in Germany transcribes and translates Eastern Bloc newspaper stories. Hackers trade information on backdoors and breaches to big computer systems in corporations, banks, research facilities. Teenage dorks make ASCII porn, the girls drawn using letters and numbers and punctuation marks.

Sometimes people reach out. The SysOp of a board in Swithenham wants to organise a meet, get everyone in the local dialling area together, who's in, they can do costumes and vote on a theme for it.

But when that happens, she drops silently off the board, erases her tracks, and vanishes.

Some of the newsgroups are about missing people. Their messages usually fall into the same desperate pattern: how the person looks, when and where they were last seen, what may perhaps have happened. Please look for. Please help. Sometimes it's abduction; sometimes people run away; sometimes nobody knows what has happened – just that the person is gone now, leaving behind confusion and fear and pain and no answers at all.

Kellie-Ann went to the store to buy a paper banner for her little brother's birthday party and never came home. Red hair, freckles; jeans and a sweatshirt with the name of a football team.

Paul was backpacking in Cambodia, supposed to meet up with friends, didn't show though they waited a week. There's a photo from an American high school yearbook. Glasses, curly hair, an awkward, friendly smile.

Stacey had an argument with her mother and stormed out of the house; said she wished her mother was dead. That was three years ago. Long dark hair, a jacket with badges, please help us find our daughter.

Jodie reads one after another, carefully, slowly. Sometimes for hours.

3

Scott gasps and his mouth fills with dry pine needles and dust. He starts to retch. The boy's knee grinds into his shoulder and the boy's hand seizes his hair and shoves his face deeper into the dirt.

What did you see?

The knee on his shoulder screws into him and it feels like his arm will break.

What did you *see*, cock breath?

Scott shouts into the pine needles, Nothing! A huge swell of rage and shame burns through him and he has to fight not to cry. Nothing! he says again.

The other boy – Ollie – says, from a distance, Come on, let's go.

I'm making sure.

Jay, for fuck's sake, the other boy says again, sounding bored. Leave it and let's go.

The weight shifts off him and Scott hauls air into his

lungs, coughing. He tries to get up but the boy grabs his arm and turns him, pinning him down. At least he's on his back. At least he can breathe. Sunlight winks through the pine branches.

Open your mouth.

Scott wrenches himself sideways and tries to tip the boy off him, but it's hopeless. The carpet of pine needles slips and gives under him and the older boy's weight is too much.

Open your fucking *mouth*.

Even in the thick haze of panic Scott knows he'd rather have his arm broken than open his mouth. He shakes his head vehemently and clamps his jaw shut.

The boy's face above his is almost calm. He watches Scott for a long moment.

The other boy – Ollie – says, sounding impatient now, Come *on*.

The calm blue eyes watch Scott a second longer. Then the boy shrugs. He works his mouth like he's chewing on something, and then spits a big gob of saliva into Scott's face. Scott gags and twists convulsively. The weight's off him and he can move. He rolls to all fours, hunched over, rubbing frantically at his face with the back of his good arm until he can open his eyes. In the scuffed patch of forest floor where he was pinned down, he sees ants half-crushed, legs twitching and straining.

By the time he's wiped the snot and saliva and pine dirt off his face and got to his feet, the two boys are gone.

You continue south.

The wind has slackened off now, but ash and grit have left your eyes red-rimmed and burning. Your shins and hands are bleeding from where you crawled out of the rubble. You have a headache; you are very thirsty.

The road surface has blistered and cracked. The strip is littered with cars. When the air slows for a moment you catch a sickly eddy of burned meat.

Above you the sky is a thick grimy mass, constantly in motion. You can't see the sun. Every so often lightning crackles but no rain falls.

A security guard lies dead in front of the downtown shopping mall. The mall is silent and empty. You try to remember what day it is.

You see: a dead security guard, a shopping mall, a parking lot, the road south.

What do you want to do now?

He keeps in among the trees, away from the path, until he's nearly down to the barrier; he wants to get home without being seen, so he can clean himself up and pretend this never happened.

But he is seen. As he follows the hedge line towards his driveway, a small sharp voice says, What happened to you?

Jodie Armitage, almost invisible in the shadows like some fucked-up ghost-child, staring at him. Scott puts his head down, looking away, and walks faster. Doesn't say anything.

Then he's round the corner into the driveway, leaving her

behind him, ignored. The cool sanctuary of the house: he ducks round to the kitchen door.

It's silent inside. No-one home. His dad is at the university, he remembers. He feels slackness in his muscles now; he draws in a deep uneven breath and gets as far as the table before he has to stop; everything has turned to a hot trembling blur; his breathing hitches.

Her voice says, again, What happened?

Scott turns, dismayed. She has followed him in – is standing there, in the kitchen, frowning at him. He says, Get out.

No. Not till you tell me why you're crying.

There's a dull burning ache in his shoulder and he can't deal with this – can't stop the tears now, and they tumble out of him. He scrubs them away, furious, ashamed, and says, Why don't you just fuck off?

She nods slightly as though agreeing with him; but instead of leaving she comes closer and says, Let me see.

For a moment Scott wants to punch her.

She says, Were you in a fight?

Something comes loose in him and the fury drains; he feels suddenly deeply tired. He says, this time almost in a whisper, Just go away.

She nods again, and stands there, looking him over, eyes resting in turn on the graze up his arm, the fucked-up T-shirt, the mess on his face. Her frown deepens and she says, Jesus. That's not a fight, that's getting the shit kicked out of you.

A small dull clench of anger, but it's gone almost at once, like the muscle for anger is exhausted now. He says, Yeah.

Who did it?

Ollie Shaw and that other kid, the one he hangs out with.

Jay Slater, she says. I know them. They're pricks.

Scott says, again, Yeah.

She says, Well, come on. Let's get you fixed up.

They go through the still, empty house. In the first-floor bathroom he washes his face with cold water, and runs the tap over his arm. Pine needles and grains of dirt swirl and twist in the sink. Jodie stands in the doorway, watching him.

Up in his room, he finds a clean red T-shirt. When he tries to take the torn scuffed one off the flare of pain from his shoulder makes his eyes water again.

Here, let me.

She helps him with the T-shirt, awkwardly lifting and holding it so he can pull free. She says, sounding impressed, Shit. You've got a massive bruise coming.

Her cool fingertips trace a shape on the back of his shoulder.

After a moment she says, You don't think it's broken or something?

I don't think so.

Yeah, or you wouldn't be able to move it at all, probably.

There is pain still, and weariness, and residual fury and shame; but also this sense of being touched, of this strange uninvited girl touching him with concern, of her small neat fingertips on his skin.

He puts on the red T-shirt with a feeling of unreality. The Armitage kid is in his bedroom, helping him with clothes, poking about along his bookshelves, pulling out paperbacks and putting them back. Finally he gets a girl up to his bedroom and it's *Jodie fucking Armitage.* Ward would die laughing.

Why did they beat you up?

I don't know. They were up by the forestry track and they thought I was watching them or following them or something.

Were you?

Well yeah. Stupid for getting caught.

You're allowed to be in the woods, aren't you? I mean, what the fuck, beating you up.

They wanted to know if I'd seen them.

Seen them what?

Getting something from some guy in a car.

You mean drugs?

I think so.

Jodie says, Just keep away from them, okay?

Yeah.

She examines one of the Dredd annuals, leafing through it, frowning slightly. After a moment she says, What's your name again?

Scott.

Like Scotch tape.

He says, with more emphasis, Scott.

Like Scotch Brite. Except not so bright if, you know. Comic books.

She puts the annual back. Just for a moment the air shifts – a lazy, unexpected exhalation from the tree line behind the houses that stirs in through the window, discernibly cooler, resinous.

She says, I'm Jodie, by the way.

Yeah, Scott says. I know.

Her eyes snap towards him: glittering, cynical, grey-green. Sharp like something mineral. Then she turns back quickly to the books.

There's a moment's silence. Scott goes to the window.

She says, Do you ever do drugs?

He glances at her. She still has her back to him. He says, No. Why? Do you?

She wanders over to the table. Some of his drawings are out: a couple of sketches of bodies tumbling through the air, as if they're falling. A sketch of his hand. A stab at a Hulk-style panel with forced perspective. She says, Did you do these?

Scott nods. Her frown deepens. He waits for her to say something about the drawings – that they're good, that they're shit, whatever – but instead she just puts them carefully back where they were, and turns to the Amstrad. She says, sounding amused, Wow. Really?

Really what?

Such a kiddy computer. I bet you have Pac-Man and Tetris and *everything*.

Scott says, despite himself, You've got a computer?

IBM, she says, and gives a kind of half-smile. Jealous, right?

Not really.

Yeah you are.

Not really.

You lie, Egg Man.

So what games do you have?

I don't do games.

Why have a computer if you don't do games?

There is other stuff, you know.

What other stuff?

Programming mainly.

For a moment he can't work out why she just called him Egg Man. Does she mean like in the Beatles song? Then he gets it. Scotch egg.

He says, Girls aren't usually into that kind of thing.

Yeah, it's not really allowed. But I have this little fake rubber dick, and if I wear that, they have to let me.

He feels the corner of his mouth tug. He says, So what do you program?

Whatever I feel like. All kinds of things.

What are you programming right now?

It's personal. Sorry.

How can it be personal?

Well, it is. Like I said. And we've only just been introduced. She crouches down and runs her hand along a row of paperbacks on the bottom shelf. Says, What are all these?

They're sort of post-apocalyptic. It's a series. It's set after the bomb and it's about surviving.

You've got a ton of them.

Yeah, I spose. It's a series, like I said.

You've got *Z for Zachariah*, too. That's set after the bomb as well, right?

Yeah, he says.

And *The Stand*. But that's not nukes, that's a plague. Well, there's a nuke at the end. But the plague is what kills everyone.

You like Stephen King? he says, surprised.

She doesn't answer. After a moment she says, So you're really into this shit. Nuclear war and so on.

Kind of.

How come?

I don't know. I just am. It's on the news. I want to know about it. Don't you?

Did you see that film on TV?

Which one?

The one where the war kicks off and, I think he's a doctor, he goes to try to help people at the hospital but they all just get sicker and sicker, him too, they're all dying from the fallout, and at the end he goes back to where his house was and there are these refugees sheltering there in the wreckage and he says, Get out of my house. Except it's not a house really, it's a ruin, they're sheltering in this ruin, and one of them just holds out some food, offers some food for him to eat. And there's no-one alive on the radio any more.

The Day After, Scott says.

That's it, yeah.

She comes over to the window and looks out. The air is heavy with heat: you can see the dark block of pines where the track goes up to the heath, and also the roofs of the houses lower down in the Heights.

Her sharp chin and grey-green mineral eyes.

Scott says, Did you really try to kill yourself?

The eyes turn to him. For a moment her face is hard, like something carved in pale stone, implacable. And then it changes and she breathes out and looks away. She says, You shouldn't believe everything you hear, Egg Man.

The afternoon sun is bright on the eerie expanse of pale concrete. Jodie scuffs her feet along it, her trainers making little gritty sounds. She glances at Scott out of the corner of her eyes as they walk. He has grass stains on his jeans and his sandy blond hair needs cutting and his eyes are grey and there's something strange about him, strange and lost.

You hear stuff – people talk, even if they don't talk *to* you they talk *near* you and so you end up hearing stuff just the same. No-one in the Heights is entirely, completely unknown.

Scott.

They're wandering through what Jodie thinks of as the Flats, which is one of those oddball segments of forgotten landscape. To get in you have to pick your way through heaps and tangles of bramble and stunted saplings on the edge of the training range; but once you're in, everything opens out into a lunar expanse of pale concrete slabs the size of football pitches. The concrete's old and weathered and split, and pink-flowered mallows have shot up through the seams. Whatever was supposed to be built here never happened. There are no structures, not even clusters of rebar; no hint of what might have been intended.

She says, Kind of freaky, isn't it?

Scott says, Yeah, it is, kind of.

She kicks a stone and it skitters away across the surface. Says, Nobody ever comes here. It's like an invisible city. Or a landing pad for the aliens or something.

After a moment he says, Why were you at my house?

Jodie shrugs. Being creepy, she says. Do you want to hear about the program I'm working on?

I thought it was personal.

Do you want to hear about it or not?

If you want.

It's basically a computer shrink. You talk to it – well, you type at it, I mean, you know – and it asks you all these leading questions from a database of psychobullshit. And then it tries to diagnose you based on your responses.

He says, Does it work?

Kind of. I need to extend the database. And I need to work on the text analysis routines so it grabs the right parts to analyse. It's fun trying to get it to sound real, you know, get it to pass the Turing test.

She imagines he's going to ask her what a Turing test is. Instead he says, You really think you could replace an actual person with a program?

Not an actual person, a shrink.

She hears him make a little coughing sound in his throat: like the start of a laugh.

She says, Well yeah, why not? It's not so hard.

How are you doing it?

She looks at him quizzically. What, really?

Yeah, go on.

Okay. So tell me your problem then.

Scott says, I don't know.

Anything, make something up.

He says, I don't know – I'm having trouble sleeping, something like that.

Okay, great. So first thing, the program looks at that sentence and it junks all the pronouns and conjunctions and extraneous words like *something like that* and *I don't know* and it tries to find the core phrase, which is *trouble sleeping*, so it assigns that a variable identifier and stores it. And now it's got two databases, one of arsehole shrink questions, one of medical condition descriptors, so it goes to its arsehole shrink questions database and it pulls out *Tell me how old you were when you started to experience X*, and it substitutes your core phrase for X. *Tell me how old you were when you started to experience trouble sleeping.*

That's pretty easy, Scott says.

She finds herself unexpectedly nettled. Says, Of course it is, doofus, that's just the first iteration. But each time you reply, it's scanning your answer for more core phrases, and assigning each of them variable identifiers, and it's also mapping those onto the database of medical condition descriptors, and then that influences which sections of the arsehole shrink questions database it uses to get its follow-up questions – so if you're giving it core phrases that show up in its medical database under depression it starts to think you're having trouble sleeping cos you're clinically depressed. And then it'll start asking you questions about depression to see if it's right, which will give it more core phrases to work with, and on and on like that until it hits a statistically-credible diagnosis.

Scott says, Huh.

So actually not so simple, right?

He says, grudgingly, That's not bad.

She's pleased that he gets it. That he understands. She suppresses a smile and says, Actually I'm kind of bored with it now. I mean, to make it really work you'd have to put in a shitload of information and, you know, who cares, right?

I suppose.

One day we'll get computers that can do all the scanning and analysis themselves and we'll just sit back and let them do it.

Or sentient computers, he says. Like the Laws of Robotics. How cool would that be?

Very, until they kill us all.

He makes that little sound again, like a half-laugh: *Huh.*

The thought worms into her head: why is she doing this? Seeking him out? Following him into his house like that? Walking, now, right next to him, telling him stuff? The thought twists in there and everything wavers: she wavers: vertigo tries to claim her. Because what does she think is going to happen here?

She realises he's said something. She drags herself back into the sunlit afternoon.

What's that? she says.

I said, how come you were in the Centre anyway?

She says, Didn't have anything better to do. I'm trying to get runtime on the mainframe but they're being dicks about it.

He glances at her uncomprehendingly. Says, But I mean how do you even get *in?*

Jodie shrugs. She digs in her jeans pocket and pulls out her security card and shows him.

Scott stares for a moment: then pulls out a similar card, holds it alongside hers. Jodie nods. Right, she says. So, what you've got is the basic access pass. Like they give to visitors. So you have to show that to the cameras and the guards in the control room verify you manually, yeah?

Scott nods. Yeah, he says.

Well mine's like a staff pass, not a visitor pass. It's got this magnetic bit here so I can just card in on the scanners. Makes it easier to come and go, you know. So I can get in the main building, use the cafeteria, hang out in the lobbies, my dad's office, that kind of thing. But it's not an *actual* staff pass. It's still restricted, which is fucked up. Apparently I'm not responsible enough to be let in the labs or the mainframe or any of the actually useful areas.

Scott seems to be thinking this through. After a moment he says, So your dad works there?

Jodie makes a face. She says, He's in charge, pretty much.

In charge?

In charge of part of it, anyway.

But what is *it?* What do they do in there?

She glances sideways at him. Says, Don't you know?

No, he says. That's why I'm asking.

I thought, cos of your books and everything...

Abruptly he stops walking. What do you mean? he says. What do you mean, cos of my books?

She stops too. Uncertain. He looks different suddenly. Angry maybe.

She says, It's, uh. It's SDI. You know SDI? They do the programming and shit for it.

Scott says, his voice flat, SDI.

It's the thing they call Star Wars, you know? The Strategic Defense Initiative. The lasers. To stop nukes from landing on us.

He says, his voice still strange and flat, I know what it is.

Yeah, well. I thought you would. That's why I thought you were in there on purpose. Scoping it out. Cos you're, you know. Kind of fascinated.

Her voice trails off. Scott is staring at her. His face is strangely blank. He says, So that's the Centre? They're building SDI?

The Americans are building it. Building the lasers. We're just writing the software. Uh, you're not supposed to know, by the way. It's seriously top secret confidential. But I already told you about my shrink program, so... what the fuck.

She watches as he exhales. Tips his head back. Okay, he says; but to himself, not to her. Okay.

What's up?

He doesn't reply. Something has changed in his face.

Jodie says, and there's concern now, Hey. Scott. What is it?

He gestures vaguely across the flats. Says, Sandhurst's just over there. And that's a primary target. But I was thinking maybe we were just far enough away. Except now your dad's building SDI right next to us.

She looks at him very carefully. After a while, as if testing the water, she says, You don't think it's actually going to happen, do you?

It is going to happen.

He sounds utterly, entirely certain. Something inside her slips. She says, You read too many stories. You're being paranoia boy.

He says, Look. In *The Apocalypse War,* the Sovs fire their nukes first cos they have this secret defence shield so they know they're invulnerable. And Mega-City One gets totalled.

What's that? Comics?

Yeah. *Judge Dredd.*

So that's just comics.

No, that's what's happening right now.

But we're the ones with the secret shield.

You don't get it. It's not secret, it's all over the news. And we don't have it cos it's not been built yet. Your dad's still working on it. The Russians know this, okay? They know this. It's *on the fucking news.* So you're the Kremlin, and you're sitting there while America and Britain build this thing that'll make us invincible right in front of your eyes. You're watching it happen. What do you do? Sit there and watch, until we're unkillable? Until we can nuke you to shit and you can't do a thing about it? Or do you hit us first, before we're ready?

He takes a breath and looks away from her. He says, Because that's what I'd do, I'd shoot first, before the other guy gets to be like Superman.

Jodie says, That's stupid. Even if we build it we wouldn't start a war right after.

Her voice sounds wrong to her. Uncertain. Unconvinced.

Maybe *we* wouldn't, Scott says. But America would.

She keeps her eyes on him. He's staring into the distance,

where the concrete ground meets the scrub of brambles and nettles and then the sky, which is colouring now towards evening.

He says, as if to himself, Or maybe no-one even needs to start a war. Maybe it'll just be an accident, you know, someone presses the wrong button or some circuit fucks up and fires a missile. Or *WarGames*, and some kid hacks into the Pentagon and sets it all off.

That wouldn't happen. They have tons of safeguards and stuff.

Challenger had safeguards and it blew up right on TV.

That was a spaceship, douchebag, not a missile.

It's not so different. Chernobyl had safeguards and that blew up. And those are just things that happened this year, I mean, since Christmas. There's probably stuff with missiles happening all the time as well, but we don't hear about it cos it's military and they hush it up.

His voice is surprisingly clear and measured. Jodie wants him to stop talking now, but he goes on: You know there's fallout? There's this cloud of radioactive fallout from Chernobyl and it's just drifting. It's reached Britain actually. I mean, it's actually here.

He nudges a stone with his toe. And that's just a stupid power-station. That's not even supposed to explode. And they've got I don't know, maybe fifty power stations and fifty thousand missiles, so you work out how long it's going to take. One mistake. That's all.

He falls silent at last. As she watches him, his tension seems to fall away. He breathes out slowly; bends down to pick up the stone. She can see it in his hand. It's pale grey, flecked with green. He flicks it away.

They stand without looking at each other for a long moment. Scott is staring at the horizon. Jodie has her eyes on the ground in front of her feet.

When she speaks, her voice comes out smaller. So you're scared?

He looks at her like he can't believe she's asked such an obvious question. He says, Of course I'm scared.

The answer drops into her head like a pebble into a pond.

When Steve Austin crashes his test plane, NASA rebuilds him and he becomes the Six Million Dollar Man. Once they're finished, he's better than before.

You can do that, in stories.

When Scott's nine or ten, there's a handful of kids in his year who are into comic books, particularly American ones like *MAD* and Marvel and DC; and of course Ward brings in stacks of Fantastic Fours after every holiday. Everyone swaps round for what they haven't read yet, so the comics end up covering a lot of ground. As a kid he's captivated by the muscular storytelling and the lean, punchy visuals that drive it; the worlds of the stories feel both excitingly unfamiliar and strangely comforting.

The comfort, he gradually sees, comes from the underlying message that's present in so many of the superhero strips: *This could be you.* All that's needed is the moment of change: the transformative instant that unlocks the hero. You may be ordinary, and weak, and scared; but it could happen – the radioactive spider-bite in the lab; the ray machine out of control; the gamma bomb on the test range. It's beguiling, this imagined possibility. The person. Then the change. Then the superhero.

Strange how many iterations of the story have radiation at their heart.

One summer he and Ward find an ad at the back of one of the comics for a bodybuilding course guaranteed to get you as pumped as the guy in the picture. The thing with the course is that you don't need any weights or equipment because it's all done using something called dynamic tension. He and Ward pool some pocket-money and send off for the course, which turns out to be a pamphlet showing you how to push with one arm while pulling with the other. They copy the exercises religiously for the whole summer, but nothing happens. Ward is furious: Dynamic tension and a shitload of steroids, what a fucking rip-off. But the truth is that Scott has, really, known all along that it's not going to work. An ad in the back of a comic book, guaranteed to transform you into someone like Stallone? They should have known better.

The change requires more than a pamphlet. It requires cataclysm.

Steve Austin ends up with a bionic eye and a Geiger counter built into his arm, and can run at sixty miles an hour. So really, Scott thinks, crashing his plane worked out pretty well.

Five years later, in a hospital waiting room, he'll remember thinking that.

Gradually he stops reading the DCs and Marvels. But he

sticks with Dredd. Dredd's different. More real, somehow, even though it's set in the wasteland of the future. More honest. Dredd doesn't have powers: just a gun and a motorbike and utter, implacable determination. With the American superheroes, the costume is a disguise for their ordinary identity, but with Dredd it's not a costume, it's a uniform; and the uniform isn't a disguise, because it's all there is. The helmet never comes off. Dredd doesn't say, *This could be you.* Dredd says, *I am the Law.* The stories are sometimes funny, sometimes grim; but at least in the Cursed Earth the radiation actually kills you.

They approach his house in silence. Scott knows something has changed. He glances at her. She has her head down. She looks troubled; upset.

Because of him.

They reach the end of his driveway; their footsteps falter and they pause there.

My dad's probably home by now, he says. So... you know.

She doesn't reply.

Scott says, Well. Uh. See you.

She lifts her head slightly. Your mum died, she says. In a car crash.

Scott glances up the driveway towards the house.

She says, her voice low, Look, everyone talks. Even I hear shit.

Slowly, he nods. He thinks, *She's going to say that she's sorry. Because everyone says that. I'm so sorry.*

But instead she steps in closer to him and unbuttons the

cuffs of her top and pushes the sleeves up her arms. Shows him the delicate white tracery of scars, like whispers; clean lines in the skin over faint blue veins.

Razor-blades in the bath, Ward said.

So that's why she wears long sleeves, even now, when it's baking hot.

He runs his fingers along the insides of her wrists wonderingly. She is soft; warm; the scars thin smooth ridges, barely discernible, Braille for an unknown language.

4

What everybody wants from her is reasons.

Why did you do it?

What were you thinking?

What possessed you?

As if those questions are answerable. As if people are reasonable. As if reasons play any part, really, in what anyone does – or at least the kinds of reasons you can articulate, spell out, point to, explain so they make any sense to somebody else.

Why did you do it? Is it a cry for help? What do you need help for? Is it just attention? What do you need attention for? Didn't we raise you and look after you and spend all that money on school and care for you? There are kids in inner-city slums who have real problems – drugs and prostitution and things you can't even imagine. What problems do you have? We did all this for you.

All thrown back in our faces.

What on earth were you thinking?

Thinking.

Not thinking.

She waits. Waits in her bedroom, lying on her bed, listening to her Walkman, until hours have gone by and her parents must be asleep.

Then, in the heavy silence of the sleeping house, she muffles the squeal of the modem with a wadded T-shirt until the necessary connections are made, and then stands by her door listening for a long time to be sure; but there's no movement.

She logs in to a Usenet board in Atlanta which skews hard towards anti-governmental conspiracy theories, Second Amendment fanatics, right-wing militias and extremist groups stocking compounds. It's not a place she often visits but she knows that there are quite a lot of ex-military users: disaffected veterans, people with grudges. It seems like as good a place as any to start.

One mistake, Scott said. One mistake. That's all.

She types

Looking for info. Nuclear near-misses. Accidents. Real events not speculation / rumour please. Has anything ever actually happened?

Answers start to tick in. Despite what she's written, all of the initial replies are speculation or rumour. But she's expected this. She waits.

And finally, at just gone three in the morning:

Yes things have actually happened. But by default they're

classified for at least 25 years. So we're only finding out now how close we've come. For example: 1957 Kirtland incident. Declassified four years ago but only hit the wire this week. Albuquerque Journal just reported it. You can FTP the text file from this server. If you want to know how the world is going to end, you should read this.

She downloads the file. It's a newspaper article, dated a few days ago, from a newspaper in the States. The headline is resolutely unsensational: *Documents Explain Kirtland Accident.*

Like it could be about a truck collision on the interstate or something.

But it's not that.

The text of the newspaper article glows softly on the screen in front of her. With a sick feeling of dismay crawling in her belly she reads it through; and then reads again.

So you're scared?

Of course I'm scared.

She turns off the computer; sits for a long time, unmoving, in the darkness.

5

On the evening news, they're burning sheep. Scott's not sure if it's the Ministry of Agriculture or a protest by the farmers or what: the story is finishing when he turns the TV on and all he sees is the pile of corpses going up in flames. It's in Cumbria, where the fallout from Chernobyl has been building steadily in the grass and soil. Nothing there is safe to eat any more.

There were stupid headlines for a while about lambs that glowed in the dark or microwaved themselves, but those have stopped. People are frightened now.

The pall from the burning animals drifts across the TV screen for a moment; and then it's gone, replaced by another story. Mrs Thatcher, talking about South Africa. Scott finishes the last of his beans on toast listening to her say that sanctions against the regime are counter-productive: the boycott hurts the black people in the townships most. Every lowing cadence of her voice signals a regretful compassion and she delivers her message slowly and clearly, as if her audience is made up of remedial children. Her eyes are full of sorrow.

Scott has the sudden urge to smash her face in. A hammer, a brick. Something to punch through the droning, implacable assurance – to make blood and bone reveal themselves, to make a human animal reveal itself. Something scared and hurt and real. Anything to shear away that perfectly armoured complacency.

He blinks. The image has been vivid and he realises he's upset.

He never used to have thoughts like this. About hurting people. He just didn't.

He washes his plate and glass and goes up to his room. It's half past six. The Music Box stays open till eight, so he's got plenty of time to head over and drop the cartoons off with Charlie.

There was a bomb, in Brighton, two years ago. Shattered wreckage and dead bodies and bleeding wounded, and Mrs Thatcher walking out unscathed. She was statesmanlike in the aftermath. She was composed and determined. Terrorism would not prevail.

That was the IRA.

Scott feels, deep in his heart, that she might be unkillable. Like a Terminator. Wales and the North are under a cloud of actual radiation right now, and all she has to say is that we should keep buying Outspan oranges and Cape apples like good little consumers.

For the townships.

He wonders what Charlie will have to say about that. The thought makes him smile slightly.

He gathers his drawings – several quarter-page panels, plus the latest instalment of the strip he's been working on – and puts them in an A4 envelope. His little packet of pay from that day's work at the Centre is still on the bed from when he got changed; he takes out the twelve quid and adds it to the money in his desk drawer.

It's starting to stack up. He could buy something soon, something serious. Maybe oil paints. Or a camera. Or a proper stereo, even, instead of his crappy little radio.

He hasn't seen Jodie Armitage since she showed him her wrists. Two days have gone by. He's kept an eye out, when he's at the Centre, and when he's walking there and back, and when he goes into town; but she's nowhere to be seen. No strange little faces watching him from windows. No scribbles of black lurking in the afternoon light. She's just absent: she was there that one day, and now she's not. Things have gone back to the way they were before.

Except that he keeps looking for her.

Mrs Thatcher as a Terminator isn't a bad idea actually. If he could draw her right. But he can picture it. What would be super cool would be to get her eyes glowing red, but the cartoons have to be in black and white.

Unless he did it on the Banda copier and used two sheets, a red one and a black one. But then you only get a few copies; and anyway, Banda red is just pink really.

Still. It might work.

He trots down the stairs and out into the evening. Maybe

tomorrow he should stop by Dixons, check out what stereos they have.

He's past the junction and heading down towards the main road when he hears her say, So what's in the envelope?

He stops. She's sitting cross-legged on a tree stump at the side of the road, half-hidden by yew hedge, deep in shadow. She's almost invisible: he has to squint to see her. She looks like an angular, baleful leprechaun, surrounded by dark foliage. A confused emotion – partly relief, partly something else, something almost resentful – expands through Scott.

He shrugs and says, Nothing. Just some drawings.

What're you doing with them?

I'll show you if you like. Fancy a walk?

Why? Where to?

The London Road.

She frowns; shakes her head emphatically. I don't do town, she says.

He imagines why not. He says, Well, yeah, okay, but it's not *town*. I mean, it's not the shopping centre or anything. It's right on the edge. Nobody's going to be there. The Music Box. Do you know it?

The frown deepens. That record place next to the biker bar? she says.

Yeah.

Don't be insane.

Why?

If you go there you're getting raped.

Scott half-laughs. It's just a record shop, he says.

Gang-raped by Hells Angels. Why're you taking your drawings to a record shop anyway?

He's about to explain about Charlie and the fanzines; but then he stops himself. Changes his mind.

No, he says. Sorry.

What do you mean, no?

Just no. If you want to find out you have to come with me. That's it. That's your side-quest for today.

Her face scrunches up in disbelief. She says, What the *fuck,* Oats. Stop being a dick.

That throws him for a second, but then he gets there: *Scott's Porage Oats.* He feels his smile widening. Look, he says. I don't make the rules. And you're never going to level up if you don't do the side-quests.

There's silence for a long moment.

He wonders why he's doing this. Pushing her like this. She doesn't want to go into town and he can see that.

He starts to think perhaps he's actually angry with her, even though he's smiling.

Abruptly she uncrosses her legs and stands up. Says, briskly, Okay. Sure. Let's go and get raped. They'd better be fucking astonishing drawings though.

You'll have to wait and see, Scott says.

He starts walking again, and she falls into step beside him: head down, scowling, scuffing her feet as she goes.

They make their way along the London Road, in a constant dull roar of traffic noise. The shopfronts here are tatty and run-down: a muddle of different businesses. The printing and copying place that Charlie sometimes uses when the Banda's not enough. A stamp collection shop with yellow cellophane across the inside of its window, to stop the stamps from fading. A tattoo parlour. The long frontage of the army surplus store, its windows full of camo jackets and jerrycans and hunting knives. Not the kinds of places you'd find in the shopping centre, which is prim and middle-class and family-friendly.

Scott darts a look sideways. She still has her head down. She seems to be not talking to him.

Up ahead, on the other side of the road, is the biker hangout: a low building made of breeze blocks painted black. Then a scrappy, weed-strewn patch of tarmac where the bikes are parked. And then the Music Box, also black, but narrower, its two front windows entirely plastered over with stickers and album covers and posters.

Scott says, We have to cross here.

She doesn't answer.

They dodge through the evening traffic like Frogger, hesitating briefly in the middle of the road. A truck roaring past sounds its horn at them and Jodie flinches.

Then they're across. They hop the verge and scramble down a little bank of loose ground and onto the cracked tarmac. The door to the Music Box is standing open, and as they walk towards it Scott can hear Janis Joplin playing.

So Charlie's in, then.

He leads the way inside, Jodie trailing behind him. There are a couple of girls browsing the racks and a punk man over at the counter talking to Charlie, seemingly trying to decide between two albums. Charlie catches Scott's eye as he comes in, gives him a grin and a wave, and goes back to conferring with the punk guy; turning one of the albums over and showing him the track list.

The interior of the Music Box is a kind of tunnel of clutter, leading further back from the black-painted frontage than you'd think from looking at the outside. Charlie has the part just in front of the till organised, more or less, so that new releases or albums she and Pete think noteworthy have prominent spots on the tabletop racks; then there are bargain bins of second-hand records underneath the tables; and the walls are given over to plywood shelves and bays loaded with more stock.

There are cassettes in stands near the counter. No CDs, though, because Pete says they sound like shit.

Scott wanders in, looking at the new releases. If he got a stereo he could buy some of these.

Jodie is hanging back, near the doorway.

Deeper into the shop things get cramped and chaotic. There are old speakers, sets of lights, music memorabilia, road cases left over from Pete's time touring, with the band's logo stencilled in yellow spray-paint on the sides; then hulking against the side wall, the huge Banda copier and its carbon papers and solvents, surrounded by reams of protest pamphlets, anti-capitalist literature, anti-Thatcher polemics, calls to arms, CND leaflets, all printed in aniline mauve on soft meths-scented paper. Then the stairs up to the little flat above the shop, and under the stairs, a tiny and often malfunctioning toilet.

He glances back towards the doorway. Outside, the road throbs with heat-haze and the traffic seems lensed and distant. The town beyond is all but swallowed up. For a moment he can't see Jodie at all, and wonders if she's ducked back out into the sunshine; but then he spots her, motionless in a corner. She seems to have drawn into herself somehow; become smaller.

The till rings and clatters and Charlie gives the punk guy his change. In the end he's bought both albums.

Scott comes over and says, How did it go at the embassy?

Charlie grins triumphantly. You should've been there. We fucking closed that place down.

Shit! Really?

Yeah, there was a bunch of us chained to the railings both sides of the street. They had to stop the traffic, no-one could get in or out or anything. Teach them what it's like to be locked up for once.

Did anyone get arrested?

They didn't dare. The fuzz just stood back and watched.

Maybe some of them think you're right.

Don't let Pete hear you say that. I'm not kidding. Hey, look at this.

It's a London evening paper. Charlie smooths it out. There's a headline and a photo – a scrum of people and placards, *Free Mandela, End Apartheid Now* – and there at the edge of the frame, caught in the moment of shouting something, blurred but recognisable, Charlie. Face twisted with furious outrage, mouth open, one hand pointing straight at the camera, the gesture emphatic and impossible to misinterpret: *you.*

Scott stares at the image; shakes his head. He says, Wow. Wish I'd been there.

You should come. There's a ton of stuff going down. Seriously. Come along sometime. Who's the little goth, by the way?

She's called Jodie.

She's your friend?

I only just met her, Scott says.

She's not going to nick anything, is she?

Scott grins. I don't think so, he says. I think she just looks like that.

He glances over to Jodie. She's made her way to the other side of the shop now and is moving slowly between the racks, eyes down. She seems tense, as if something inside her is coiled up tight.

Seems, in fact, like it is costing her effort – a physical, painful amount of effort – to remain here. Scott feels suddenly uncertain.

Got anything for me? Charlie says.

He lays the envelope on the counter, pulling out the drawings. Okay, so. These are for *Wakeup Call*. There's two of them, but you can choose which you like most.

Charlie looks at the panels; nods. These are cool, she says. This one for sure, don't you think?

Scott nods. Yeah, he says. I thought so too. And this is for *One Voice*. You said do something really bold, so...

Charlie takes the paper from him. Her eyebrows go up a bit. Wow, she says. Yeah, that's bold. That's kind of porno.

Well, Scott says.

Hey Stella! Charlie shouts over the music. One of the girls browsing looks round.

Yeah?

Scott's drawing porno now! Charlie shouts.

Well what a surprise, the girl shouts back.

Scott blushes; shakes his head. If it's too much I can do it again, he says. You know, tone it down a bit –

No, no, no, Charlie says, laughing. No, I get it. She has to be that way for the joke to work. I'm just saying... man. You gave the girl some serious boobs, that's all.

Yeah, Scott says, feeling flustered. I suppose. Sorry.

Anything else?

I did you a title for *Shocks of the New,* Scott says, showing her.

That's ace. Cheers.

And another one of these, he says, taking out the strip. He's saved it for last. He says, apologetically, I mean, I know Pete thinks they're weird...

Charlie shrugs. They are kind of weird, she says. I like them though. I think Pete just can't tell if they're sposed to be funny or, you know, sad.

Well, Scott says. Yeah.

She turns the strip so they can both look at it together. There are four panels, with a little title crammed in vertically alongside the first one: *Afterwards.* In the first panel, the farmers are planting cabbages. In the second panel, the cabbages have grown, but have mutated in the radiation; the farmers are worried. There's a speech bubble: *it's happening again.* In the third panel, some of the cabbages are escaping and the farmers are chasing them to and fro. The cabbage roots have become tendril legs, like tentacles. In the final panel, some enormous mutant cabbages are eating the farmers; the caption reads *time for the harvest.*

Scott says, after a moment, You don't have to use it.

No, I like it, Charlie says again. Don't worry, I'll find somewhere for it.

Cheers, Scott says.

And these other ones are great.

So what's next? Scott says. He realises that Jodie has sidled up closer to them; she's looking at the leaflets on the wall next to the till. Or pretending to.

Charlie thinks for a moment. Then says, Okay, well, something for the mail order list would be cool. It doesn't need a message or anything, just a picture's fine. Maybe just a grotty student room full of albums and shit and someone with headphones in the middle of it kind of blissed out?

Sure, Scott says. Got it.

And something for CruiseWatch. They're staking out the missile routes and they want more people involved. So I was going to put round a flier, just a single sheet that we could post up or hand out to people?

I had this idea for something like *Terminator,* Scott says. So, imagine Maggie and Ronald Reagan and they're walking over this field of human skulls, like at the start of the movie? And maybe there's mushroom clouds in the background. And I thought they could be holding hands, almost like they're skipping along. Cos I was thinking she's kind of like a Terminator, really.

Yeah, Charlie says, cautiously. I get it. That's a good idea. But I think Pete was thinking maybe just like a big picture of the missiles themselves? Cos if people just glance at it, they need to think *nukes* straight away, you know what I mean?

Scott nods. All right, he says. Okay, fair enough. I can do that.

I mean, you should do your Terminator thing too. We can use it somewhere else.

The girl who Charlie shouted at earlier comes over. Let me see the porn, then, she says. Charlie shows her the drawing. The girl examines it, then looks at Scott.

You draw pretty well, she says. For a little pervert I mean.

Charlie guffaws loudly. Scott shakes his head. Thanks? he says.

Jodie watches them talking. Scott and the girl behind the counter. She looks like she's at least twenty. Scott said her name was Charlie.

He's laughing and showing her the drawings he's done. And the girl's leaning close to look at them. Scott's talking, pointing at things on the pages.

Jodie examines some of the pamphlets near the till. Molesworth Peace Camp. The Anti-Nazi League. Down With Murdoch.

The girl's wearing a T-shirt that says *Extreme Noise Terror,* the words tight across her breasts.

She's very, very pretty.

She has dark-red hair, curling round her face and down past her shoulders. Her body is an adult body: curved, relaxed, easy. Scott is leaning closer now as they talk. He keeps looking at her.

(Of course he does.)

Walking here, in the open, in sharp daylight, has been even harder – even more corrosive – than she thought it would be. She has kept thinking *soon we'll be there. Soon it'll be okay.* But now they are there, and it's not okay. She's trapped. The way home is endless: too far to manage. Impossible. She can't leave. She can't leave and she doesn't want to stay and she hates this.

Scott laughing aloud at something.

Why has he brought her here?

You continue south. It is night.

As you walk the wind is constant, blowing fine grit into your face. The sickness you have been feeling is worse. The ash underfoot deadens sound. You are very tired. Cars are strewn at intervals along the road.

The highway surface is uneven and blistered and you stumble in the darkness. Above you the sky is lost in endlessly drifting clouds of dust. You have not slept in a long time and your mind wanders. Your mouth is parched. The potassium iodide you took has dehydrated you and you are beginning to become desperate for water. Even with the cloud cover, the desert night drains the warmth from your body with every step and you are shivering uncontrollably.

If you do not find shelter you will die soon.

What do you want to do now?

On the way back, as they're passing the multi-storey car park, Scott looks round to say something; and realises in dismay how pale she is. She looks like she might be about to puke up in the street.

When they get back to the Heights, to where the road forks, he slows; then stops walking. Jodie stops too. He looks at her uncertainly. His earlier feeling of buoyancy – recklessness – has gone entirely.

She says, What?

Her voice hard: almost bitter.

He says, Yeah. Look. I'm sorry, okay?

Sorry about what?

You said you didn't want to.

It's fine, she says.

No, it's not. It was, uh. What you said. You were right. I was being a dick.

Her gaze is sharp like glass. She says, I'm used to that.

Well I didn't mean it.

Yes you did. You're pissed off with me.

Scott falls silent. He feels the silence stretching out between them: more and more of it: like a wall going up. If he waits too long there will be no way over.

He swallows. Clears his throat. He says, Okay. Yes. You're right.

So why?

I don't know. It's just – we talked. We talked and you, you showed me your – you know, your arm. And then you just vanished. I mean, I've been at the Centre every day, and I was – I thought you'd be – I don't know. So I thought, okay, maybe that was it. Maybe it was all a mistake and... that was it.

He can't find the right words. He isn't even sure what he's trying to say any more. He feels stupid and helpless and no words will come.

At last he says, I thought I'd see you again, that's all.

And when you did see me that made you pissed off?

Scott doesn't know what to say to that.

Jodie lets out a long ragged breath.

And then, to his astonishment, she puts her hand out and touches him lightly on his forearm: just for a second, with her fingertips.

She says, Okay. Look. Actually me too.

Scott stares at her in real confusion. He doesn't understand what she means. You too – ? he says.

You're not the only one who gets scared sometimes, you know. Anyway, fuck it. You were a dick, I was a dick. Where does that leave us?

Gratitude creeps up inside Scott, and with it, a lopsided smile.

Normally I just quit and start again, he says.

She thinks about it for a moment. Nods. Says, Then let's do that.

6

At first it's hard to make any sense of it – just a chaotically seething carpet of movement. And it's unsettling, being in the midst of it; you have to keep shuffling and moving your feet before the ants get onto your shoes.

But after a minute or so, sense does emerge.

They've gone a long way up the sand and pebble track that runs from just outside Scott's driveway off through the pines. Another few minutes would have taken them out onto the heath and the training range. The Army runs all sorts of exercises up there, and in among the heather and scrub gorse Scott often finds spent smoke grenades, charred flash-bang cartridges, scattered nests of rifle and machine-gun bullet casings, some dull brown with age, some bright and brassy.

But they have stopped short of the heath, at a point where the track's still running between heavy pine woods.

The ant war is happening right across the path, the ants

coming from both sides, meeting in the centre. Scott crouches down, staring closely.

Jodie says, Look at those ones. What is that? What're they doing?

Scott looks where she's indicating. He says, Carrying away dead bodies I think.

Are they their own side, or the other side? I mean, is it – She stops, brushing her jeans and trainers for a moment; then goes on: Is it they're trying to help their fallen comrades, or are they taking prisoners or trophies or what?

Scott says, They're dead, so...

Jodie moves her feet a little. And again. She's looking round about her, frowning. After a long moment she says, No-one's winning.

Scott says, Probably technically one side is. You just can't tell cos there are so many of them, and they keep on coming.

She says, Why are they fighting anyway?

Scott says, Yeah, I was wondering that. I think they're just too close to one another. Look.

He straightens up and points. To one side of the track, dimly visible in the gloom under the pines, is a stumpy brown cone heaped up a couple of feet high. He points the other way. The other side of the track, another.

He says, They start small, just a queen laying eggs, and I spose they can't tell then whether there's another nest nearby or not. But as they get bigger, they reach out further, right? They kind of sweep a whole area around the nest for food. And if they find a smaller nest in their zone they have to fight it, kill it off. But these ones, they're more or less the same size, and they're far enough apart that they haven't really met each other until now, they've just been growing and growing, and now they *have* met they're both pretty big nests.

Jodie straightens: shuffles and stamps her feet back and forth a bit. The whole track, for several yards in each direction, is crawling with movement. You could walk through it and not notice, but if you stop, and look, it's suddenly there, like static on a TV screen: hundreds, maybe thousands, of big red-brown ants struggling silently among the grains of sand and bits of grit and stones and pine needles. Damaged ants, twitching. Corpses.

She says, So just bad luck really.

I suppose, Scott says.

How come they're just fighting out here on the path?

It'll be happening in the woods too, probably, Scott says. But you probably couldn't really see it there. It's only cos it's out on the track that you can see what they're doing.

She watches intently for a moment. It's carnage down here, she mutters.

Yeah, Scott says.

After another moment she says, Maybe we should move now. It's a bit fucking creepy, actually.

Scott nods.

They head back down the forestry track towards the Heights. Jodie walks slightly ahead of him, kicking at stones as she goes.

Her hair at the back is close-cropped. The nape of her neck is pale. From behind she looks pretty much like a boy.

Then they're at the padlocked rail, and out onto the gravel and patchy, tacky tarmac, with the yew hedges rising up around them.

In the gloomy hallway he calls out, Dad? Are you home?

He and Jodie wait for a moment. There's no reply. Scott goes along the hall to his father's study and opens the door; but the room is empty. The notes on his father's desk don't seem to have been moved since the last time he was in here.

Scott knows that the paper is a lie. That there is no work, not really. Not for months now. But he still asks how it's going whenever they talk. Somehow it seems like the kindest thing to do: to let his father keep believing that he, Scott, believes.

I think he's gone out, he says uncertainly; but when he turns round, she's nowhere to be seen. Jodie? he calls.

You've got a piano, he hears her say, her voice coming from the room opposite the kitchen.

Scott goes to the doorway; stops there, on the threshold. Jodie has lifted the lid on the piano; she traces her fingers along the keys without playing them. Then closes the lid silently. She picks up one of his mum's art books from the table for a moment; opens it; puts it back.

You play, then? she says.

No, Scott says.

Her face twitches quizzically. She gestures at a corner of the bookcase and Scott sees his own certificate for Grade 7, which his mother had framed for him last year. It has his name on it. *With distinction.*

He says, evenly, I mean I don't.

A fleeting expression of awareness, of understanding, crosses her face. She nods very slightly, and comes out of the room without saying anything else. Scott closes the door again behind them.

They take glasses of cold orange squash up to his bedroom. Scott's notes from the trip to the Music Box a couple of days ago are scribbled on a piece of paper stuck to his cork-board: *Student in bedroom, messy, lots of albums. CruiseWatch, picture of missiles, really big, threatening.*

Jodie huddles down on the floor by the end of Scott's bed, leaning against the wall there. She picks up one of the *2000 ADs* and starts leafing through it. Her expression is one of faint derision.

Scott glances at the cover. He says, You shouldn't start with that one.

What?

You're in the middle of the story. If you start there, nothing's going to make sense.

She arches her eyebrows at him. You read these cos they make such good sense? she says.

Scott shrugs. She goes back to flicking through the pages of the comic. After a while she says, You can draw and you can play the piano, then.

So? Scott says.

So fuck you, Oats. Fucking show-off.

Scott's not quite sure whether she's joking or not. But he

thinks she is. He pushes his chair back from his desk; drinks half his squash. You can program, he says.

She gives him a sideways look. I meant to ask you. How long have you been doing cartoons for, you know. CND protest march lesbians?

Since last summer.

How come? How did you start?

You know the art shop?

She shakes her head.

Well, it's further on. It's past the old cinema. But it's really good, it's got good stuff. Paints and brushes and inks and these really good technical drawing pens, and – yeah. Anyway. So I was going there, and I kept hearing this music from across the road, and one day I just... went in. Not for any reason, really, cos I don't even have a record player. But anyway, me and Charlie got talking. Cos they had all these leaflets and things, and some of them had cartoons on them, and I just thought... maybe I could do that. Cos I'd been drawing cartoons for a while. And a lot of the leaflets were about trying to stop the war, trying to stop the nukes, so... I said, if you want cartoons for any of these, I could do you some. That's what I like to draw anyway, pretty much, so, why not use it, put it to use, you know? And, yeah. She said yes.

Do you get paid?

No. It's not like that. I just do it because it might help. Also it's pretty cool. I mean, I know it's not *published* published. But it's something. People see them at least.

She turns the page in the comic. Peers at it closely. She

seems wryly amused. She says, And because you fancy Charlie, right?

Scott shakes his head slightly. He says, She's got a boyfriend actually. And she's twenty-two.

Neither of those was my question, Oats, she says. She lowers the comic and fixes her eyes on him. I mean, come on. She could be a Page 3 girl, looking like that.

I dunno, Scott says. He can feel himself frowning slightly.

Of course she could. Easily. Are you really saying you don't find that attractive?

Why do you care who I fancy? he says.

I don't. You can fancy who you like. I'm just interested, that's all. Investigatively interested. I don't talk with many boys. I thought you could help me, you know, understand how you work.

How boys work? he says. Again, he finds himself unsure if she's joking or not. And this time he's less certain.

Yes. What you want in a girl. What gets you hard. I mean, is it just the obvious stuff, the clichés, like big tits and long hair and lips and all that?

Scott feels a twinge of irritation. He says flatly, Yeah. It's the obvious stuff.

So then you do fancy her.

Well what kind of boys do you like? he says.

I don't.

You don't fancy boys?

No.

Scott hesitates. He says, So are you – I mean, do you fancy girls then?

No.

So you don't fancy anyone.

Got it, she says. Give the Egg Man a sticker.

Well if you don't fancy anyone, you shouldn't be worrying about what boys like, should you? Cos then it doesn't matter if you're not. You know.

If I'm not what? she says.

Not a cliché, Scott says.

Her eyes are steady on his. Scott feels the heat of a blush rising up his neck; onto his face.

After a moment, she says, Well that's an excellent point, Oats. You can have another sticker.

I just meant –

No, she says. I couldn't agree more actually.

She turns the page of the comic. Lowers her head to read.

He waits for her to say something else; but she doesn't.

Some minutes go past. Scott starts putting away the pencils and inks on his desk. He stacks up the loose paper and some old drawings and puts them on top of his sketch pads. He thinks about turning the radio on; but decides not to.

Outside, the sun is setting behind the pine trees. As the air cools the ants will return to their nests: depleted, damaged. He wonders how much longer they'll manage to continue the war.

She's still ignoring him. He switches the Amstrad on. The disk drive chunks and whirrs and chirrups as the machine boots up. While it's working, he takes a jar of inky water over to the sink and rinses it out; puts it on the windowsill to dry.

She'll go home soon and he'll have his room to himself again.

He sits at the computer and puts the game disk into the second drive slot.

The program loads. There's a thin beep. The screen goes black.

He hears her say, from behind him, What is that?

Don't worry, Scott says without looking round. I know you don't do games.

He hears her toss the comic aside. She gets to her feet; comes to peer over his shoulder at the empty screen. After a moment she says, Well?

Scott hits a key and in the centre of the blank screen the opening text appears.

You wake suddenly.
Everything is dark.
There is a constant, deafening roaring sound. It's everywhere. It seems to press down and crush you.
The air is thick with dust. You can't breathe. You strain and tear your way through rubble until something gives way and you feel hot air on your face. The roaring is much louder, buffeting your eardrums, painful, incessant.
You are hurt and damaged. You have no idea what has happened.

Scott says, Except I bet you do, right?

Jodie says, You've got a *game* about nuclear war? Jesus fucking Christ.

It's called *Dispersal*. I think because of the fallout.

Oats. Seriously. Get help.

Help would be good, Scott says, making a face. I can't

beat it. I mean, I've tried over and over, everything I can think of. You always die. Always. I think I've played it... I don't know. A hundred times maybe. And I never make it more than two days. Not once.

Maybe that's the point, she says; and then intones in a robotic voice, The only winning move... is not to play.

Scott glances at her, surprised. Yeah, he says, Well. I wondered about that too for a while. But nothing else about it is like *WarGames*. It's not like you get to fire the missiles or anything, you just crawl out of the rubble. And why make a game if you can't actually play it? Why make it unwinnable? I'm missing something, I know I am. I just can't find what.

So what do you usually do?

I try to get away from the blast site. Get something to help with the radiation sickness – iodine tablets are good, and you can find pharmacies. It's set in some American city and there's a big interstate just to the south, but the EMP knocked out all the cars, so you're on foot. The first day I usually get supplies, I try to wash off the fallout, I look for shelter for the night; but the start of the second day I'm sick no matter what I do or what direction I go in, and by the end of the second day I'm dead. Every single time. That's weird, right?

It's kind of weird, she says slowly.

Scott taps the screen with his finger. Says, And there's no score or anything. It doesn't even tell you if you did better or worse than last time. So there's no way to learn, not really.

Maybe it's just a shit game. Where did you get it?

At school. One of the sixth-formers got it from a bulletin board I think.

Yeah. So maybe it's just some kid's project, and it doesn't work properly. What else have you tried?

I've tried staying where I start, just not moving from the rubble. I've tried running into the desert. I've tried hiding out in a car and a truck and a shopping mall and all kinds of places. I've tried following the road and not following the road. I've tried everything.

It lets you do all those things? she says. It's got options for all that?

It doesn't have options like a, b, c. You just type what you want to do and it lets you.

It parses it? she says, frowning now. This thing fits on one disk?

Yeah, Scott says.

Then that's not some kid's project, she says. She stares at the screen at where the cursor is blinking. She murmurs, reading aloud, What do you want to do now?

And then abruptly she leans across Scott and types, rapidly,

search for survivors

She hits Enter. Immediately lines of text appear:

You screw your eyes up against the roaring wind and dust and look around. But you see no human figures. There seems to be no-one alive here.

Scott says, See? It's cool, isn't it?

You're so fucked up.

Yeah. I know.

She keeps looking at the screen. The frown deepens on her face for a second. Then she shakes her head slightly; glances out the window. Says, Yeah, well. I have to go.

Okay, Scott says.

Jodie gets her bag; hands Scott her empty glass. Thanks for the juice, she says.

On impulse he says, Look. Do me a favour. If you're going to read them at all, do it right. Otherwise you'll never know if you like them or not.

He casts about the room, gathering the right comics; slotting the one Jodie tossed aside into its correct place among them. He ends up with a stack four inches thick. He holds it out to her.

She takes them from him with a wary look. Man, that's a shitload of comics, she says dubiously.

You don't have to if you don't want, Scott says. I just thought – if we're going to hang out...

Is that what we're doing?

Just leave them if you don't want them, he says.

No, it's cool. It's not like I have anything better to do.

She stuffs the wad of comics into her bag; gets her Walkman out. And then she says suddenly, You know what, give me the game too.

What? he says.

Give me the game disk. I'll find out what's going on, why you can't win.

How are you going to do that?

By being exceptional, she says; and for a moment a small, bleak smile flickers. You know. Like the opposite of a cliché.

Scott doesn't know what to say. He goes to the computer and ejects the disk and gives it to her.

See you, she says; and he hears her footsteps thump down the attic stairs and away through the empty house.

Challenger had safeguards and it blew up right on TV. Everyone knew by the time school was over – in fact, the first jokes were already going round by then. *NASA: Need Another Seven Astronauts.* And Ward laughing like crazy.

They show it on the news: the smoothly arcing shuttle abruptly blooming into silent flame, coming apart in a rushed, savage disintegration: spirals of debris twisting in the bright winter sky. On the shuttle is a schoolteacher who has won a competition, beating ten thousand entrants to join the crew. The BBC rebroadcasts CNN's footage, which lingers on the faces of her parents in the crowd, watching as their daughter's dream of flight is blotted out in fire and smoke.

Scott watching also, blankly, the January house dark around him.

The spaceship unfurls across the blue.

The images are replaced by the newsreaders. A NASA spokesman is saying, Obviously some kind of major malfunction.

There's analysis; conjecture. Little is known. The astronauts are dead. There is no more information.

Scott makes his way to bed that night knowing only that the shuttle and the seven people on it are gone. Nobody will rebuild them, make them better than before, not even NASA.

Nobody will ever really know what their last moments held. If they knew they were dying.

And in bed, huddled in the dark, the attic very cold, something gives way and he begins to sob; uncontrollably, wrenchingly; as if he will never stop.

She puts the stack of comics on her bed. Remembers how Scott handed them to her: *I just thought – if we're going to hang out...*

There was something tentative in the action: strangely vulnerable. As if it were a peace-offering.

He wants her to like them.

After dinner is done with, after her parents have gone to bed, she starts reading.

To begin with she gets nowhere. There are a whole load of different stories with different characters, set in what seem like totally different worlds. Even though Scott has apparently thought that things will make sense to her if she starts from the top of the pile, it turns out that many of the stories are serials that have already started. She's dumped in randomly, in the middle of events, surrounded by people she doesn't know and references she doesn't get. Also, the style of the strips jumps about all over the place. Sometimes the artwork is sleek and polished; sometimes it's gritty and haggard.

She perseveres. No-one has ever lent her a four-inch stack of comics before.

By two in the morning she's starting to make sense of the different worlds. *Rogue Trooper* leaves her cold. Too straightforward. *Strontium Dog* she likes better, though there's something unsettling about the nervous, sketchy artwork. The world of the Judges and the Mega-Cities, with Dredd at its heart, she finds initially rather simplistic – it's cops and robbers, just in the future – until, halfway down the stack, the one-off weekly strips give way suddenly to a sustained narrative. The style of writing and drawing changes. Dredd takes on a new, almost terrifying aspect: vengeful, damaged.

But it's Anderson she's captivated by.

The first image of her is early on in the sequence: a woman suspended, frozen, in a block of transparent plastic. A museum exhibit for tourists to gawk at. Judge Anderson: brilliant, lost, a genetic freak tolerated for her mind-reading abilities and – in the end – the only person strong enough to contain the pure evil force of Judge Death. Her mind becomes a receptacle for that evil; so long as Anderson is kept dormant, cocooned, Judge Death is trapped as well.

There's a plaque below her motionless body that reads *A monster dwells within her.*

And Jodie, to her complete astonishment, finds that her throat is clenched with emotion. She has to force herself to look away for a moment; to find a way to breathe before looking back.

Anderson is beautiful: long hair and a slender, curving, perfect body.

(Like Charlie.)

But inside there is something awful.

She keeps reading. Every so often her finger traces the contours of the drawings, with a kind of bewilderment.

. . .

Scott wakes.

It takes an uncertain amount of time to reassemble himself.

He is standing at the piano.

Two flights of stairs down from the attic. Two doors to open and perhaps close again – this one is closed. The piano lid to lift. A sudden lurch of fear – has he been playing it? Has he been playing the piano in his sleep, like some freak savant?

But in fact there is no resonance of sound in the room, no sense of strings struck and damped but a frame still faintly thrumming. The piano is a deadweight, lifeless. And his hands are slack by his sides.

He stands and waits, but there's no sound in the house either. And the air in this room is entirely still.

He folds the lid silently and pads out into the hall, closing the door. The house stands blankly about him, cobweb-coloured walls, stairs greyly stepping away into black. A little thin light from the kitchen. As he walks past the dining room he catches sight of his own reflection in the full-length French doors that lead to the garden: a pale, hollow, naked figure, elongated, like a laboratory specimen. A dead boy preserved in perspex.

7

The hedges that border the Centre, and which mask the twin fences from view, have leapt up in the summer. Colin's been working his way round with the hedge trimmer but there are places where the new growth is as thick as your thumb. He gives Scott a pair of long-handled parrot-beak cutters and a billhook, and lets him take one of the little mower tractors with a trailer behind it for the trimmings.

Driving the tractor is actually pretty cool. The land around the Centre undulates and there are several places where you can get to the top of a hillock, put the clutch down and just roll, way faster than the tractor can usually go. He doesn't let Colin see.

Once he settles to the work of pruning the hedges, it goes steadily. There's something tranquil and measured about squeezing the handles of the cutters, snipping off the saplings, and laying them into the trailer bed. And things do look a lot neater.

Every now and then he catches himself: registers how weird this is. Working away in the hot sunshine, like he was on a farm or something. Sweating. Arms streaked with dirt and sap and starting to ache. And then, a couple of hundred yards away, the implacable concrete span of the Centre, where in silent air-conditioned rooms, scientists and programmers are edging the world towards extinction.

Chernobyl has been on the news again this morning.

The thing that bothers him most – that he can't get out of his head – is all the confidence. The arrogance. It's everywhere, on both sides: people so entirely sure, so entirely convinced, that what they're doing is the right thing; that it can't possibly go wrong.

He thinks of the books on his shelves. It doesn't have to be nukes. Comets, aliens, plagues; all wipe the slate equally clean. But really, it's the nuclear stories. The ones after the bomb.

Dredd out in the irradiated wastes of the Cursed Earth.

He can't leave them alone. He's certain it will happen. Chernobyl is just the harbinger, the voice crying in the wilderness. What comes next is the war.

Something about it is overwhelming; and enthralling.

Quit and reload from the beginning. Admit that humanity fucked up and just... start again.

Everything broken. Everything different. Equal.

The thought is terrifying. The thought is hypnotic.

She is much better now. Everyone says so.

In fact all the questioning (and there was so much of

that, so much that at times it felt like it would never end) has died down now, replaced by a cautious, watchful silence whose guiding principle appears to be, Don't rock the boat. Leave her alone. She's much better now.

They've been through a bad patch but they're out the other side.

(She is not out the other side of anything.)

A truce has been established: they are a family again.

(Because she has become so much better at lying.)

And she has thank God stopped trying to hurt herself.

Anderson can see into people's thoughts. What would she see, if she could look into her mother's head? Her father's? Would there be anything in there that you could understand at all?

Still. Even though she is *so much better*, there are still questions left hanging, unanswered. Because no-one can work out what went wrong in the first place. What led from the keen little maths champion to whatever it is that she is now.

She remembers the shrink they got for her saying, We should try to join the dots on that. Only it turned out that there weren't any dots; there was no chain of event following event following event, not that they could find, anyway; there was just what she can only think of as a disconnect, a gap, buried, unseen, unexpected, unprepared for, something black and wrong, inside her, that one day slipped and opened. A gap through which she fell.

It was only later, on her own, that she did find two dots, and join them.

They didn't send her to the shrink when she hurt herself.

They sent her when she hurt someone else.

Do you ever do drugs? she asks Scott, the first time she's in his bedroom.

And he says, *No. Why? Do you?*

The Valium used to be in one bottle in her mother's nightstand. Now it's a clutter of bottles – nightstand, bureau drawer, kitchen cupboard, bathroom cabinet – scattered throughout the house, some with just a couple of little yellow pills left rattling in the bottom where her mother has misplaced the bottle and then had the prescription refilled. She misplaces the bottles more and more; there's no way she keeps track of them all. The thing to do is to choose bottles that are more than half full, and take only a few at a time.

It's not even like the Valium is anything to do with what happened with Jodie. Her mother's been knocking the stuff back for years: back when Jodie was nine years old and used to have yellow bunny wallpaper and was doing so well at school and won that prize in the County Maths Challenge.

In Dixons they're playing the Communards. Scott walks slowly along the wall where all the stereos are set out. There are different sizes of portable boomboxes, and then a lot of all-in-one hi-fi tower units with speakers; and finally a few separates, but they're too expensive.

Despite Pete saying how shit they are, he knows he wants something with a CD player.

He goes back and forth a few times until he's narrowed it down to two of the tower units. They both have auto-reverse tape and CD. One has a graphic equaliser with five bands; the other only has three, but it's a bit cheaper so he might have some money left over to spend on discs. Also, he thinks it looks cooler.

He wonders how important the graphic equaliser really is. Everyone at school seems to think they're a really big deal but he's not even sure what they actually do.

Jodie might know. She's always got her Walkman. Maybe music is a big thing for her.

He realises he has no idea what she listens to. He's never asked. Probably some kind of goth stuff. Fields of the Nephilim maybe.

Don't Leave Me This Way finishes, and now it's Madonna, *Papa Don't Preach.* Some kids are messing around with the controls on the boomboxes, cranking everything to the max.

He wishes he hadn't said the thing yesterday – the thing about liking girls with big tits and long hair. The thing about clichés. He wishes he could take that back.

He's not sure why he said it. It's not even true.

Why does she piss him off so easily? Because she does. Every time they start having an okay conversation, something seems to jar and snag and just... go wrong.

He thinks about how he would have felt if she'd said she only liked boys with big muscles and eight-inch cocks.

The store manager comes over and tells the kids to stop pissing about with the boomboxes. Scott looks again at the two stereos. In a week or two he'd have enough money. So he still has time to decide how important the graphic equaliser really is.

. . .

The back door is ajar. She pushes it open and calls, Hello? Egg Man?

And then, after a moment, a little louder, Scott?

There's silence from inside the house.

She goes into the kitchen. The air here is cooler. Everything seems dark after the brilliant afternoon garden.

She calls again, Hello?

There's no reply. She shifts the strap of the heavy bag of comics on her shoulder slightly, listening.

He might be upstairs.

She trots up the staircase to the first floor; then up again, more slowly, to the attic. Knocks on Scott's bedroom door.

She knows, by this point, that there's no-one home. You can tell if there's someone in a house: she's not sure how, but you just can. The air, perhaps: moving, or not moving.

She's been inside houses before, when no-one's home.

But not Scott's.

She opens his bedroom door. The window in the attic is standing wide but the room still swelters. She looks around.

The bed is made and the room is cluttered but not untidy. Outside the window there is bright afternoon sky and the dark swell of pines.

She slings the bag of comics off her shoulder and puts it on Scott's bed: on his dark-blue duvet.

He's not here and she knows that conclusively now and she knows also that what she ought to do is go back downstairs, and out of the house, and wait. Wait for him to come home.

Instead she walks over to the table near the open window.

It's scattered with comics and sketch pads and fibre-tipped pens. On some of the sketch pad pages Scott has been copying panels from the comics, the same figures over and over, repeated with variations. Dredd. McGruder. Anderson.

Jodie turns the pages. Now he seems to be working on a political cartoon. The one for the Music Box: the one Charlie wasn't sure she wanted. He's done studies of Margaret Thatcher's face, Ronald Reagan's face. They're good. She recognises them at once. Then a faint, uninked pencil outline of two figures seemingly dancing across a field of skulls.

She turns to the next page and stops dead.

There's another sketch of the two figures in the field, but it's gone wrong and he's put a line through it.

In the lower corner of the page is another, smaller drawing: totally different. A doodle almost. Like he might have done it without thinking, or while considering what to do next with his political picture.

It's done in pen and ink, the lines bold and crisp: sharp-edged black and white. The image is of a child in a bath, seen from above; the head tips back against the rim of the bathtub, the knees and elbows are splayed, and black ink pools in a thick swirl through the water. The eyes are closed. It could be a boy or a girl; the sex is obscured by the spreading black.

A boy or a girl, but in fact she knows it's her.

She is suddenly acutely aware of how much of an intrusion this is. Slowly she closes the sketchbook; and, after a moment, tries to put the other papers back the way they were. She steps away from the table; takes her bag off the bed; smooths the duvet flat with her hand.

Somewhere downstairs a phone starts to ring, and she jerks round guiltily.

The phone rings and rings in the empty house. She stands there frozen, waiting for it to stop.

She is skinny and unformed. Half finished. Not a kid any more but not anything else either.

And the thought slips its way in, oiling back and forth: You are irrevocably and permanently unfinished. You're just a botched product on the island of misfit toys. This is all you get.

She knows she will never be beautiful. Not like Anderson, or Charlie. Her body naked looks like it's been drawn by an angry child: angles and straight lines, awkward juts and hollows, ribs, shoulder-blades; that still-unfamiliar fierce exclamation of dark hair scribbled between her legs – everything is hasty and inept. The only tranquility, the only sense of care and order, is in the thin uneven lines that lap her thighs where no-one will ever see them: red and living, or pale as the surface of the moon; secret and unknown. Her body's nearest approach to serenity.

Scott comes round the side of the house, eating the remains of a sandwich he's bought from the corner shop on his way home. To his surprise, Jodie's sitting there on the step of the kitchen doorway, waiting for him. She's got her canvas shoulder-bag leaning against one leg and her headphones on and she's leafing idly through one of the *2000 ADs*.

Hi, he says.

She pulls the headphones off and says, Where have you been? You were done at the Centre ages ago.

I went into town, Scott says.

Yeah, well. I brought your comics back.

He walks over to her. Did you read all of them? he says.

Mm-hm.

You read really fast.

They're comics, they're not *Titus Andronicus.*

What did you think?

She squints up at him. They were surprisingly okay, she says.

Told you, Scott says, pleased. Do you want to come in?

No. Actually I was thinking we should go to my place.

He tries to keep the surprise out of his voice. Yeah? he says. Okay. Why?

I found out why you can't win your game. But I can't show you here. We need my computer.

Scott says, Awesome. Really?

Really, she says, standing up. So come on then.

Could I have a shower first? I, uh, kind of stink.

It's good you can tell, she says. But I think we're just going to have to live with your rankness for now. My dad works late today but my mum's going to be back at seven, so – now is good.

Scott, amused, says, What, I can't be in your house if your parents are there? Are you not allowed to have friends round?

Her jaw clenches. She says sharply, Look, do you want to do this or do you want to stand here fucking about? Cos we can just not bother, if you prefer. It's your game.

Okay, Scott says, taken aback. Sorry. Sure. Let's do it.

All right then.

She starts towards the driveway, walking fast. Scott goes with her, falling into step at her side. They turn out from the driveway and start along the road towards the junction.

Her footsteps are punching into the gravel as she walks.

A minute goes by in silence and then, gradually, the clench of tension in her neck and shoulders eases a little. Her footsteps fall into a slower rhythm. She glances at Scott and her expression is sheepish, as though she's been mentally replaying the conversation and starting to regret it.

Okay, look, she says. That was an over-reaction, right?

A bit maybe, Scott says.

I'm just – my parents make everything complicated. I don't want to do that. This is better. Trust me.

I get it, Scott says. It's okay.

It's not as if I'm, you know. Actively ashamed of knowing you.

Well, cool, Scott says slowly. Thanks. It's nice when people aren't actively ashamed of me.

Although you could walk downwind maybe.

Shut up, Scott says. There isn't any wind. Anyway it's not like it's that bad.

It's pervasive though, she says. She's smiling now.

Shut *up*, he says again. But he's smiling too.

Jodie sings little fragments of something, half under her breath, as she busily powers up the computer and loads a series of small utility programs. The modem beeps into life and dials, connects in a rush of noise, and mutes itself. A hard disk chatters intermittently.

Scott, sitting on her bed with his shoes off and watching her, says, So what did you find out, then?

Wait and see. But you'll like it.

Why the modem?

You have to have a network connection or it won't work, she says, sounding distracted; she's typing commands now.

Scott says, puzzled, I don't have a modem and it works fine for me.

No it doesn't, she says. That's the problem. That's why you're not getting anywhere.

Now she's doing something with a screen of text and numbers and commands, none of which means anything to Scott.

It's still odd to realise that she understands computers so much better than him. Charlie would say he's a male chauvinist pig to think that; but still, it just feels wrong.

He looks around the bedroom again. He's struggling, slightly, to make sense of the house in general: of Jodie's room within it. The house itself – the house of someone programming SDI, someone working on the missile defence system – is bland and tasteful and blank. The wallpaper is a neutral off-white, with almost-invisible stripes of a slightly different, slightly less neutral off-white. There's cream-coloured carpet in some rooms and tan-coloured carpet in others. The furniture is stylish in a way that Scott finds cold: there is a lot of dark polished wood and pale upholstery. It's a house that doesn't seem to be breathing.

He has followed Jodie up the stairs expecting some kind

of shocking, stark contrast: a room painted jet black, or the walls slashed with red. A chaotic explosion of mess. A ton of heavy-metal posters, maybe; though he still doesn't know what music she listens to.

In fact her room is also neat, and blank. There's a bed with a matching grey duvet and pillowcase set. A bookcase with a few books, a few computer manuals, and a long row of magazines about programming. One shelf is reserved for a series of little prizes and awards, the sort of things they give out at the end of term at school, or for chess tournaments.

He looks at them when she's busy with the computer. The dates are all from 1981, 1982. Four or five years back. Nothing since.

Don't touch those, she says absently. Scott moves away from the shelves.

There's a dresser and a wardrobe and the desk with the big computer on it, and that's it. That's everything.

And there's no mess, no clutter. No stuffed toys or clothes on the floor or pictures on the walls.

She sleeps in here but you wouldn't really know it.

He feels a sudden sting of loneliness, even though she's right there, sitting at the desk, close to him.

She's typing something now. He says, a little awkwardly, So? Who'd you like the best? In the comics I mean.

She hesitates; typing still. Then says, I don't know. Dredd was cool of course. Or maybe Anderson, she was okay.

Scott says, What do you mean, okay? Anderson rocks. She's totally awesome.

Jodie says, without looking at him, Do you mean because of the mind powers, or because of the tits?

Cos of the mind powers of course.

Oh come on. Are you saying you'd still think she was awesome if she was fat? Or hunchbacked? Or some sweaty bloke called Trevor in a string vest with BO. Still awesome?

Scott's about to reply, but he stops himself. He can feel the conversation trying to twist the way it twisted the other day. After a moment he says, Look, I'm not saying Anderson's not hot. I'm just saying when it comes to cartoon women, you can do a lot worse than Betty Rubble.

Jodie stops typing, looks round quizzically. Then the hint of a smile. Says, See, that's why I let you in my bedroom, Oats, you're a classy guy.

He says, Betty doesn't have mind powers but she can cook.

You're funny. Fun-nee. Better hope Barney doesn't find out.

Scott says, trying hard to keep a straight face, I don't think Barney satisfies her.

There's a strange look in her eyes: a cautious relief. As though this is somehow going better than she'd hoped.

The computer beeps. Scott sees the familiar text appear on the screen:

You wake suddenly.

Okay, Jodie says.

Are you going to tell me why I can't win now?

Yep, she says. You can't win cos it's not a game.

Scott shifts to the end of the bed, where he can see the monitor more easily. He says, So what is it?

Took me forever to work it out, she says, with grudging admiration. The version you've got? I found that all over the place. You can download it, stick it on a disk, pass it round at school. Which is how you got hold of it. But that's not the actual program. Not even close. It fits on a disk because it's the chopped-down lobotomised version of the real thing. *That's* why you die in two days, no matter what; because there's no memory available to hold more than two days' worth of data. So the lobotomised version has some parameters that've been altered, to make sure you never get beyond day two. The big one is the radiation sickness, which is basically overclocked like crazy so you can't avoid dying of it. In the original program it's geared much more slowly, in real time actually, so you can get a lot further. I mean a *lot* further.

You found the original program? Scott says.

She nods at the screen. Running it now, she says. Well, kind of. That's another thing. What I'm running is just the front end. Most of this is actually somewhere else.

What do you mean, somewhere else? Scott says. Where?

I don't know. Some ARPANET mainframe probably. I got suspicious because when I first tried playing it, it was super slow, sometimes there was tons of delay between me typing something and it responding. Not like on your Amstrad. I thought it was bugged or something so I did an interrupt and took a look at the code and it turns out the delay was all packet lag. There's hardly anything running locally. All this computer is doing is a bit of basic input handling, then a big whack of communications stuff that sends your responses off over the modem to the main program, which is sitting somewhere else. But whatever that main program is, it can handle seriously complex input. Makes my shrink program look utterly retarded.

Why do it like that? Scott says, struggling a little to follow. Why not just let people run it themselves?

Well. Two reasons, I think. First, I reckon it takes a pretty hefty machine to run the core program, and you can't guarantee what firepower people have got, right? I mean, you've got Baby's First Computer and okay, that can run the lobotomised version, but no way could it handle the real deal, even if you added a hard drive and memory and everything. The CPU's just too primitive. Mine too, in fact, and mine's actually, you know, good. So the core sits on a minicomputer or a mainframe somewhere, and just the front end comms stuff gets handed out to the user. More efficient that way.

Okay, I get it, Scott says, though he's not entirely sure he does. What's the other reason?

I think it has to be centralised in order to collate all the players.

Scott says, There's more than one player?

Oh yeah.

How many?

I'm not even sure there's a limit. It varies. I can't get access to the mainframe so I can't tell how many people are dialled in. But I walked for a couple of hours last night and I saw about twenty or thirty people. I spoke to a couple of them, too.

You can *speak* to them? Scott says incredulously.

She's grinning now. Yeah, she says. You can speak to

them, try to help each other, share food, whatever you want. The program keeps track of all of it, in real time.

So what do you all do? Do you compete for some kind of leaderboard or something?

Jodie shakes her head. You're not listening, she says. I told you, it's not a game.

What is it, then?

It's a simulation. It's old. From the 70s I think. But it's heavy duty. There's proper accurate modelling of the fallout, wind patterns, radiation sickness progression, all kinds of other vectors for injury and illness, dehydration, starvation. You can die all kinds of ways, believe me.

Why? Scott says. Why is it all about death?

Because that's what it's modelling. It's not called *Dispersal* because it's tracking the dispersal of radiation or fallout or anything like that. It's tracking the dispersal of people on the edge of the strike zone, trying to escape. The patterns they make as they run. Where do they go, what do they do? Most importantly, where do they die? That's what it's mapping. It's a military sim.

Fucking hell, Scott says quietly.

I think maybe what happened was, some general or some government guy said, We need to know where people are going to end up after this. So we can, you know, put the hospitals and the triage centres and the mass graves in the right places. Cos you'd need to know that, right?

Yeah, Scott says. I, uh. Yeah. If there's just bodies piling up in the streets, then you have disease as well, so...

So it's a valid thing for them to want to know. They have computer models for how radiation disperses and how fallout drifts and all that stuff. But people aren't clouds of fallout or rays of radiation, they're humans. They're irrational. How are you supposed to model human behaviour on a computer, mathematically? Especially human behaviour in a crisis which no-one's experienced. There's no computer that can do that. So what I think happened was, someone thought outside the box and said, Okay, we can't make computer models of humans. So let's use real humans instead. Use the computer to simulate the environment, then let people experience it in real time and see what they do. Write it well, make the text emotive and scary and, you know, convincing. So they start to believe almost. Basically, make them imagine that it's actually happened, and see what they decide to do, how they try to survive, where they decide to go. And then the program will keep count of how and when and where they die. And that lets you know where to, you know. Bulldoze the pits for the corpses. Or whatever.

Scott nods slowly. He stares at the winking cursor on the IBM screen.

What do you want to do now?

He says, If it's military, then whoever programmed it knew about the radiation and how it would work. I mean, it'll be accurate. So it can do its job properly, map what happens properly. Right?

Jodie nods. That's the idea, she says.

So. Can you beat it? Can you get away? Or do you still always die, just – you know. Further out. Later on.

You're still trying to win the game? she says.

Scott shakes his head impatiently. No, he says. What I'm asking is, did *they* think – the people who made this, the people who *know* this shit – did they think anyone could actually survive?

She meets his eyes evenly. Says, I don't know. I think you'd have to play it for days and days, over and over. And maybe you'd still never find out. I mean, I can ask around on the boards. Find out if anyone's ever, you know.

Yeah, Scott says. Okay. He realises he feels numb.

So, she says after a moment. Do you want to – ?

She indicates the computer: pushes her chair back a bit, to make room for him at the keyboard.

No, he says. No, it's okay. Maybe, uh. Maybe another time. Anyway, it's nearly seven. Your mum'll be home soon.

They leave the house together in silence.

She crouches in the middle of the path, looking carefully around. Scott walks on ahead. She traces one finger through the grit, drawing a little groove with levees of mica, schist, sand; making a circle around a single brittle ant body, crisp in the evening sun. Says, What the fuck?

Scott is some way away, off the track. He says, This one's dead.

Jodie comes over, scrambling the bank and padding onto the carpet of pine debris. In the dim half-light of the trees she examines the stunted nest, its surface unmoving. Scott takes a stick and disturbs the mound a little: a small avalanche of pine needles, but nothing emerges.

So the other guys won?

Looks like it.

They clamber back; cross to the other side of the path. One of the trees here is leaning at an angle and the gap in the cover brings a thick shaft of sunlight down, hazy with dust. The second nest is just beside it. Scott goes down on his haunches and stares.

No, he says after a moment. This one's dead too.

Shit.

They're both quiet for a moment. Somewhere not too far away a magpie chatters angrily. Then Jodie says, You know, this is seriously fucking metaphorical.

Scott glances at her. He says, Yeah. It really is, isn't it?

Which ones were us and which were the Russians?

Scott shrugs. I spose those were the Russians, he says, pointing. Cos that way's East.

Jodie hugs her arms around her knees and stays still for a moment. She's no longer looking at the nest; her gaze is fixed on the yellow block of light, or maybe beyond it. Scott watches her: the small movements of her ribs as she breathes; the sharp points of her shoulder-blades sticking out; her dark eyebrows drawn close, frowning.

She gets up, moving around restlessly; there's a fallen branch, bone dry, and she puts her foot on it, cracks it in two. Says, We need a fucking plan, man.

A plan? Scott says.

For when it happens. We can't just wing it and hope. It's no good crawling from the fucking rubble and searching for survivors. We need to know what we're doing. We need to prepare.

He isn't sure – quite – if she's kidding. Being ironic. He says, with a half-smile, What kind of plan were you thinking?

She doesn't answer. She walks away among the trees a little way, feet scuffing through the pine needles. She puts out one hand and runs it over a tree trunk. Scott sees the hand clench suddenly into a fist against the bark. She shouts back at him, loudly, emphatically, We need – a fucking – *plan*.

8

He is finishing his breakfast. *The City and the Stars* nestles against the cereal bowl but he hasn't turned the page in ten minutes or more. On the television, there are more reports about the fallout from Chernobyl; but he's not listening.

In the hallway, the phone is ringing, on and on.

What does he have, actually *have*, except for comic books and sketch pads and science fiction and apocalypse stories?

Three weeks' wages from the gardening job, cash, saved in his desk drawer. Just over two hundred quid. That's something.

And knowledge. He knows stuff. What to expect. Symptoms and timings and what foods might stay safe and reduction in exposure per inch of concrete.

And they did that first-aid course at school. He can stop someone bleeding. He can make a tourniquet. He knows resuscitation.

It's not nothing.

The holiday job was his mother's idea. Last year's school reports kept returning to variations on a theme: Scott seems to be drifting. Lack of focus. Not engaged with the subject. Not fully committed, except in Art. His mother's thought was to find something substantial for him to work towards – to demonstrate the connection between application and reward.

And in the end he agreed. Oil paints, or a camera, or even a stereo.

And she went and spoke to someone she knew, who knew someone at the Centre, and he landed this gardening job, even though he's only fifteen and that's not really allowed.

Working towards a reward is good psychology, he supposes.

In the hall, the phone stops. The house falls silent. And then, insistently, the phone starts ringing again.

His father was home earlier, when Scott came downstairs; was making himself a cup of coffee. But he must have gone out, or surely he'd answer it?

The phone has kept ringing, on and off, these past few days; or weeks maybe.

Scott pushes his chair back and pads through to the hall and picks up. He says, Hello?

Jeremy?

Jeremy is his dad's name.

He says, It's Scott.

Oh – Scott. It's Caroline here. Caroline Fielder.

Scott doesn't know what to say for a moment. David and Caroline Fielder are friends of his parents, good friends; the kind who, in another family, might have ended up being called Uncle David and Aunty Caroline. David was at university with his mother, and they kept in touch. And since then, birthday presents every birthday, and visits of course, to and fro, and once – a long time ago now, back when he was perhaps nine – a shared holiday in the south of Spain, outside Granada, where the adults sat drinking red wine behind the villa they'd rented and talking about Arabic poetry and the architecture of the Alhambra and research grants while Scott and Leah splashed about in a raised swimming-pool made of breeze blocks painted blue. Leah: another only child, blonde and academically precocious and a little spoiled, sometimes brattish. As the holiday wore on, Scott remembers finding more and more excuses to go off and play on his own.

But all the memories are of the two families, complete. Four adults, two children. He can't, for several uncertain seconds, work out how to fit the remaining pieces together into this new, current, picture.

Scott? Are you there?

He says, Yeah. Dad's – I don't think Dad's at home. I think he's gone out. Do you want him to call you?

Sweetheart – how are you? Are you okay?

Scott says, Yeah. I'm okay. And then, inconsequentially: I'm kind of tired. I got a holiday job. I'm doing gardening for this place, cutting the grass and hedges and stuff, so... it's a lot of work, but...

That sounds nice, though. Being outside.

Yeah.

I haven't seen you in such a long time.

Scott feels a panic rising in him. He says, Yeah, I know.

I wish –

He says, without thinking, You should come round. You know. I could make something. Cook something I mean. Dad would like that.

What?

For dinner. It would be nice. I could cook something. I cook now. What do you think?

The words coming in a rush.

And silence down the line, for the longest time.

Scott says, again, his voice uncertain and constricted, What do you think?

She cards her way in through the side entrance, which is neither the main one on the public road nor the back one that Scott uses to get to the gardening sheds. This gate is used mainly for deliveries: replacement parts for the machines, supplies of data tape for the tape storage drives, even the daily postal deliveries and collections, which are handled by the same personnel who do them for Sandhurst.

The gate's not the one nearest her house – that, as for Scott, is the maintenance gate – but she doesn't want to risk meeting him. She wants this to be a surprise.

Once in the grounds, she loops her way to the automatic doors that lead to the staff cafeteria and the space designated Lobby B. She cards in here, too. One of the programmers she knows – a guy called Fletch, one of the American team – is coming from the cafeteria with a tray on which are clustered eight or nine mugs of coffee.

Hey Jodie, he says.

How much caffeine do you people need? she says.

All the caffeine. The secret is to let it sit for a good three, four hours, to get that nicely stewed flavour.

Have you seen my dad? she says.

He's in Main Dev. We're about to start the weekly shit-list, but we'll be done by eleven. Maybe.

Okay, she says.

When you see him, tell him to give me a raise, Fletch says.

Give me time on the mainframe, she says sourly.

Never happening, kid. Have fun, he says, juggling the tray awkwardly while he lets himself into Main Development.

Jodie smiles slightly. She goes along past the secretarial area and into the corridor where the admin offices are. Her dad's is at the end. It's locked. (Because of Main Dev. Because of the shit-list.)

She finds Molly and asks to be let in. Says, I think I left a tape in there.

Molly lets her in and goes back to her desk.

Jodie leaves the door standing wide like she's not bothered at all. She goes straight over to the big cupboard with the drawers under it; and opens the third drawer; and takes the radiation rock from its little cardboard box. It is small; heavy; one side roughly granular and gritty, the other translucently faceted, pocked and crazed like badly-fired ceramic. Jodie holds it up to the light from her dad's window and the interior flares with an irregular, fractured green glow.

She slips it into her bag, closes the drawer, pops the tape out of her Walkman, and walks back out to Molly, brandishing the tape triumphantly.

Cheers, she says.

You're welcome, Molly says, and goes to lock up behind her.

It's that simple.

The chainsaw won't start, and they need it to take down a dead fir tree overhanging the corner of the car park. Colin brings it back inside the mower shed and sets it on the workbench. He checks the fuel line, the choke, the spark gap, muttering to himself as he works. When he drags the starter there's still nothing. Colin says, Fucking thing. Hand me that, will you? No, the other one.

Scott says, What's wrong with it?

Needs easing, Colin says, unscrewing the air filter and squirting starter fluid into the carb. You want to watch yourself, cos too much of this and it'll blow back like a cunt, pardon my French.

This time there's a loud bark and a dense guff of blue smoke and the chainsaw judders to life. A second later the smoke alarm in the shed ceiling goes off.

A sharp unhappy look almost of panic crosses Colin's face: he kills the chainsaw abruptly, dumps it on the bench, and shuffles fast to a grubby tan telephone on the wall which at the same moment starts to ring loudly. Colin picks up and says, Hello? Yeah, gardening block. It's nothing. It's just engine smoke, we're fine.

Then a pause, and then, Oh for fuck's sake, really? Can't you tell them to cancel it?

Then another pause, and then, Well. I'll put the kettle on, then.

He hangs up; rubs his neck for a moment. Scott says, Is everything all right?

Can you rinse them mugs out? We're going to have company.

Scott rinses out the tannin-stained mugs and Colin puts the kettle on; and before the water has boiled they can hear sirens, getting rapidly closer. Scott goes to the door while Colin methodically counts out tea-bags.

Three fire engines heel round the corner of the Centre from the direction of the side gate, jolt up the kerb and come jouncing across the lawn to the mower shed, fanning out, sirens blaring and lights flashing; and from the Centre itself, surreal in the hot yellow afternoon sunlight, two hazmat-suited figures with oxygen tanks on their backs and blankly mirrored helmet visors approach steadily down the slope like spacemen in a 60s B movie.

Colin mutters to Scott, Welcome to the fucking circus.

Scott passes round the tea to the fire crew.

The lead fireman radios back to base, confirming a false alarm. The men in the hazmat suits do the same, and then pull their helmets off and uncouple the oxygen cylinders and set them in the shade and sit down. No-one seems in any rush to go anywhere now and no-one seems particularly bothered about the mistake with the chainsaw. In fact, Scott gets the sense that perhaps this isn't entirely unwelcome: a break in routine, a chance for the crews to ditch some air-conditioned ready room and stretch their legs in the sunshine a while. Colin stares a little wryly at the ruts the fire engines have carved in his lawn.

The men sit around talking and joking and sometimes laughing, and the fire engines tick quietly, and Scott watches through the grimy cobwebbed window from inside the shed and wonders what exactly he is doing here.

By the time everyone has left – slowly, more carefully this time, but they still tear some more turf up on their way back to the road – it's too late to tackle the dead fir. Scott helps Colin to put the tools away. As they're shutting the shed up he asks, Why did they send three fire engines, just like that? And the men with masks?

Colin nods towards the Centre and says, There's all kinds in there.

All kinds?

I dunno. Chemicals and radioactive and who knows what.

I thought it was just computers.

It's computers *and* it's all kinds. So if the alarm goes off they don't piss about, they send the lot, automatic. You can't even phone and stop it, they just come.

Scott says, Right.

Colin walks over and nudges one of the tyre ruts with his toe. Says, These're going to have to be filled in and reseeded and gone over and rolled. We can start that tomorrow. Slow fucking job that'll be.

Scott says, I – I can't come tomorrow.

Colin says, Oh?

Scott says, Actually, I can't come any more. Not after today.

Colin says, again, Oh? And then: I thought you were going to do the whole summer.

I know. But.

What happened to staying power? A lot of kids would give their left bollock for a job like this.

Sorry. It's... it's stuff at home.

Colin looks at him narrowly. He says, You should've told me before.

I know, Scott says. Sorry.

If I'd known it was your last day, I was going to get you something.

Scott, surprised, says, Well. I got fire engines.

Colin snorts. He goes back to the shed, unlocks the door, and disappears inside for a while. When he comes out he hands something to Scott. It's a clasp-knife with a wooden handle and a carefully-honed five-inch blade. It looks old; like it might have been Colin's when he was young. Colin says, You can have that. Don't fucking cut yourself.

Scott opens the knife and touches the edge gently and then closes it. He says, I won't. It's really cool. Thanks.

When the gamma bomb goes off, the next panel renders Bruce Banner's figure in a series of ink-line striations like shrapnel: staggering, caught on the edge of the protective trench but not yet in it; half-falling.

The caption reads

Dr Bruce Banner is bathed in the full force of the mysterious gamma rays.

The moment of change. The Hulk is born.

Cosmic radiation swamps the prototype spaceship carrying Reed Richards and his crew. Irradiated spider venom courses through Peter Parker's veins. The Children of the Atom. Nukla. Doctor Manhattan. Godzilla. Radiation changes all of them.

Sometimes he thinks of reworking the story. The six or seven panels when Banner is in the military hospital, where everything takes a lurch sideways, away from reality: just tear that page out and, instead, write the truth.

Dr Bruce Banner is bathed in the full force of the mysterious gamma rays.

Except the gamma rays are not mysterious. Their effects are well understood. Scott knows exactly what would happen.

Acute radiation sickness follows a progression. There are three more-or-less clearly defined stages. Prodromal. Latent. Overt.

The prodromal stage comes first, immediately after the radiation exposure. You experience headache and nausea, followed swiftly by vomiting, abdominal cramps, diarrhoea. It can last minutes or days. If the initial dose of radiation has been high, you'll also experience anxiety, confusion, loss of consciousness.

Then the initial symptoms subside. This is the latent stage. You feel better. Your health seems to stabilise or even improve. The latent stage can last from a few hours to – in some cases – several weeks.

But the apparent improvement is an illusion; a cruel trick. You feel better but your cells are dying. Progress to the third stage is invariable.

The final stage is the overt stage, sometimes called the manifest illness stage. How exactly it progresses depends on the nature of the initial radiation dose. If you've been exposed to a concentrated dose of penetrating radiation across much or all of your body, the overt stage will take the form of central nervous system illness. You'll have tremors and convulsions, cardiovascular and cerebral failure; then fall into a coma. You'll die swiftly and inevitably: within two or three days at the most.

If you've had a lesser initial exposure, you'll suffer gastrointestinal illness instead of central nervous system illness. You'll have recurrent nausea and vomiting, resulting in electrolyte imbalance; intractable diarrhoea; blood plasma volume reduction; vascular collapse. You'll die through complications or infection.

An even lesser initial exposure, or a repeated series of small exposures, will result in bone marrow illness. Your lymph nodes will fail; your spleen and bone marrow will atrophy and your body won't be able to make blood cells properly. After three weeks, both antibodies and platelets will be severely reduced. You'll start to haemorrhage internally, especially in the bowels. Your skin will start to slough off and haemorrhage. You won't be able to fight off infection; and this, or complications from internal bleeding, is what will kill you.

Dr Banner has been exposed to a concentrated dose of penetrating radiation in a short, intense burst – the direct blast of a nuclear device. His will be brief prodromal and latent stages, lasting a matter of hours, before progressing briskly to the tremors, convulsions, coma, and death typical of central nervous system illness. The way the Hulk panels are paced, Scott thinks, you wouldn't need more than three pages; you could probably do it in a single spread.

He's on his way home, turning the clasp knife round in his hands, when he runs into Ewan and Chris, loitering just around the corner from Ewan's house. He knows both boys, sort of; Ewan was friends with Ward for a while, though they fell out in the end; and Chris's sister Kellie was in the youth drama group Scott used to go to. They look round as he approaches.

Hey, Ewan says. What've you got?

Scott hands him the knife.

That's fucking cool, Ewan says approvingly. Did you get it at the Surplus?

No. It was a present.

Nice. You could fuck someone up seriously with that, Ewan says.

He makes a few passes with the knife at Chris, who jumps back with a yelp: Fuck off, Ewan! Fucking psycho dickhead.

Nice, Ewan says again; and reluctantly passes the knife back to Scott. Hey, is it true you got in a fight with Ollie and Jay Slater?

Not sure I'd call it a fight, Scott says wryly. I got beaten up by Ollie and Jay Slater is more like it.

That's not on, Chris says. Two against one isn't on, plus they're older than you. Cowards.

It's on now, Ewan says, indicating the knife. Scotty just evened it up. Jay fucking Slater should try it now. He'd probably piss himself if you pulled a knife on him.

Chris shrugs. So would you, he says. Come on.

Yeah, but the difference is, Jay Slater's a cunt, Ewan says seriously.

Scott finds himself grinning. He says, What're you guys doing out here anyway?

Ewan glances around. He says, Kellie's been invited to a party. Susan Lewis's birthday party. It's on Saturday. A lot of the girls are going. And she says Susan's up for inviting pretty much anyone, okay?

Okay, Scott says a little blankly.

Well. Susan Lewis's house backs on to Aston's place, right?

So?

Ewan glances around again, even though the road is deserted. He lowers his voice, too, conspiratorially, so that Scott has to lean in a little to hear him.

So, this weekend, Aston's parents are away. He's got his house to himself. The plan is, score yourself an invite to Susan's birthday. That way it's all legit, okay? Your parents can call her parents and, yes, sure, it's all fine.

He stops suddenly: his eyes dart at Scott. A moment's uncertainty.

Scott knows why. Because he said *your parents.*

Okay, he says briskly. I get it. And then what?

Well, man, that's the classic part, Ewan says, obvious

relief in his voice. Because then you just slip away. Through the hedge at the back of Susan's garden. Slip slip away to the *real* party. It's going to be fucking *radical.*

And Aston's okay with this? Scott says, in mild disbelief. He knows Aston: an awkward, intense seventeen-year-old who's into D&D in a big way, and who Scott would never have imagined suddenly having the urge to open his house up to unlimited drunk teenagers.

Chris sniggers. I don't think it really matters whether Aston's okay with it or not, he says. It's all over the Heights now. It's *happening.*

Scott shakes his head. Well, cheers for the heads-up, he says.

Get yourself invited to Susan's birthday, Ewan says. That's the key element. That's central, okay?

Got it, Scott says. Anyway, see you.

He's a few paces down the track when Ewan calls after him, Hey, Scott.

Scott turns. Yeah?

You were on the London Road, right? Near the stamp place. Couple of days ago.

Scott nods. Yeah, he says. I was going to the Music Box.

Was that Jodie *Armitage* with you?

Scott blinks. He says, Uh, yeah, actually. Yeah.

What the fuck, man? The freakshow? How come? Do you know her or something?

Scott hesitates.

He says, I don't know her. She was just there.

. . .

He comes into the kitchen, leaves the door standing open, goes to the fridge. He hears footsteps in the hall and his father's voice: Scott?

Yeah, it's me, he calls back.

His father comes into the kitchen. He looks agitated; distressed. Scott closes the fridge and steps instinctively towards him. Dad? Are you okay?

Did you talk to Caroline?

Scott nods. Yeah. Yeah, she called, and I... I spoke to her.

Did you invite her here?

Yeah.

He sees the same flash of dismayed panic fleet across his father's face that he saw on Colin's when the smoke alarms in the mower shed went off.

Why did you do that?

Scott says, You weren't here.

You should have waited until I was back and asked me then.

She was on the phone, Dad. What was I supposed to say? Besides.

Besides?

They're your friends. Don't you want to see them?

Silence for a moment. His father doesn't reply. Scott doesn't know what to do.

Finally his father says, in a low, worried voice, I wish you'd asked me, that's all.

It's David and Caroline, Dad.

Silence again. Scott is out of his depth. This is all wrong.

He says, I thought it would be a good thing.

And, after a moment, again, They're your friends.

His father stares past Scott at the kitchen door and the patchy dapple of afternoon light in the garden. Scott sees his own confused pain written just as clearly in his father's face.

What frightens her most is not death so much as the grey death of spirit. The way the adult murders the child they used to be. If she lives to be twenty – thirty – forty – will there be anything left of her at all?

You continue west.

It is dark and there are no longer any gaps in the clouds. The only light comes from your torch beam, fanned out in front of you, glittering on the desert sand. The only sounds now are the wind howling between the rocks and the crunch of your footsteps.

You have seen no other living human beings since leaving the highway.

Your feet are bleeding. The uncontrollable trembling in your hands and jaw has passed but you feel nauseous and lightheaded and the desert air tastes bitter in your mouth.

In your backpack you have:

2 pints water

1 can opener

1 can pork and beans

4 packs potassium iodide tablets

2 sealed sterile hypodermic syringes

4 ampoules diethylenetriamine pentaacetic acid

1 copy On the Road *by Jack Kerouac*

What do you want to do now?

. . .

Later that evening there is the trudge of footsteps coming up the attic stairs. The door is open to try to get some air moving through the room. The footsteps stop. Scott, pushing his chair back from the desk, looks round to see his father hesitating at the threshold.

May I come in?

Course.

His dad walks over to the desk; says, What are you doing?

Scott turns the paper slightly to show him. A series of small, quick uninked pencil sketches covers the page: two figures struggling in a wood, a dark mass of trees crowding around them, one figure on the ground, the same scene repeated from different angles and perspectives, close to, further away, above as if looking down, ground level and strangely exaggerated, the prone figure reminiscent now of the tethered Gulliver, as if seen from an insect's point of view.

His dad seems to hunt for something to say. After a moment: Gosh, there's a lot of – movement, and energy, isn't there? You've captured the sense of movement, I should think.

I should think tacked on there almost unconsciously, qualifying the statement, because really, Scott knows, his father's not certain: in fact his father is hopeless with this kind of thing. He feels a small bloom of affection; says, playing his part, You're not working this evening?

Oh – I should probably get back to it. But – I wanted to

say that it's all right that you invited Caroline. You were quite right. I shouldn't have... Anyway. I'm sorry.

It's fine. It's – don't worry about it.

His father smiles very slightly. He taps the drawing with his finger and says, A lot of movement. That's good.

Then he squeezes Scott's shoulder quickly and goes back out the door and softly away down the stairs.

9

Out on the heath the heather and furze are crisp and tinder-dry; Scott's footsteps, ahead of her, kick up little gritty puffs of dust from the track. Earlier, on the wider path, they could walk side by side, but now it has to be single file. They walk steadily; he appears to know exactly where he's going.

Once she sees an adder curled under a gorse bush: she touches Scott's arm and they both stop, watching the snake for a long minute, until at last it flicks its tongue, smoothly unwinds itself, and slips away into the roots. Once Scott points out bullet cases strewn by a hummock of grasses – a place where the training soldiers have laid down covering fire or perhaps set an ambush. Once there are some torn and crumpled pages of a porno magazine beside the path. Scott looks quickly away – pretending interest in something on the horizon – but a deep uncontrollable flush rises over his neck as they go past. Jodie slows, staring for a moment in frank curiosity. She's hardly ever seen any porn, only Page 3 really; never anything hardcore.

The woman in the picture is wearing a Girl Guides uniform, open to show her breasts.

The man's penis looks unpleasant.

She realises that she's pleased Scott is embarrassed.

They walk on in silence for a minute, but it's not the same easy silence as before, when they saw the adder; they are no longer comfortable with each other.

Anderson would know what he's thinking.

The land has been trending slowly upwards, and now the track reaches the break point: there is a ragged bank, below which the ground drops away steeply, the track deepening into a narrow, winding gully. The gorse and broom bushes are much thicker here, freckled with bright yellow flowers, growing densely and tall and shading down into stands of trees; and the underlying land follows a series of uneven crests and furrows right on until the pine forest starts in earnest.

Scott says, a little out of breath, Want to stop for a bit?

Yeah, she says.

They scramble down to where a section of bank at the edge of the gully has given way, leaving bright bare sand below the matted grass roots and a tumble of clods half-blocking the way forward, and sit on the lip with their legs dangling. There is coarse scrub-grass under them. Scott picks at pebbles in the exposed sand. He glances at her; the blush comes back, and he looks away.

Jodie says, after a moment, I didn't know the Guides had a badge for that.

Surprise on his face. Then half a grin: still awkward but laughing too, and relieved to be laughing. He says, Yeah. Sorry.

Why are you sorry? It wasn't yours, was it?

No.

Well then.

She slings her bag into her lap and takes out a thick, uneven wedge of bread, some cheese wrapped in foil, and a pack of Hubba Bubba. Scott says, sounding impressed, You brought lunch?

I thought we could be like Topsy and Tim.

She unwraps the gum and gives half to Scott. Scott takes a sharp-looking clasp knife from his pocket and cuts the bread in half. Jodie watches his movements: neat and precise and curiously satisfying; and in the faintly humming air the sound of the crust parting is crisply audible. They eat their pieces of bread in silence, watching butterflies looping erratically around the bushes.

She wonders what Scott's penis looks like. Whether it would look less unpleasant.

The thing of putting it in your mouth, like in the picture, makes her feel a little panic-stricken.

She puts the thought away. Says, Got something to show you.

Yeah?

Yeah. Here.

She digs in the bag, finds the radiation rock, and hands it to Scott. Says, There you go.

What is it?

You tell me.

He doesn't reply at once. She watches him from the corner of her eye as he turns it this way and that, staring into the grey-green depth of it. He holds it to the light.

Jodie says, You can do twenty questions if you like. Only yes or no.

Okay, Scott says.

Go on then.

He smiles slightly and says, Is it volcanic glass?

No.

The smile vanishes.

Jodie, delighted, says, Ha! You thought you'd got it in one. Such a clever little geologist.

He says, frowning, Is it some kind of glass at least?

Yes.

Is it really old? Like millions of years old?

No.

Did it come from a lightning strike on a beach?

No. That's four.

He opens his mouth to ask something else, and then stops; his expression alters. He says, Did it come from a desert?

Yes.

Did it come from America?

Yes.

From New Mexico.

Yes. You know what it is, don't you.

Yeah. I read about it somewhere. When they tested the first atom bomb in the desert, it melted the sand, turned it to glass. It's got a name, but...

Trinitite. Because it was the Trinity test site.

How did you get it?

It belongs to my dad. Someone on the hardware team gave it to him when he was over there.

Fucking hell, Scott whispers. Is it radioactive?

Yes. A bit. Not enough that anything's going to drop off, though. Just more than background.

Scott says, almost to himself, Maybe now we'll get superpowers.

Yeah.

You know when they did that test, the first atom bomb, there were a whole load of scientists who thought – I mean, who *really* thought – that there was a good chance it would ignite the atmosphere? Just send a wall of flame around the whole planet and wipe everything out. They actually worried about this. They thought it was possible.

But they went ahead and did it anyway, she says.

Yeah. Exactly.

He stays staring at the rock for a moment; and then suddenly his gaze darts straight from its green-grey depths to Jodie's eyes, as if he's been struck by a thought. He seems on the verge of saying something.

She says, What?

Nothing.

Tell me.

No – nothing. It's just... it's kind of beautiful.

I know.

He hands it back to her. Jodie puts it away in her bag. She says, Would it happen here, do you think?

What, on the heath?

Yeah.

Scott breaks a handful of sand off the side of the gully and crumbles it into powder. He says, I suppose so. If the bomb was close enough. But on the Trinity site, that was right under the blast. I don't think we'd be right under the blast here, unless they missed their target. They'd be going for Sandhurst mainly, I think. So all we'd really have to worry about is the pressure wave and the radiation and the fallout.

That's all?

Yeah.

All tickety-boo then.

He jumps down into the gully and says, Come and see.

Come and see what? Just fucking tell me. I showed you an actual radiation rock.

It's not far now.

He starts down the gully. Jodie scrambles down the bank and follows him. A couple of dozen yards and the ground flattens out into a tangled delta of overlapping watercourses, all bone dry, mallows and wild buddleia and pale straw-coloured grasses straggling up everywhere. There's a crowd of gorse and bramble bushes and, beyond them, the trees. Scott ducks off the path, threading his way between the tall gorse, following a narrow rabbit run; Jodie, following, mutters What the fuck, man.

Nearly there.

Sudden gloom as the pines blot out the sun and the temperature drops distinctly. Scott stops walking; turns back to her, a curious almost shy expression – half anticipation, half uncertainty – on his face. He steps aside slightly, pressing himself into the bushes to make way for her.

Jodie comes forward. There's a structure half-buried in

the scrubby undergrowth. Dull grey concrete angles, mottled with lichen; but at some point in the past there must have been a landslide of sorts in the hill above because the back part of it is covered over with a slumped mound of sand, its outline obscured by brambles, mallow, birch saplings, tangled clumps of sheep's fescue.

The concrete is low and blocky and obviously military. Most of it's deep in shadow, but one corner still catches the sunlight and Jodie puts her hand on it to feel the warmth. There's a narrow concrete apron extending a few feet out from it on which the larger plants can't get a foothold, so the exposed part stands in relative isolation. In the end wall is a narrow horizontal slit, perfectly dark.

They go silently together around to the far side. Here, a stubby projection extends out of the main block, a rectangular concrete tunnel with a low doorless opening facing them, a short passage, and a right-angled turn leading through a second aperture into the body of the structure itself.

Scott is beside her. Jodie looks at him quickly but neither of them seems to have anything to say. Silently she ducks into the short passage. Scott follows. Three paces in and she turns and crosses the threshold to the interior.

Inside, there's a dense bright bar of light from the horizontal opening, which she presumes must be a gun slit. The air in here smells cooler and almost mossy. They are in a small, rectangular chamber; and as Jodie's eyes adjust, she sees that in the far corner of the back wall there is a further doorway, showing black. She steps to it and peers through, but her eyes are still dotted with after-images of the harsh outdoor sunshine and it takes her a long while to realise that this is, in effect, the same room repeated: another small, rectangular space, only with no external access, and its slit window clogged by the landslide.

The whole bunker is a square block, maybe eight yards along each side, divided internally by a thick concrete wall into two rectangular spaces, plus the side entrance passage.

Scott steps in beside her. He has to crouch slightly.

She says, What was it?

He says, Army training. A gun emplacement. So, you know, one lot of guys defends it with machine guns and the other lot attacks. They do that kind of thing all the time. Over the other side of the heath there's two of these, only bigger and out in the open.

You think they're still using it?

No. You'd be able to tell. No-one's been here in years. I think they forgot it.

She says, unable to keep from sounding impressed, So how did you find it?

I don't know. I come out here a lot.

You have hidden fucking depths, Egg Boy. Really well hidden, but.

You said we needed a plan, Scott says.

Yeah.

So this could be the plan. What do you think?

You really think nobody knows?

If anyone came in, they'd scuff up the moss and the lichen outside the doorway. And I checked. Seriously. No-one knows.

Jodie says, That's not bad. That's... that's actually kind of awesome.

Their voices, in the cool darkness, sound close and strange.

Scott says, Do you want to go back out?

Yeah.

In the afternoon light she examines the bunker and its surroundings again. The overgrown snarl of brambles disguises it completely from anyone looking down from the hill; the gorse and broom bushes hide it from the gully, which isn't even a proper path in the first place. Scott's right. It's forgotten. Invisible.

She puts her hand on the warm concrete again and says, Would it work, do you think? I mean, is it good enough?

Scott says, with certainty, Yes.

10

Has anything ever actually happened?

The answer becomes more and more like a bad joke. Because the Kirtland accident is just the start.

She reads how, in 1974, a schoolteacher in a small town in the USSR can't help noticing how many of the children in her class have leukaemia. She starts asking questions. This is how she first hears of an incident which occurred seventeen years earlier, but which is – in many senses – still in progress; still unfolding.

The incident in question is an explosion in the nearby Chelyabinsk-40 plutonium processing plant. The explosion has happened still earlier, in 1957.

The same year, in fact, as the Kirtland incident in America.

The realisation stops Jodie cold. That date again, glowing unblinking on her computer screen. 1957.

It takes a moment before she continues reading about the schoolteacher and the sick kids.

Chelyabinsk-40 doesn't appear on any maps. Built after the Second World War to serve the Soviet nuclear weapons programme, its existence is a closely guarded secret, even though the local people know perfectly well that it's there.

The liquid nuclear waste from the site is first pumped into the Techa river. Then, later, underground storage chambers are constructed, with cooling systems and other safeguards. The cooling systems and safeguards fail in 1956, and nobody fixes them. The waste tanks are thick steel, sealed in layers of concrete, buried eight metres deep; that is deemed safeguard enough.

She keeps reading, drawn along. Who has written this? It seems to be some kind of a governmental report; but which government, to what purpose, she's not sure.

Whatever its origins, there is almost an inevitability to the information.

In 1957 a tipping point is reached. The waste storage system spontaneously detonates – shredding the steel tanks, erupting through the eight metres of soil, flicking a 160-ton concrete capping slab into the sky like a tossed coin. A radioactive plume pours out, spread by the wind, eventually casting its pall across twenty thousand square kilometres. Scientists will later call this the East-Ural Radioactive Trace.

(She looks this up. It still exists. It's a real thing.)

The surrounding area is evacuated, but the process happens slowly, and it happens late. In fact, it takes a week before anything is properly underway; a week during which black rain falls and people start to become sick. It is the most devastating nuclear accident the world has yet seen, although the world, properly speaking, doesn't know it yet, because everything is kept secret, kept hidden, denied.

Seventeen years later, in 1974, the small town where the woman is teaching falls within the East-Ural Radioactive Trace. Hence the leukaemia silently eating away at her class. Hence her increasing interest in the repercussions of nuclear weapons and nuclear power.

Hence, eventually, her change of career, from teacher to journalist.

Jodie checks the woman's name. Lyubov Kovalevskaya. She looks for recent articles by her, recent news about her.

She is, it seems, now under investigation by the KGB for having recently questioned the safety of the Chernobyl nuclear power plant.

Jodie reads, *The failures here will be repaid, repaid over the decades to come.*

She steps inside the Music Box. Out of the sunlight. Her heart beating so hard it hurts.

There are several people. She ignores them: keeps her head down, eyes on the floor.

She's gone alone. Fast. As quick as she can manage. She feels propelled by a strange, unfamiliar determination. Almost like gravity. Almost like she's falling.

Charlie is behind the counter and something loud is playing on the sound system. Jodie lifts her headphones off her ears.

She goes towards the pamphlets and fliers. She wants to

walk casually, to wander towards them, unconcerned. But in fact her steps feel jerky and nervous and not quite under her control.

Hiya, Charlie says, glancing over.

She sounds friendly. Maybe slightly amused. Jodie looks at her. Charlie is smiling: an easy, open smile.

Jodie says, Hi.

You're Scott's friend, yeah?

Jodie nods. The nod feels like a twitch. Why the fuck can't she just relax, like anyone else. Smile, like Charlie. Be normal for once.

One of the customers comes over with a record they want to buy. Jodie locks her gaze on the fanzines and posters and pamphlets.

There, right in front of her, is the new one Scott has drawn. A fanned-out cluster of nuclear warheads bristles out of the page, pointing right at you. He's done them with thick black shadows and heavily-inked outlines. Underneath in heavy capital letters, CRUISEWATCH NEEDS *YOU!*

Small text below that. Typed information.

She pulls one of the sheets from the rack: holding it.

The customer is leaving now. Charlie says, It's good, isn't it? He's fucking talented.

I know, Jodie says. And then, after a moment, What's CruiseWatch? Is it like CND?

Yeah, a bit. Kind of. You know they move the nukes around? From place to place. Station them in different places, go on manoeuvres, that kind of thing?

Jodie hasn't known this. But she says, Yeah. Sure.

Well these guys get in the way. Try to draw attention to

what's really happening, you know? Because it's all done in secret. At night. They don't want people to know. These things are rumbling around the roads while everyone's asleep. So CruiseWatch just... try to shine a light, basically. Fuck things up for Maggie and her missiles.

Jodie peers at the information on the flier. She can't make sense of it. Her heart's still beating too hard and the little words are dancing. She says, So do you know when they're going to move them?

Not yet. But we will. There's people who know people who know stuff. We get the word a few hours before it happens, and we just have to go.

Jodie looks at Charlie closely. You're part of it? she says.

Yeah. Absolutely.

Another customer comes over to the till, but they don't stay long; they're just saying goodbye.

Jodie says, Can I have this?

Of course you can, Charlie says, sounding surprised. That's what they're for. Take a bunch, give them to your friends, okay?

Jodie blinks. She finds herself staring at Charlie with genuine curiosity for the first time.

Charlie's easy smile falters; falls away. She says, a little uncertainly, Are you okay?

Jodie nods. She lets out a breath; looks around the shop. The other people have left. It's just her and Charlie now.

She doesn't really understand why she's come back here. She's not making sense to herself any more.

She understands Anderson. *A monster dwells within her.* But there's no monster in Charlie.

She wonders if all she's really doing here is looking for permission to hate her.

She says, Why do you do it?

Do what?

Try to stop the missiles.

Because they're evil. Nobody should be able to press a button and destroy the world.

Yeah. I don't mean that. I mean you. Why do *you* do it. I know why Scott does it. But you're not scared. So why?

Charlie hesitates. It's just wrong, she says. It's – all of it. It's keeping people in their place, and making sure they don't think too hard, or making them always think about who's their enemy maybe. You said Scott's afraid and that's it, that's what they do. Scare everyone so they shut up. Scare everyone so you can make money. I mean – it's bullying really. It's just bullying and we let them get away with it. And we shouldn't.

Jodie runs her fingertip along the edge of the paper. She says, Yeah, I bet you get bullied all the time.

She can hear the scorn in her voice.

Charlie doesn't reply. After a moment, Jodie forces herself to look up: meet her eyes. To her astonishment, there's real, candid anger there.

Charlie says, steadily, Look, I don't know anything about you, okay? Except you're Scott's friend and I like Scott. He's cool. But when you first came in here I was sure you were going to nick something. I was waiting for it, to be honest.

Well I didn't, Jodie says.

Yeah. I got it wrong. So how about we both stop judging

people off of how they look when we don't know anything about them.

Jodie feels an unfamiliar heat rising in her. Shame, perhaps. She nods, just a little. She looks at the flier again: at Scott's drawing of the missiles. She says, I'll just take one, okay?

She walks out of the shop, back into the sunlight, folding the piece of paper in half, and then in half again, as she goes.

Sally was wearing a green anorak and jeans. She went with friends to the Beresford Arcade but left them later in the evening after an argument. One of the girls remembers her saying *I'm sick of you and I'm not coming back.* Forty-nine days later she's still missing. A message from her family, begging her to come home; another from the Kent police asking anyone who saw her that night, or saw anyone acting suspiciously near the town centre, to call.

Trent stole his stepfather's dirt bike, two hundred dollars in cash, and a Colt pistol his grandfather brought back from Vietnam. A patrolman found the dirt bike the next day, ditched to the side of Highway 149. Of the boy, there's no sign, and remains no sign, as days become weeks become months. His face is earnest, a little hollow around the eyes; he is fourteen but looks much younger.

Some of them must be taken, of course. And some must be found, eventually. And some must just give up and go back home.

But some must manage it. Manage to keep hiding. Change their names and their stories and become someone else. Or maybe just find some way to step off the world entirely and just – be gone.

Stupid thoughts. Of course that's not what happens. You don't get to step off the world, she knows that, it's just a story she tells herself, a *what if,* a daydream. The reality for most of these kids isn't going to be escape; it's going to be, at best, some kind of coercion or abuse or being in some way taken advantage of, being used, in a world suddenly without family or friends or anyone to help them or to lean on. At worst – well, she's read the message boards. She knows what some people want.

But she keeps reading anyway, because once she's started she can't stop, can't look away.

Sometimes it feels like drowning. Or (because precision is important, you're supposed to be precise) it feels like what she imagines drowning must feel like.

Their conversations across the dinner table.

The way her mother's face shifts between the expression she has when she believes she's alone to the expression she has when she is aware of company: the way the shift has become slower, more of an obvious effort: as if the mask is getting too heavy to lift into place. Or as if she is simply too tired to care what gets seen any more.

The way, sometimes, her father looks at Jodie with such a piercing clarity of disappointment that she can hardly believe he's not aware of it, that it's not deliberate, that it's not a conscious assault.

And everything becomes thick with fog; and dark; and the water closes over her and pulls her down; and she can't find her breath any more.

One day her heart will stop right there at the kitchen table while her father talks and talks, unchallenged, and her mother stares past him into the garden, and when they pump her out in the autopsy they'll find her lungs full of cold black water.

When the blade licks at her skin, and slips through, and the pain is brilliant and hot as a wire, and beads of blood pop out bright and vivid, then there's no fog at all: everything is crystalline and present and sharp enough to taste right in your mouth. The blade slips along with an eagerness that frightens and amazes her, the flesh parting, parting, and the pain that wells with it is awful and sickening and she can't leave it alone.

The ritual, from taking the little packet of blades from its hiding-place right through to rinsing out her flannel in the sink, watching the brownish stain swirl away, is as familiar now as a friend.

(Or, because precision is important, as familiar as she imagines a friend would be.)

When it's done she hides the blades away; hides her body away; carries the aching throb of the cuts with her over days, a week or more, depending on how deep she's made them; black clothes so even if the blood comes through again nothing will show. And gradually they scab and heal, livid at first but then fading, easing, finally changed to gleaming white scars the colour of silver birch bark or the moon, paler than her skin, pale as paper; against which the next time's blood surges – carmine, astonishing, incomprehensible, wonderfully strong.

11

The London Road swelters: in the middle distance the surface trembles and shimmers crazily with heat-haze into which traffic recedes blurrily. Scott trudges past the frontages, sweating, with more than two hundred pounds in his jeans pocket. The print and photocopying shop is running an offer on business cards. The yellow cellophane that covers the stamp shop window is reflecting a weird amber glow onto the pavement outside. From the other side of the road there's a big throaty roar of engines and three Harleys pull out from beside the biker bar. From the open door of the Music Box, he can hear blues playing.

He thinks for a moment, a little ruefully, about the stereo. Then opens the door to the army surplus place.

Inside, in the dim canvas-smelling air, he takes his time, checking the prices. Some of the items are on sale, so it's worth looking carefully. He starts with a big drab-coloured backpack and starts to weigh it down with supplies: two lightweight two-season sleeping bags; a camping stove and extra gas cylinders; a set of mess tins; a battery lantern; water purification tablets; potassium iodide solution. When it's full he can barely lift it. He lugs it two-handed over to the till, sets it down, and starts unpacking the contents onto the countertop. A scrawny-looking guy wearing a ghillie jacket over his T-shirt walks over from the air-rifles and goes behind the counter.

Uh, hi, Scott says. Do you sell Geiger counters?

The scrawny guy shakes his head; says, We used to. Now, all the ones they're making are going straight to armed forces. Well, them and government. They're taking the lot. So there's nothing coming onto the market. Anyway, they cost a lot more than a backpack, my friend.

Scott says, Oh. Okay.

Shows you just how worried they are. Right now you can probably get an anti-tank launcher easier than a Geiger counter.

He casts a fresh glance over the purchases Scott's laying out on the counter and says, So this isn't a camping trip, then? You're getting ready?

Yeah.

Should've known it from the iodine. Sensible lad. You think it's coming?

Scott nods.

The man says, Yeah. Me too. You need a knife?

There are heavy, black-steel Commando knives with serrated back edges lined up under the counter. Scott eyes them wistfully; but he's low on money now. He says, No thanks. I've got one.

Once he's paid he stows everything back into the pack, hoists it onto his shoulders and goes back out into the glaring white sun; slogs down the alleyway between the side of the cinema and a plumbing supplies place, doglegs his way through the loading bay at the back of Dixons, and comes out in the pedestrian part of the town centre.

In Boots he goes to the medicines section and picks out a small all-in-one first-aid kit; half a dozen tubes of burn relief cream; rolls of bandages and sterile gauze and surgical tape. By now the canvas straps of the backpack are beginning to cut into his shoulders. His movements are clumsy and lumbering and he feels out of place, like everyone must be watching him.

In front of the display of Durex packets he stops abruptly. A small hot clenched feeling takes hold.

There are all sorts of packs, different colours. He has no idea what the difference is. He's never bought condoms.

Perhaps there are different sizes?

This is stupid.

They're not going to fuck or anything. How would that happen? It's not like she's his girlfriend.

And he ought to be getting back now anyway.

His feet don't move.

They put the supplies Scott's bought inside the bunker, setting them neatly in the back room, working by torchlight. The sleeping bags. The cooking stove. The gas cylinders. A little line of basic survival equipment. Now they need food. Water. Lots of it. More medicines. Batteries and lanterns. The list of things they realise they don't have gets longer and longer the more they think. Scott writes it all down, neatly and methodically, in a little pocket sketchpad.

They go out through the low concrete passage, into the afternoon; stand there for a moment. Jodie puts the torch away in her bag and Scott puts the pad with the list in his back pocket. He leans against the warm concrete and closes his eyes, letting the heat seep into him.

Maybe I should've worked another week, he says. We need a shitload of stuff.

I've got some pocket money, she says. Don't worry.

Okay.

He's quiet for a moment. There's something he wants to ask – has been wanting to ask right from the start. But it never seems like the right time.

Now doesn't feel like the right time either, but he still says, almost without intending to, Why did you do it? If it wasn't – you know. Wanting to die.

He opens his eyes. Her shoulders are hunched. She obviously knows exactly what he's talking about. She says, the familiar spiky edge back in her voice, I don't know. Why do you care?

I keep thinking about it.

Well stop.

He says, awkwardly, I can't.

She doesn't reply.

Scott steps away from the concrete, scuffs his foot through the weeds. He says, Sorry.

Jodie seems to make an effort: says, in a steady voice, I really *don't* know, okay? I'm not just saying it. Sometimes I do things and I don't know why. Only nobody understands that. Because everything has a reason. Everything happens *because*. If you say you don't know, people don't believe you; and if you keep saying it, they just get angry. But it's the truth. I don't know.

Scott says, No, I get it.

You don't, though. You can't get it unless it happens to you. So you don't get it. Nobody gets it.

It does happen to me, he says quietly.

She gives him a look of flat contemptuous disbelief and says, You cut yourself?

No. Other things.

What things?

He's nettled by the suspicion in her voice. He says, Maybe you wouldn't understand.

Her face softens a little. She says again, but less harshly this time, What things?

I wake up.

She's staring at him: no longer sceptically. Just waiting.

He says, I wake up in the kitchen. In the hallway. Outside in the road sometimes.

What, sleepwalking?

He nods.

Since when?

Since – you know.

Fuck.

Yeah.

You don't know it's happening?

Of course I don't. Not till I wake up. One time I was in the garden. Once I was in the car. I'd taken the keys and unlocked it and I was sitting in it.

Fuck, Jodie says again.

Both of them are quiet for a moment. Then she says, That's different though.

He nods. Yeah, I know. But – it's not completely different.

It's different. You can't help it. It's not a choice for you.

There is something indefinably wrong; just out of reach; something about what she's just said. Scott frowns – about to reply – then stops. In his head the words replay.

She looks away from him; she seems to shrink into herself a little.

He says, Did you do it again?

There are bees humming through the gorse flowers, just beside his head.

He says, More than once?

Jodie's eyes meet his. Grey and green; uncertain; afraid.

But not on her wrists. The scars there were old, as white as paper. He says, quietly, Where?

She reaches down and puts her hands, hesitantly, on the insides of her thighs; left and right; just below the crotch of her jeans.

When he looks back at her face he sees with dismay that her eyes are bright with tears.

She says, low and uneven, sounding absurdly like a child: Don't tell.

While Scott goes into town with her pocket-money for supplies they can't scavenge, Jodie combs her house, methodically, carefully, for things that won't be missed. Tins of soup, tins of spaghetti hoops, tins of beans, peach segments, fruit cocktail: pulled dusty from the backs of cupboards and now knocking heavily against each other in an old school duffel-bag.

And Valium, in ones and twos; never enough to notice.

So that's good.

And the place Scott's found is great: brilliant, really. The walls are thick and solid and Scott knows exactly how much concrete you need to stop radiation; he says it'll work, and she believes him. They block the open gun-slit with rocks, gathering them and stacking them and packing the gaps with sand until it's solid. One afternoon, they trek over to the unofficial rubbish-tip next to the Flats, where they use a length of metal to lever the lid off a chest freezer, snapping its hinges. It takes them two hours to lug the thing across the heath, sweating like crazy, but once they get it there, it's perfect: it fits across the entry door to the bunker neatly, and they find a way to hold it in place with a line of rocks, sliding it awkwardly to one side when they need to come and go. Scott's confident that the rubber lip will help prevent fallout from drifting in.

So. The shelter is good.

The problem is timing.

She's spotted a flaw, one that she thinks Scott – despite all his depth of imagination – hasn't seen; and which she hasn't told him.

Because what should happen is: the warning. Getting to the shelter. The bombs falling. And you're safe.

But what actually will happen, most likely, if it's a first

strike, if there's no build-up, if it really does come out of nowhere – they say out of a clear blue sky, which could be exactly what happens – well; if it happens like that, it will be: the warning, but too late. Then the bombs falling. And then getting to the shelter, some time later.

Because the shelter's more than four minutes away from the Heights, even if you run like fuck.

So that's less good. Much less good.

Scott thinks even if Sandhurst gets a direct hit, the initial blast wouldn't reach them here; so they'd be exposed, but not for long. It's the fallout that's the real concern, and the shelter would protect against that.

But still.

What if he's wrong? Or the nukes hit just a bit off target? Or they're bigger than everyone thinks? What if, running, they make it to the shelter but then start to die – horribly burned, with radiation cooking them from the inside?

She doesn't want to think it but someone has to.

In her parents' bathroom she opens the big, mirrored medicine cabinet. There's an open bottle of sleeping pills and two unopened ones behind it. She takes both the full bottles and rearranges all the other tubes and packets slightly to cover the gap.

One full bottle each would be enough. More than enough. In case they have to.

The condoms do fit, once Scott's worked out in the privacy of his bedroom how to roll them on. They have a little teat at the end that you're supposed to pinch flat, and some sort of slippery stuff on them. In fact, the whole thing feels pretty good, slick and unfamiliar and kind of exciting.

He thinks of the magazine pages on the heath. The first picture of a blow-job he's seen, even though it was only a hasty, startled glimpse. But still. A real blow-job.

There's a bit in *The Naked Ape* about it: he has read the chapter on sex over and over. *The lips and tongue are also applied to many other areas of the partner's body.*

And Jodie's sharp sardonic voice saying, I didn't know the Guides had a badge for that.

Once contacted, the partner's genitals may also become the target for repeated actions of this kind.

And her feet kicking back and forth as they sit on the edge of the gully.

When this occurs, the male concentrates largely on the female's clitoris, the female on the male's penis.

It's not like she's his girlfriend. But.

The ridges on her wrist.

The nape of her neck in the sunshine.

Her mineral eyes meeting his, green flaring in their depths.

And he doubles up with a stifled gasp, the little flat teat instantly pulsing out into a bulb; twitching; a miniature heartbeat.

As they're leaving the heath late the next afternoon, both of them grimy with dust and sweat, he says suddenly, What are you doing on Friday?

I'd have to check my diary. Why?

I'm – we're – having some friends round. They're these friends of my dad's.

Jodie says, looking at him curiously, That's nice. That's really suburban of you, Scott.

I was thinking, maybe if you wanted...

His voice trails off, and he slows his pace; then stops. He bends to the track and picks up a pebble; rubs the dust off it; shows it to her: pale and smooth, almost a perfect oval. He seems to be hunting for the right words. After a moment he tosses the pebble away and says, Do you want to come?

She says, stupidly, Come where?

Do you want to come for dinner. On Friday. I'm going to cook. Then he adds, as if inspired, You could help.

Help you cook, she says, trying not to sound incredulous. She has not been prepared for this at all.

Yeah. If you like, I mean.

Wow.

What?

I mean, it's great that I get to meet your dad's friends and everything, but now you're going to let me *help you cook* as well...

Scott gives her a wry grin. He says, Yeah, okay. I mean – don't worry about it. It's going to be awful anyway.

Why's it going to be awful?

Cos he doesn't want them there.

Then why did he invite them?

He didn't. I did, kind of by accident, and then when I told him... And I don't think they really want to come either. The whole thing is just fucked up but no-one's backing out and I promised, so...

You invited them by accident? she says. This wasn't a sleepwalking thing was it?

He gives her a grudging, almost-amused look. Says, Don't.

Cos that would be killer. Waking up each day and never knowing what parties you'd arranged the night before. Life would be a constant surprise.

Stop it. For all I know it's happening.

How did you invite people by accident anyway?

I just did. I didn't know what to say to her on the phone and I just... And I don't even think they want to be there either. So – basically it's going to be a disaster.

You're really painting a picture.

And I just thought you might...

Fit right in?

He laughs aloud. Shakes his head. Says, Yeah. Exactly. I was just thinking, if by some miracle it actually started to work, Jodie could step in and... fuck it back up.

She's grinning with him. She says, Well. Thanks but no thanks. Not really my thing. Not really my *bag*, you know.

Scott starts walking again. They go down, in silence, onto the patchy tarmac; and on to Scott's house. Scott says, See if you can get more tins.

Yeah. I know. And water.

I can do the water.

Okay.

A pause. Jodie says, And I was thinking.

Yeah?

We should have a signal.

For what?

For... if it's happening. For if we need to go. Like a code that only we know and if you say it, you know it's the real thing. Mayday mayday, kind of.

Wouldn't we see it on the news if it was going to happen?

I don't know. Isn't the whole point that it might come out of nowhere? A surprise attack. First strike. And then we only get four minutes.

Scott says, slowly, Yeah. I suppose.

And in any case, one of us might see the news and the other one doesn't, or something like that. Or one of us might hear something.

Hear something?

I don't know. At home maybe.

He thinks about that. Says, Oh. Right.

Yeah. So – don't we need a thing only we understand? That's quick? So if you say it, we just go – we don't ask a thousand questions, we don't stop and fuck about, we just *go*. We run.

He's nodding. He says, Yeah. You're right. We should have that.

So what's it gonna be? Not an ordinary word. Something unusual.

What about Trinity? Like where your radiation glass comes from.

Okay. That's not bad. Trinity then. That's it. And you don't get to piss about, okay. We don't joke about it, we don't use it unless we mean it. Unless it's real.

I get it, Scott says. It's a good idea.

You have to swear. I mean it. Do you promise?

He nods seriously; says, I promise.

12

She hasn't told him about the article in the Albuquerque Journal. She hasn't told anyone. She has, though, printed it out on her dot-matrix, and slipped it between the pages of one of her programming magazines.

Documents Explain Kirtland Accident.

The article has its origins in a rumour that has been circulating on and off in the Albuquerque area for twenty-nine years.

The rumour being that there was some sort of military mistake, in 1957: that some weapon got launched or fired or dropped by accident, in the desert, and the whole thing was hushed up and classified by the military.

Finally, this summer, four months after Chernobyl, seven months after Challenger, some reporter resurrects the rumour and gets interested. What kind of weapon. What kind of accident. More than enough time has passed now for the incident to be declassified, if it actually happened. He submits a request for information.

What he finds out is, firstly, that the rumours are true; and, secondly, that the weapon involved was a ten-megaton hydrogen bomb.

A ten-megaton hydrogen bomb, Jodie learns, is the single biggest nuclear weapon the world has ever built, even now, in 1986. The equivalent of ten million tons of TNT. More than six hundred Hiroshima bombs, all in one go.

This is the warhead that gets dropped, by accident, out of the bomb bay of a B-36, as the plane is leaving Kirtland Air Force Base, just outside Albuquerque.

The nuke falls out of the plane. It falls and falls. The bomb is the size of a school bus and its parachutes fail to deploy, so by the time it hits the ground it's going at enormous speed.

The way Jodie sees it, this now becomes a binary proposition followed by consequential results. The binary proposition is that the bomb will either detonate, or it won't. If it detonates, it will take Albuquerque with it. The fireball alone will be three miles wide; the blast radius will extend ten miles beyond that. Everyone in the city will die, because killing a city is what this bomb is designed to do.

In fact, of course, this doesn't happen. There are conventional explosives in the bomb, intended to compress its nuclear core to the point of criticality, and some of these detonate; but by some miracle, that's all that happens.

The consequential results of it failing to detonate are: the matter is hushed up and classified for twenty-five years. Then ignored for four more. Finally surfacing in a local newspaper report that doesn't even gain global exposure, unless you count the copy folded into the pages of her FORTRAN magazine.

But it's the other possibility that has been circling and circling in her head. The consequential results of the bomb exploding.

They drop it by accident. Its chutes fail to deploy. Its conventional explosives detonate on impact (blowing a crater in the desert twelve feet deep).

So it doesn't seem that big a stretch to imagine that there could have been a little bit of further bad luck, and the nuclear payload could in fact have been triggered.

So. Follow the argument through. Trace the line.

What would have happened if one day – out of a clear blue sky! – Albuquerque had just *vanished,* disappeared in a roaring cloud of nuclear flame?

Further consequential results. Branching now. Different possibilities. But, she thinks, trending primarily in one direction.

Because the first people vaporised are the ones who know this was a fuckup. The command unit on the ground; the plane crew in the air; the guy in the bomb bay who stumbled against the wrong lever (seriously, she can barely believe this, but that's how it happened – he tripped and stumbled and that was all it took). All those people are gone. Along with the city. All that's left is a fireball and a mushroom cloud the size of six hundred Hiroshimas and no-one, no-one at all, to say who did it.

And it seems very clear to her that, at this point, the lives of everyone else in the world are staked on the US military realising that this was a fuckup and not a first strike that they failed to detect. That they don't hit the reply button by reflex. That the soldiers in the chain of command don't follow their training. Don't think like soldiers. Think, instead, like humans.

Of course if they do press the button, it's game over for the whole planet, right there in 1957. America fires; Russia retaliates. The end of human civilisation. Because that's what's on the table when you drop the biggest nuclear weapon in history out of a plane *by mistake.*

She knows now that Scott was right about everything. He just doesn't have a modem so he hasn't been able to check, confirm it for sure.

Has anything ever actually happened?

Kirtland in 1957 leads her to Chelyabinsk in 1957. In America, the bomb plummets towards the ground. In the USSR, the East-Ural Radioactive Trace begins its slow work of slaughtering schoolchildren.

And it's not over. There's more.

She sticks with 1957: not just because you have to start somewhere, and not just because information from that year is now finally hitting declassification. More, it's because the year feels like it has significance now. Horrified fascination takes over. She wants to know what other mistakes have there been, that no-one talks about, that have been shuttered and coded Eyes Only and hidden away in the dark?

She reads about the plutonium fire in the Rocky Flats nuclear weapon production facility just outside Denver, Colorado, which releases a plume of radiation into the air.

She reads about Britain's Windscale military nuclear

facility, which in 1957 overheats, catches fire, and burns for two days before being finally extinguished. All that time the plant vents a huge, trailing cloud of radioactive gas, which drifts across Britain and Europe. There is particular fear of thyroid cancer. Milk from cows in the contaminated area is destroyed.

She reads how the facility is, even now, sealed up and abandoned; how it will have to remain sealed for at least another fifty years before anyone dares go inside to start decontamination.

Windscale is the worst nuclear accident Britain has seen: it is believed, by the West, to be the worst nuclear accident the *world* has seen, but this is only because the West is as yet unaware of the far more severe Chelyabinsk explosion – which, though it remains a guarded secret at this point, has in fact occurred eleven days earlier.

She can barely believe it. Like 1957 was a cursed year. A year of disasters.

Or maybe not at all. Maybe just a typical year. Because she now believes Scott might have been right about this, too: that accidents are happening all the time. These are just the stories that are, finally, coming to light; being allowed to crawl into view.

She makes more printouts and gathers them between the leaves of her programming magazines. Facing pages now contain, on the one hand, neat linear sets of computer instructions, perfectly ordered, satisfyingly nested, guaranteed to produce identical results every time they're run. And on the other, a haphazard chaos of human error: a palsied, insane throwing of the dice, over and over, without order, without understanding. Trying again and again for the double-sixes that will light the world on fire.

Voices from the sitting room. Jodie tries to slip by unnoticed but Mrs Williams is there with Jodie's mother and Mrs Williams sees her at once: Jodie! There you are! We were just talking about you.

Which they may have been; but not, of course, what gets said behind her parents' backs – here it will have been only carefully-modulated concern and slightly mistrustful sympathy (because, really, it's all so incomprehensible, isn't it? That you can do everything, absolutely *everything*, for someone, and yet this is the result).

And Jodie knows, straight away, that she can't face this: not now. Not the precise, bland questions about how things are *going*, how school is *going*, is she *feeling all right*; and not the silent background scrutiny (those clothes; that hair of hers; isn't she thin; doesn't she look ill?). It's simply not bearable. She makes her decision in the space between one heartbeat and the next: with Mrs Williams right there, her mother will have no choice. She says, brightly, Is it okay if I go out this evening? I'm having dinner at a friend's house.

13

Scott has the back door open and the radio on, picking up the trailing edge of Capital Radio with a fair amount of static breaking through the tracks. On the counter are what might be the makings of a salad: cucumber, onions, tomatoes, all of which he's diced very finely and put into heaps on a chopping board. Beside them is a brand-new bottle of olive oil, just opened, the little plastic wrapper from its top screwed up beside it. On the table in the middle of the room are some serving plates of different sizes, edged in a sombre grey-blue, formal; empty for the moment.

Jodie watches him from the doorway as he moves around the kitchen unaware: his unconscious orderliness; his precision and concentration.

He checks the oven; and when he turns she clears her throat and says, Still want a hand?

Obvious surprise for a second, and then he says, sounding pleased, Yeah, sure. Of course.

She comes in: slings her bag and Walkman down on the countertop and says, What can I do?

Uh... I don't know. There's not much left, really. You could chop some more cucumber.

Are your dad's friends here yet?

They're coming at eight.

She sets to with the cucumber. Scott watches closely; after a moment says, Smaller bits.

People have teeth, you know. They can chew.

It's supposed to be small.

Is piles of very small vegetables your whole dinner plan?

He shrugs and says, unfazed, Pretty much.

This is some shitty music, you know.

Yeah, I know.

She works steadily, trying to match the size of the pieces Scott has chopped. There is a strangely dreamlike quality to the room: this side-by-side domestic work; Scott's focused but companionable silence; the knife moving with regular neatness through the cucumber, tap tap tap on the board. The half pill of Valium she took on the way here is easing through her now, smoothly familiar. She adds her pile of dice to the plate. Scott checks his watch and turns off the oven; takes out a baking tray covered in small cubes of bread, toasted gold and twinkling slightly with oil. One or two are burned brown and he picks them out to throw away. Jodie eats one of the remainder – hot, crunchy. He's salted them too.

Jodie says, You got any booze?

Uh, yeah. In the fridge.

There's white wine and red wine and beer and a nestled

cluster of soft drinks cans. Jodie says, Shit, man. You've put the red wine in here.

Scott says, I know. I want it there, don't take it out.

You're not supposed to serve red wine cold, you spaz. Even I know that.

Just leave it alone, he says firmly.

Jodie shrugs. Your funeral, she mutters. She helps herself to a can of Coke, finds a glass, and fills it halfway. Says, Where's the vodka?

We don't have vodka, Scott says. Sorry. There's brandy, in the cupboard there, he adds doubtfully.

Man. Brandy and Coke. Is that a drink?

I don't know. Try it and tell me.

She adds brandy to the glass and takes a cautious swallow. Says, Well, it's something.

You're not going to get shitfaced are you?

Don't worry. I know what I'm doing. I'm kind of a professional at this.

There are other things in the fridge: several plates covered with foil; a mixing bowl also covered; a plate with different cheeses laid out. Jodie watches Scott covertly. There's something different about him: a concentrated tension that has been relieved a little by her arrival, but which hasn't entirely dissipated. Like he's trying, trying hard, not to fuck something up.

There's the sound of a car crunching up the driveway and Scott looks briefly panicked: but it's still only half seven.

It's my dad, he says.

Right.

A moment later a man comes into the kitchen holding

two bottles of wine. On seeing Jodie he stops, his expression changing from faintly awkward hopefulness to a simple blank surprise just like Scott's a few minutes earlier.

Scott says, Dad, this is Jodie.

Jodie says, Hi.

Scott's father says, Hello.

The fleeting surprised expression – unexpected guest; Scott friends with a girl – fades pretty fast and his face comes back to a slightly worn, quizzical politeness. He says, coming properly into the room, Pleased to meet you, Jodie.

Scott says, It's okay if she stays for dinner?

Well – I – yes. Of course. I bought this, by the way, I thought perhaps...

Scott glances at the bottles. He says, Oh, okay. Thanks. I already got wine though.

Ah. All right, Scott's father says; and then, a moment later, Is there anything I can do to help?

Uh, not really I think. It's nearly ready. Jodie's helping.

Jodie says, He won't let me eat anything.

Scott's father raises his eyebrows. He says, Thou shalt not bind the mouth of the kine that treadeth out the corn, you know, Scott.

Scott ignores this. He takes glass grapefruit bowls from the cupboard and carefully divides the little crunchy bread pieces between two of them. His father watches this nonplussed; then says, Right. You seem to have everything under control. I'll just... Should I lay the table?

It's okay, I've done it.

Well. All right then. I'll just...

And he goes through into the still depths of the house, leaving them to it. The song on the radio changes.

Jodie says, Your dad just called me a kine, whatever the fuck that is.

He didn't mean it, Scott says absently. He's always like that.

Really?

Yeah.

A pause. Then he says, What's it like then, brandy and Coke?

It was a bit rank at first. Now it just tastes like Coke.

Do your parents let you drink?

My parents don't let me do anything.

He grins at her quickly and says, Get me one too.

He works neatly and steadily. Jodie, aware of not really being needed, puts his drink beside him and then hoists herself onto the work surface by the door and sits there watching him. The song on the radio changes again. Peter Gabriel comes and goes in crackly gusts: *Games Without Frontiers.* Outside, the real heat has backed off a little and the familiar smells of the Heights in summer – tarmac and creosote, pine sap, chlorine – are slackening.

The yellow plastic clock high up on the wall creeps round towards eight.

Jodie says, Remember you said it could start with an accident?

What could start? says Scott; and then, Oh, yeah.

You said someone might push the wrong button. And

then you said there's probably loads of shit happening we never hear about cos it's military and they hush it up.

Did I say that?

Yeah.

Okay.

I think maybe you were right.

He glances at her and says, Why? Did something happen?

Just something I read. I'll tell you later. But basically... maybe you were right.

He gives her a look. At least we're ready, he says.

Yeah.

The music on the radio stops and the news comes on. More than three million people are unemployed. The Conservatives are back ahead in the polls. Something about video nasties and Mary Whitehouse and the government. Something about AIDS in America.

Again there's the sound of a car pulling up outside. Scott turns the radio off and visibly gathers himself. Doors slam, there's the crunch of footsteps, and a moment later the front doorbell rings. Scott's father emerges from somewhere within the house to answer it.

Scott wipes his hands on a tea-towel and takes a big breath: lets it out. Contained and determined. Looks at Jodie with a sideways smile and says, Thanks.

For what?

Dunno. Being here.

There are voices in the hall. Greetings being exchanged. Scott goes through to join in. Jodie is alone briefly and the back door is still wide open and now sharply, sharply, she's tempted to slip out and be gone.

But gone where. And besides: Scott.

She takes another gulp of her drink; sets it down and follows after him.

They're all crowded in the hall. Scott's father, looking rather flustered and unprepared: Scott, contained and almost grave: and then a kindly-looking woman who is smiling at Scott, and behind her a girl Scott's age or a little older, slender and blonde and assured. Introductions get made, though she's the only one who needs them. The woman is Caroline. The girl is Leah. Scott's father, it turns out, is Jeremy. And she is Scott's friend Jodie.

There's supposed to be a husband with the guests, but he's unwell; he sends his apologies; it must be the bug that's going round, Caroline says; and Jodie, surprised, sees in one of those odd instants of penetration that this is a lie – and that Jeremy knows it is.

They go through to the sitting room. Scott busies himself fetching drinks: he seems determined not to relinquish the role of host, and once Jeremy and Caroline have both realised this and accepted that they're not supposed to assume any responsibility, everyone relaxes slightly. The two adults talk. It's a little stilted to start with – small talk about the weather, the heat, their jobs; polite inquiries after David, the husband. Leah sits attentively listening. Scott comes back with the drinks: tall glasses brimming red, with ice and slices of orange.

Jeremy says, Gosh, is that Pimm's?

No, Scott says. Try it.

Jeremy and Caroline sip their drinks. Caroline's face changes – a complex flush of recognition and surprise – and she says, It's sangria. Scott, what a nice idea. Thank you. It's delicious.

Scott blushes slightly. He says to Leah, What would you like? There's Coke and lemonade and orange juice.

Leah says, I'll try the sangria if I'm allowed. What do you say, are we allowed sangria?

Caroline says, Make it a bit weaker than this, then.

Jodie says, My Coke's beside the toaster.

The conversation continues. She's aware at one point, when Scott is answering some question about his gardening job, of Leah glancing curiously her way, as if trying to fit a Jodie-shaped piece into the pattern of Scott's family and life, and failing. Those cool blue eyes linger briefly and then return to the main flow of the talk; but she sees a tiny, privately amused smile tug for a moment at Leah's face.

She has hair like the girl in the shampoo ads on television.

And proper breasts, the size of apples, under her casual white blouse.

Jodie takes another swallow of her drink; the brandy burning dully in her stomach. Glances at Scott; but he's listening to Caroline. Soon after, he excuses himself and goes out of the room: she hears cutlery; plates being moved. The conversation shifts to Leah's O-level results, which have only just arrived, they got the post yesterday; which are excellent and about which she is appropriately bashful; and her A-level choices: History, English and Latin, a demanding combination, so many essay subjects, but one she says quietly she feels comfortable tackling. So she must be at least sixteen.

Jeremy appears delighted with the academic news and decisions; Caroline proud but also preoccupied. Every time her eyes rest on Jeremy there is something tentatively questing in the look which she can't entirely suppress. Jodie is beginning to get the sense that Caroline wants to say something about Scott's mother: wants to offer comfort to Jeremy somehow: but can't work out how to broach the subject, if indeed broaching it is even possible now.

Scott appears in the doorway and says, slightly awkwardly, Dinner's ready if you want.

Jeremy ushers them through to the dining room at the back of the house, and then stands staring: the room has been emptied, the tall French doors to the garden are open wide, and the dining table and five chairs have been set out on the grass in dappled shade. Jeremy gives Scott a look of frank astonishment and says, How did you get the table out there?

Bit by bit, Scott says, with the trace of a smile. Very slowly.

It weighs a ton. You should have asked me. I could have helped.

I wanted it to be a surprise, Scott says; and he turns to show Caroline where to sit and so doesn't see the fleeting expression of wonder that crosses his father's face. Jodie sees it, though, and something in her belly clenches for a moment like a fist.

. . .

She is exceptional. She comes top. She wins prizes. She will do better than the other simple, easy children. They will be worn down by the world: she will not.

But she is self-contained. Closed off. Isolated. Is that normal? Sometimes she doesn't seem quite normal. She is difficult to like.

She is difficult to love. Sometimes.

A small dark creature in one far corner of the room while the other children play side by side. She soaks everything in without giving anything back.

Her eyes are disquieting. Those oddly green, glittering eyes, which sometimes seem so empty of any kind of compassion.

Sometimes you can't help wondering.

She is stubborn and ungrateful. Wayward. In trouble at school, several times. More and more.

She watches you like a cat, implacably. You catch her doing it. It's like having an animal in the house, something wild. Not shrieking and frenzied and chaotic wild, but tense, ill at ease, wary wild; as if always ready to bolt.

She is unfamiliar.

Like someone else's child. Like a fey child. A changeling.

And when she cuts herself, cuts her wrists, and the bathwater swirls red with blood, she cuts away also in the same moment the last possible chance you might have had. You have nothing else to give to this any more. She's gone now.

. . .

Jeremy is pouring more drinks and the evening sunlight is speckling the tablecloth. Scott serves everybody bowls of chilled red-orange soup and shows them how to sprinkle the diced onions and tomatoes and cucumber and the little toasted cubes of bread into it before eating.

Jodie tries a spoonful somewhat charily, but the flavour, fresh and vivid and spiked through with onion and vinegar, is delightful. She says, Hey, Scott. Actually not bad. What is this, then?

Caroline says, It's gazpacho.

It's kind of a Spanish meal, Scott says. You know, cos it's so hot.

Caroline says, It's just like we had that summer – Jeremy, you remember? We had the villa outside Granada? And there was a little restaurant in the village with a terrace and we used to drink sangria and they made gazpacho –

She stops; blinks; looks at Scott. Says, Is that why? Did you make it because you remembered?

Scott nods. Says, I thought... because, we were all together, and...

After the tiniest pause Caroline says, again, Scott, what a lovely idea.

A wave of confusion and sadness across Scott's face; and gone; and Jodie ashamed for having seen it.

And Jeremy saying, It tastes just the same. It really does.

And Caroline saying, How did you make this? Did you have a recipe? I bet this isn't in Mrs Beeton.

Both of them, Jodie understands, talking to cover the moment, to give Scott some time.

Scott eats a mouthful and when he looks up he's back in

control and he says, Actually it is, but it's not a very good recipe. It tastes a bit boring. So I phoned Mrs Martinez.

Jeremy says, Mrs Martinez from school?

Scott nods.

We have her number?

Yeah. Cos of the extra French classes.

Leah says, Your French teacher's called Mrs Martinez?

Scott says, I know.

Jodie says, Not sure that's the real issue anyway.

Leah looks at her: says, What's the real issue?

The issue is, he made this twice. An unsuccessful trial run and *then* he calls his French teacher who's actually Spanish for help. That's seriously anal.

Scott says, I can get you Heinz out of a tin if you'd prefer.

Leah grins. She has braces on her teeth. When they come off, everything about her will be perfect.

The adults are talking now – reminiscences of the holiday; of the time the car blew a tyre; the vineyard visit; the long slog up the hill to the Alhambra but how worth it it was.

And Caroline says, Do you remember Emily picking oranges from the trees inside?

They weren't up to much, Jeremy says.

I think they were only supposed to be decorative. Or maybe they needed watering. Don't oranges need an awful lot of water? But she was so determined.

They're talking about Scott's mother.

Jodie, not drunk but definitely a little blurry round the edges now, with that heightened sense of perception that comes over her after a couple of hits of vodka (or even brandy and Coke, it turns out) is starting to understand now:

to see how Scott has set this up, why he was so focused and tense, what it was that he has been trying not to fuck up. And while it's pretty obvious that the adults have seen through the whole thing, the end result is the same, conscious or unconscious. She feels a swell of fondness for him, or something stronger than fondness: for the care and thoughtfulness and determination of him.

And Caroline is saying to Leah, We thought we'd lost you! We were searching everywhere! I was absolutely beside myself.

Leah saying, Scott said it was hide-and-seek. He said we were all playing. How was I supposed to know he was an evil little twat?

You hid really well, Scott says, deadpan.

We nearly called the police. I thought you'd been kidnapped or fallen down a well.

Really well, Scott says again.

I seem to remember Scott being sent to bed with no dinner that night, Jeremy says.

Worth it, Scott says, grinning at Leah, who narrows her eyes at him, pretend-angry for the trick he played years ago, back when they were kids together and he found her insufferable.

After the gazpacho there is Spanish omelette and a potato salad and a green salad and the plates of cheese. Scott brings loaves of ciabatta bread hot from the oven – explaining diffidently that they're Italian but the closest thing he could get at the supermarket – all brought to the table together, you help yourself, and everyone talking, the last vestiges of reserve falling away now. More sangria for the kids – the young people, Jeremy calls them, acknowledging that this is now a table of equals, or equals of a sort – and the chilled red wine from the fridge for the adults: again, delight at the unfamiliarity of it, the beaded condensation on a *red* wine bottle, but actually isn't it refreshing? And under the table Jodie kicks her trainers off and works her socks down and wriggles her toes in the grass.

The sun dips lower and the whole rather overgrown, unkempt garden becomes swathed in shadow and seems to draw in closer around the table; but the air remains still and balmy and in a moment of inspiration Jeremy brings candles from somewhere in the house and lights them so that everyone is suddenly golden and lustrous and the dusk is pushed back. Caroline points out the first star, low in the sky; and Scott says no, it's actually a planet, it's Venus; and Leah is teasing him about being a science geek and does he still read those books and comics; Jeremy joining in now, chiding Scott for his dereliction of real literature. Jodie sits there listening and worming her toes into the soil, eyes darting from face to flickering face around the table. She feels warm and soft and sharp at the same time.

Jeremy saying something about aliens and spaceships.

Caroline saying something about more a boys' enterprise than a girls'.

Scott smiling a little awkwardly and shrugging it off.

Leah saying thank goodness sci fi doesn't form any part of her A-level syllabus.

Jodie tips her glass up but there's nothing left. She puts it deliberately back on the table. There's a lull in the conversation and into it she says, You know what bugs me?

Jeremy says, smiling, What's that, Jodie?

I mean – aliens and all that. It's just not believable. You get some guy, he's the hero, and okay maybe he's a credible character, you can believe in him, but then they wheel on the baddies and it's just – oh, right, now we've got aliens.

Exactly, Jeremy says. There has to be a willing suspension of disbelief for literature to connect wholeheartedly.

Scott is looking at Jodie with evident reproach but she ploughs on, unable to stop now, with a kind of reckless confidence: There's this story – Scott, you'll know this one – and the guy is lost and he's trying to get his team back home but they just keep meeting one sort of trouble after another; there's these enormous creatures who eat humans so they chew up some of the crew, but the rest escape from them, only then when they get off that planet they run into these monsters who try to basically erase their brains, and when they get away from *them* they're caught in a black hole, and there's some bad guys with tractor beams who try to pull them in so they can't escape and all sorts, one after another. How are you expected to read that without laughing your arse off?

Quite, says Jeremy. It is all a little improbable. Alienating, one might almost say, for the reader.

Presumably not for all readers, Caroline says in a conciliatory tone.

Leah is staring hard at Jodie. She says, That's the Odyssey.

Caroline says, What?

It's the Odyssey. That's the Cyclops and the Lotus Eaters and Charybdis and the Sirens.

Everyone looks at Jodie, who says, Oh, yeah. Sorry. I get confused sometimes. Sci fi, the classics, whatever.

Jeremy opens his mouth and then closes it again. Caroline says, looking amused, I think that's a rather good point Jodie just made, don't you, Jeremy?

Jeremy says, I'm not sure. What exactly would be your point, Jodie?

I don't know. That you can have monsters and adventures and totally unbelievable random mad shit and if it's in a comic it's pulp, but if some ancient Greek guy wrote it three thousand years ago it's the foundation of literature.

Caroline laughs aloud and says, You see, Jeremy? Not everything is Henry James.

And in any case, there are things you can do in sci fi that you simply can't do in conventional books, or only in a very limited way, but they're still important qualities of human experience, right? So Kipling says, okay, if a human baby is brought up by wolves, basically he becomes a wolf. And that's *The Jungle Book.* And a big part of that is an exploration of what it might mean to be in that situation: how your viewpoint alters, how you see the world, all those kinds of things. But that's as far as you can go in that kind of conventional story because the known world doesn't allow you to put the question the other way round. But Heinlein can, because he's writing science fiction; so he can say, okay, I get the man-cub idea, but what if a human child is brought up by Martians? And what if, instead of wolves who are more basic animals, these Martians are way more advanced than we are: way older and cleverer and with a totally different way of looking at life and time and existence. What if we're like wolves to them? Or like insects? What does that human child become then?

Leah says, An alien?

Jodie shrugs; says, Scott's the expert.

Scott shakes his head and says, A god, basically. He can't become a proper Martian, he doesn't have the capacity. But he can exceed what any other human has managed. One of us but different.

Jodie nods and says, So Heinlein's playing with the whole Christian thing, a man's body but this kind of god-like mind that makes him totally different, but the thing is it's really just a matter of perspective. Mowgli in reverse. It's like Arthur C Clarke saying any sufficiently advanced technology is indistinguishable from magic, only Heinlein's applying that to sociology and politics and religion and sex, instead of machines. Any sufficiently advanced process of thought is indistinguishable from godhead. And this is just Heinlein, remember, we haven't even touched on Asimov or Philip K Dick or Bradbury or Atwood or Le Guin or Gibson.

Caroline says, What book is this?

Stranger in a Strange Land.

Caroline says, I should read that.

It's good, Scott says.

Caroline looks at Jeremy, smiling. She says, Well? What do you have to say to that, Jeremy?

Jeremy says, I concede the point entirely. Scott and Jodie can have Mr Heinlein if I can have Homer.

Deal, says Scott. He shoots Jodie a quick glance of direct unguarded admiration; then gets up and starts gathering the plates, refusing to let anyone else help him. Jodie watches him.

She thinks, a little at random, *He deserves to be happy.*

There's fruit salad for pudding. Soon after this, the stars are out properly; Jeremy asks Caroline if she's not a little chilly now; Scott points out Deneb and Vega high in the sky, and Arcturus low down, just grazing the black silhouette of the tree line; and then they move inside, bringing the chairs but leaving the table – Jeremy says it can wait for tomorrow. In the kitchen, Jodie swiftly puts together another drink, adding the brandy when no-one is looking. Caroline says what a fantastic meal it was: thank you, Scott; Jeremy and Leah say the same. There's some bustling about and Jeremy offers coffee and Caroline says yes. Leah says, I kind of want to see these books now, and Jeremy says, You kids can go and – I mean, you don't have to stay with us. I'll make the coffee. Scott, well done. That really was super. I had no idea.

And so Jodie and Leah and Scott go upstairs to Scott's room while the adults hang back, looking for filter papers in the kitchen drawers.

14

In the attic Scott turns on the bedside lamp and the desk Anglepoise but brings it low down, so the light is moody and subdued. Leah, watching him, says, You know your dad nearly said you kids can go and play.

I know, right? Scott says. He really did. I've got Lego if you want.

Radical, Leah says. She glances at Jodie. I loved what you did by the way, that thing with the Odyssey. That was seriously cool.

Jodie finds herself confused by the praise. She says, Cheers.

Leah looks round the room; then says, You know what this party needs? Excuse me a moment.

And she goes back down the stairs.

Scott says, She's right, though. That was cool.

Well.

You never told me you liked Heinlein.

Jodie says, I don't. I mean, I don't know if I do. I never read any.

Scott says, What?

I just read the back cover last time I was up here. And a bit of the introduction, somebody wrote an introduction all about the symbolism and all that. She points to the bookshelf: There you go – *Stranger in a Strange Land,* then Asimov, Philip K Dick, Ray Bradbury, Margaret Atwood... I was just pulling names out, really. I thought, no-one else is going to know, except you maybe.

Scott follows where she's pointing and says, So you were just making shit up?

I still meant what I said. I didn't like them making you sound stupid for liking this stuff. I liked the comics. It's not stupid.

Have you read the Odyssey?

Fuck no. We did a project at school when I was eleven. I drew pictures of the monsters. Don't tell Barbie though.

Scott starts to laugh hard. He says, You're totally evil. My dad thinks you're some kind of fucking genius now, did you see how he was looking at you? You have to keep doing that.

Jodie shrugs and the confusion deepens; she doesn't think she's ever heard Scott laugh properly before. Leah's footsteps come back up the stairs: she's carrying a bottle of white wine, three juice tumblers and a corkscrew. She says, They're in the sitting room talking. Thought we might take the edge off.

Scott says, Nice.

Couldn't find your wine glasses so we're slumming it.

Leah uncorks the wine with a practised movement and

pours it for them all. They find places to sit: Jodie on the floor by the bookcase, Leah and Scott opposite, leaning against the bed; Leah holds her tumbler up and says, Toast to the chef.

Jodie drains her glass straight off and says, More please.

Leah passes her the bottle and says, When did you learn to cook, anyway?

It's not really cooking, Scott says with a lopsided smile. It's just putting the right things on the plates.

Bollocks, Leah says. It was cooking. Better than I could do anyway.

Jodie's eyes move between Leah and Scott.

Leah says, Can I ask something? Why did you do it? That meal, I mean.

Scott just looks at her.

She says, Only... it was – kind of specific.

After a fractional moment, he nods.

Leah says, This is something to do with your mum, right?

Scott fiddles with his tumbler, turning it this way and that. He says, We never talk about her. I mean – my dad – it's been more than half a year now, and he never says anything, he never... I don't get it. He goes into himself and it's like he's forgotten I'm here. I meet him in the house and I swear to God sometimes he's surprised. I swear to God. And we never talk about her. Never.

Leah says, quietly, Why not?

How should I know?

Do you think it's – maybe, how he's grieving? He can't bear to?

I don't know. Because we never talk. So I don't know.

But you're grieving too, Leah says, slowly. Can't he see that?

I don't know.

Jodie fills her tumbler. She has the sense of having slipped very slightly adrift from the room: of being apart from what's happening. She's an observer now. She sees Leah put her hand on Scott's knee where it's drawn up in front of him, and squeeze: compassion, reassurance. She sees Leah say, You have to talk about it.

She sees Scott nodding.

Leah saying, But you started that. You did it. Plus it turns out you can put the right food on plates, which isn't nothing.

Jodie blinks and the room floats very slightly upward. She rests her head against the books, pulls her gaze back to Leah and says, experimentally, So you guys were friends when you were kids?

Not exactly friends, Leah says, grinning. She takes her hand off Scott's knee and sips her drink; adds, I think Scott thought I was boring. Did you think I was boring?

You were a bit boring. You were such a good little girl.

No. Girls mature earlier than boys, everyone knows that. I was just more mature than you.

Jodie watches, fascinated.

Hey, do you know Toby? Leah is saying.

Who?

He's friends with Ollie. Ollie Shaw.

Scott makes an equivocal movement with his head. Right, he says.

Jodie remembers touching the bruise on his shoulder; here in this room.

Well anyway, I can introduce you. Are you coming to the party?

What party?

Jodie draws wine in through her teeth and makes it tumble around in her mouth for a moment.

Leah says, It's tomorrow. Me and a couple of friends from school are going. I can get you in. It's supposed to be this birthday party, but trust me, it's the real thing.

Scott says, vaguely, Yeah, I heard about that. Susan Lewis's birthday, right?

Exactly. You should be there.

Jodie says, almost a whisper, I know what she tastes like.

Leah darts her a look of genuine shock, almost instantly hidden. She looks, momentarily, less sure of herself.

Jodie laughs just a little. She gets up – not even slightly unsteady; look at that self-control! – and says, Where's the loo?

Scott says, First door on the landing.

Jodie makes her way down in the half-dark. She stands for a moment listening, but hears nothing from the ground floor. The house is too big to carry any conversation this far, she supposes, or perhaps Jeremy and Caroline are keeping their voices low.

In the lavatory the light is very bright and white on porcelain, mirrors, tiles. She gets a handful of water from the tap and takes the other half of the Valium.

As she sits to pee, the bands of scars on her narrow thighs span like wings; silver and brown and red striations of colour; tattered delicate fans; or the leaves of a book, old, ancient, from the days when you had to cut the pages raggedly free yourself with a knife.

She loses track of time a little.

Then she is downstairs, in the kitchen. The white wine Scott and Leah are drinking tastes acidic to her. She makes another brandy and Coke with the dregs from the bottle.

She wanders across the hall; then through the dining room and through the open French doors and out to where the table is standing, empty on the grass, in darkness.

The air out here is cooling now.

She drinks a little. She wants better for Scott. He deserves better.

Further along the house, one of the windows is open, lit up yellow from within. She can hear Scott's dad's voice. Then Caroline's voice.

Carefully, silently, she walks close and stands beside the window, close in against the wall.

After a while she hears Jeremy say, I was thinking, some time ago, about not knowing how to be much of a father. Not having had the practice, is how it came to me.

He's doing it for you. He's got it covered.

Yes.

Silence for a moment. Jodie closes her eyes to hear better.

Caroline says, I think all he wants is to remember her. Talk about her. Have people... recognise that she was there.

Yes.

You haven't been doing that?

No. Not really.

You have to. He needs it.

Yes, I know. I do know. I just... it hasn't seemed... I didn't know how.

Another silence.

Caroline says, How's work?

I'm on sabbatical. So... it's more or less in my hands.

You're doing research?

Yes.

How's it going?

It's not really *going*.

Silence. Jodie hears the faint clink of a coffee cup being set down.

Caroline says, He's a good boy, Jeremy.

Scott? He is. I know.

You can't ever tell him. You may want to one day but you can't.

I know that. I wouldn't.

Jodie frowns to herself. *Tell Scott what?*

She hears Caroline say, How long did you know? I mean, before...

Some time. A few months. We talked, in the Autumn.

Talked?

Yes. She told me.

Silence. Jodie stands in the darkness, waiting.

Jeremy says, How about you? Did David...

No. I found out myself. He really wasn't very good at hiding it. I found out.

How are you? Both of you?

Jodie hears Caroline take a breath. Hears her say, Not good.

No. I suppose not. He's not ill, is he.

No. He couldn't face coming here. Couldn't face you, I imagine. Or his own conscience.

Then – thank you. For coming anyway.

Caroline says, quietly, Honestly I've been dreading it.

So have I.

But it's not actually so bad, is it? Talking.

I suppose not, no.

Did you hate her? When she told you?

Silence. Jodie presses the back of her head against the brick. The house is still warm. They're talking about Scott's mother. About Scott's mother and Leah's father.

She remembers Scott, coming off the heath: *He doesn't want them there.*

And, *I don't even think they want to be there either.*

She hears Scott's father say, Hate is a very strong word.

I hated David. For a while. I hated Emily too. Sorry.

No, Scott's father says, sounding very tired. Don't be sorry.

I am sorry though. Things change. Even in a few months, things change. I mean – I still hate him, but I think I know I won't hate him forever. And there's Leah. So I suppose we'll find a way. Work through it. People do that, don't they?

Yes.

Silence. Jodie waits; piecing things together in her head.

Jeremy says, I'm so glad you came.

Me too. Good for Scott.

Yes indeed.

Silence.

Jeremy's voice says, I never said sorry.

Caroline's voice says, Sorry? For what?

Jeremy's voice says, For letting her down. I must have let her down. That seems clear enough. Not much of a father; not much of a husband. Sometimes I can't stop thinking about it – what I would say. If she were still here.

Caroline's voice: You want to forgive her.

Jeremy's voice: I want the chance to try.

Leah is sitting on the bed, cross-legged, looking through a sketchpad. Scott has put the radio on: the reception's better up here and the music comes out fresh and clear.

Jodie goes slowly across the room. No-one seems to have noticed how long she's been gone. In fact, no-one seems to have noticed that she's been gone at all.

Her movements feel clumsy and sluggish. The words that slipped through the open window should have escaped into the night, been lost like fireflies. But instead she sucked them in greedily and they lodged inside her: settled in her gut: died there. The dead mass of them is dragging her down like cargo.

Leah taps the page and says, These are so good. How did you learn to draw like this?

Scott shrugs.

Leah says, They look like real people. Everyone I draw looks like attack of the sausage men.

Scott says, It's just practice.

He slips past Jodie and down the stairs. Everyone needs the loo.

Jodie comes over to look at the pictures. Dredd; a straggle

of mutants; Chopper against the Mega-City One skyline. On the next page, a self-portrait: Scott's face, half in shadow.

Leah says, He's actually not bad looking now.

Jodie says, You think?

Yeah. Are you guys going out?

Jodie thinks about that for a moment. She says, No.

Oh, right. I just thought.

No.

Do you want to come along tomorrow?

They'd call the cops. Seriously.

Leah looks at her. Says, So it was you that, uh...

News travels.

Fuck.

Yeah, says Jodie; Fuck.

Scott's footsteps on the stairs. Jodie reaches out – on impulse – and touches the smooth perfect curve of Leah's cheek. Leah shrinks away, flinching.

Scott comes into the room.

Jodie stretches; goes over to the window. Night air is easing its way into the house in whispers. She says, Listen, folks, I gotta go.

Scott, taken aback, says, Really? Why?

Ah – you know. There'll be all fucking hell to pay if I'm not back by ten. Eleven, I mean. Shit. Anyway. I should go.

Leah says, evenly, Are you sure?

Jodie says, Yeah. See you.

On the dark stairs winding down through the house Scott catches up with her and says, Do you have to?

Yeah, I really should.

Well – okay. See you tomorrow?

What?

We need to take the rest of the supplies over.

Maybe. Maybe we should give it a rest. Nobody's going to start World War Three this weekend you know.

She goes down to the landing below. A wedge of white light spilling out of the lavatory. Scott still following her. Jodie turns to him, frowning.

I can find my own way.

Yeah, I know. I just – kind of hoped you'd stay longer.

Anyone would think you were afraid of her, Jodie says.

What?

You don't need to be. She's nice. She likes you.

Jodie –

Seriously. She does. And you like her.

Scott says, looking bewildered and increasingly angry, I don't.

You do. You just don't know it yet.

I don't, he says, harder. What's this all about?

Egg Man, listen to me, all right? Listen to me. It's not *about* anything. I'm just – going home. I'll see you. Good night now. Stop following me like a fucking puppy dog, okay?

He stays on the landing.

Downstairs, from the sitting room, the low murmur of voices continues to dredge the past. She goes through the kitchen. There's one of the open bottles of red wine on the counter, more than half full; she plucks it from its place without breaking stride and is out the door.

15

Leah's mouth tastes of wine. Scott pulls away from the kiss slightly; she has her eyes half-closed, as if dreaming. She pulls him in again and this time as they kiss she traces her tongue across his lips. Something in Scott's belly lurches like he's stepped off a cliff.

She whispers, It's okay.

She slides one hand between his legs; when she finds his erection she makes a small moaning sound in her throat. Scott feels like he can't breathe.

She whispers, Scott. Come on. It's all right, we'll hear if anyone's coming.

She kisses him again, her hair in his face. Her hand presses on his cock through his trousers, moving more firmly now. Scott pulls away again.

She whispers, Touch me. I want you to.

Scott says, Wait.

She says, It's all right.

He drags himself away completely; stands up, wincing, his hard-on jutting painfully against his jeans. Leah's eyes are wide open now and the dreamy blissed-out look is gone. She says, What is it? What's wrong?

Scott says, helplessly, I don't want to.

She says, You do. Look at you. Of course you do.

Scott shakes his head. He mutters something half-formed: Sorry, I'm just – it's not –

The words don't come out properly.

He stumbles away from her expression of blank incredulity, and down the stairs, his head reeling.

Jodie tilts the bottle; cold red wine fills her mouth in a wash. She's wedged into one of the pie-slice vertices of the playground roundabout, legs splayed out over its rim, feet dragging on the ground. The bottle, between gulps, nestles between her legs.

There are stars overhead. It's a pretty night.

The eye finds movement. Her eye finds Scott, small and distant, on the path going past.

She pushes with her foot and the roundabout turns to follow him. Pushes again, and it creaks; and he stops at the sound. Sees her.

Jodie says, to herself, Fuck fuck fuck.

He comes across the grass quickly, Jodie trying to reel him in to her constantly-lifting frame of vision. He is angry. Arms and legs. All his movements are angry. He stops, a yard away, facing her. Jodie says, You, my friend, should not be here. This is the island of misfit toys and *you* – do not belong.

Scott says, his voice trembling, Why did you do that?

Jodie says, I didn't do anything.

You did. You know it.

(She does know it.)

She says, I just wanted to go home.

You're not home.

The island is my home.

Stop it.

Fucking hell, Scott. Sort yourself the fuck out. She's pretty. You're pretty. I bet she has her Girl Guide badges in everything. What's wrong with you?

He says, sounding appalled, You wanted us to – you wanted that?

No. You want that. I just – got out of the way.

Scott doesn't seem to know what to say. He stares at her. There is so much blame in his eyes that she has to look away. She says, So? What was she like?

I don't know.

The playground is angled and drifting. She doesn't want to look at him. She fixes her gaze on the swings. She hears herself say, Jesus Christ, why not?

Because I don't like her. I like you.

You're such a moron. I thought you were clever.

I'm not a moron. Don't say that.

You are a moron. Why wouldn't you want her?

I just told you.

Jodie starts to laugh; and once she starts laughing she

can't stop for ages, until her head hurts with it and her eyes are watering and everything's bright and shiny. She says, Nobody wants me, Oats.

I do.

Then you're a moron.

She pushes the roundabout with her feet but Scott grabs it, stops it with a lurch. Jodie feels suddenly sick – sick like she might throw up. She struggles to sit vertically: to breathe hard. The laughter is all gone.

He says, furiously, Why are you being like this?

Everything swims: tears start sharp and quivering in her eyes: a kind of wail comes from her – Go *away*. Leave me alone.

Scott says, No. I won't.

Just *fuck off,* will you?

No.

Jodie's stomach rises. She scrabbles for a handhold and pitches forward off the roundabout – the bottle spinning away, fanning its dregs – hands and knees on the rubberised tarmac – a hard gush of vomit spluttering out of her; and again; and again – all the drink and the meal, all that meticulous care – until she's retching on bile. Scott watches: doesn't move to help.

When it's done she sits falteringly back; then gets hold of the roundabout and pulls herself to her feet. She feels light as air, void and untethered.

Scott says, You need to go to bed.

She says, You need to fuck off. Please. Just fuck off, Scott. I thought you were cleverer than this. Leave me alone. I don't want you, okay? I don't want you, I will never want you. So go away. Go. Go away.

The universe spins. She rests one hip unsteadily against the cold metal of the roundabout, gathering herself; in the periphery of her vision Scott recedes, walking away, just like she told him, going away, disappearing, swallowed up by darkness.

16

He wakes late and eats cereal in the kitchen alone. On the radio, the midmorning news report says that the Soviet Union's investigation into the Chernobyl incident has concluded that the plant technicians were to blame; that the mandated safety protocols had not been followed.

There is a bitter resentment coiled inside him; he finds it hard to swallow the food, hard to get it down. When the news finishes he turns the radio off, slings the bowl in the sink, and goes back upstairs.

His father's car is gone and the house is silent.

He doesn't understand what has happened to him.

In his bedroom he finds two unwashed tumblers and the nearly-empty white wine bottle. The sketchpad Leah was looking at is splayed face-down on the desk, three of the pages bent back on themselves. He tries to smooth them flat but the creases won't go. He closes the pad and puts it on the shelf.

He takes the glasses and the bottle and puts them at the head of the stairs to take down later.

The end of the evening, seeing them off at the door, is a jumbled disconnected blur; but in among the adults saying their farewells and embracing and promising to do this again soon he remembers Leah saying Bye, Scott, thank you for a lovely dinner, in a clear expressionless voice; and remembers meeting her eyes for one dead second, and seeing in them not just a studied reserve, but also a sort of pity.

She's pretty. You're pretty. What's wrong with you?

And he thinks, savagely, *Something. Something's wrong with me. Obviously.*

He should have stayed.

Not much of a hangover.

Not much of a memory of getting home, either. Some stuttered impressions of the driveway; the front door; her bedroom. Unclear how much of that will have passed unnoticed but so far, no-one has said anything.

She remembers hoovering up water straight from the tap for a while in the middle of the night.

She remembers Scott walking away and leaving her there.

You continue north-west.

There is a gatehouse ahead. The razor-wire fence stretches to either side. By the gatehouse barrier is a dead man wearing army fatigues.

Beyond the barrier is a stocky concrete structure, set low into the landscape, and a sloping entrance tunnel, leading down.

You feel very sick; the ache in your joints and head is now severe and continuous.

What do you want to do now?

Go inside

You pass the gatehouse, staggering slightly; the pain makes putting one foot in front of the other agonising. The wind blows fine white ash and grit into your face as you approach the concrete tunnel. It is dark here and your eyes adjust slowly. There are two more bodies, huddled to one side against the wall. Ahead is a heavy steel and concrete blast door, leading to the missile silo beyond.

The door seems to be sealed shut.

You can just make out, painted on the steel, the Domino's Pizza logo and a stencilled message reading, Your ICBM delivered in under 30 mins or the next one is free.

What do you want to do now?

Try to open the door

You fumble with the silo door, but there is no way to open it. As you try, you are conscious of your hands shaking. The shaking becomes a series of convulsions. You stagger and fall to the floor. You can no longer see the door. You can no longer see anything.

Briefly you can feel your limbs trembling, knocking against the concrete.

Blackness sweeps up around you.

Thank you for participating in this exercise.

Start again? Y / N

Lunch is casserole. Jodie pushes it around her plate. Usually at lunch Radio 4 is on – something funny, then the news, then a magazine programme talking about the week's events – so they don't have to make conversation. But today the radio's silent. Her father seems preoccupied, picking at his food like she is. And she's aware of her mother glancing at her more than usual: a wary scrutiny.

Where did you go last night?

So there it is at last. Jodie says, I told you. To a friend's for dinner.

What friend?

Jodie puts her fork down. She says, Just a boy I know. He lives in a house. Where we had dinner.

Her mother says, Why?

Because he asked me to.

Yes, but why?

These are, Jodie knows, the questions that couldn't be asked last night, in front of Mrs Williams. She says, I thought Dr Grange said we shouldn't ask judgemental questions.

The phone starts ringing. For a moment it looks like no-one will move; but then her mother goes to answer it; and, after a muffled exchange that Jodie doesn't hear, comes back to tell her father it's for him.

A call from the Centre, clearly, since he's gone a long time and then returns only to say brusquely that they need him for something, he'll be back later. The front door bangs behind him.

(Important shit. Man shit. Shit that takes priority over whatever kind of shit *this* shit is.)

Her mother takes Jodie's plate and scrapes the remaining food into the bin.

She slips from the table.

Where are you going? her mother says.

I thought Dr Grange said –

Asking where you're going isn't a judgemental question, Jodie. It's just a question. I am still allowed to ask questions, aren't I?

Jodie says, I'm going out. I'm going for a walk. It's such a lovely day.

What happened last night?

Nothing happened. Dinner happened.

You'd been drinking.

There was wine with dinner.

Jodie –

I don't know what else to tell you. I went out. I had dinner with a friend. I came home.

A friend. When did he become a friend?

Jodie is silent. She counts her heartbeats up to seven.

Her mother says, letting out a breath, Jodie, I'm only trying – I'm just trying –

What are you trying?

I'm trying to...

I thought you'd be pleased that I had a friend.

Jodie.

I thought having friends was healthy. And that's what we

all want, isn't it? A healthy daughter we don't have to be ashamed of.

Her mother closes her eyes for a second; then goes back to clearing the table. She says, quite quietly, Do you ever stop to think how what you do affects other people? Do you ever – pause, and consider that? How you hurt everyone?

Jodie stares at her. Says, I don't hurt everyone.

Her mother takes plates to the sink. She has her back to Jodie. She says, You do, Jodie. You do it all the time. All the time. This is why none of the other children like you any more.

This wasn't what she was expecting. Perhaps a row: being shouted at for coming home drunk. Not this. Why is she saying this?

She struggles for a moment, trying to say something; but the words won't form. For several seconds nothing comes out. In the end she mutters, That's not true. Scott likes me.

And an oily, sick feeling uncoils inside her; because of course this isn't true any longer.

Does he. Is that what he said?

Yes.

Why do you think he said that? Why do you think boys say they like girls?

Jodie looks out the window. The sunlight in the garden is very bright. A thin keening pain is in her head now.

Her mother is rinsing the plates.

Jodie says, as evenly as she can manage, Well, I'm going out for a walk. Why don't you take a pill and have a little rest. You'll feel better.

Her mother doesn't answer.

Jodie walks out of the kitchen. By the time she's in the hall she's walking fast, fast, for the front door.

The air outside hits her like a furnace. Her eyes screw up tight. She wants to run. She won't run. They would see. Someone would see. Her footsteps on the tacky road surface are as quick as she can make them. She keeps her head down.

She has no idea where she's going.

Scott stands alone in the garden. He's got the dining table back indoors. There are divots and indentations where the furniture stood. There's a candle stub lying in the grass. It's late afternoon now and the sun is getting low over the trees, slanting straight into the garden, straight into his face. He has spent all day tidying up; washing dishes.

He could have stayed.

He goes back inside the empty house.

He could have spent the two hundred quid on a stereo. A stereo with a CD player. Instead of some sort of fucked up playing-at-houses, a game for little kids, something he should have grown out of years ago.

Wretchedly he thinks: *Her blouse was undone. She wanted me to touch her.*

And instead he blundered out of the room. And got to watch Jodie Armitage puking her guts out in a kids' playground.

Touch me. I want you to.

Would that have been all? Touching?

No. Almost certainly not.

He wanders through to the kitchen. Juice from the fridge.

He could have had sex. Woken up this morning not a virgin any more.

He is, above all else, always scared.

Scared of the war.

Scared of waking up not knowing where he is.

Scared of waking up naked and ashamed and having people seeing him and laughing.

Scared of what happened to him with Leah.

Scared of being alone.

Scared of dying.

He's paralysed by it and he hates himself.

In the kitchen, he sees Jodie's Walkman on the countertop. The headphone cable is snarled up. She's left without it.

He stares at it. Suddenly he has a penetrating, almost painful intuition that the tape inside isn't the Cure or Joy Division or anything cool like that, but something small and simple and childish.

He knows he could press play, right now, and find out.

The strength seems to go out of him.

He drags a freezer door up across the heath with her, sweating every step of the way.

He touches the white ridges of her wrist.

He cuts bread for them to share. He sits by her side playing computer games. He watches her when she doesn't know.

He sees her in his mind every time he masturbates now, the shape of her ear, her neck, her green mineral eyes. When he comes, she's always there.

Scared of everything.

Fucking coward, he says quietly; and the house soaks the words up without response. He says, much louder, almost shouting, Fucking *coward*.

The air moves slightly.

What would he do, if he wasn't scared?

One thing. Name one thing. If nothing mattered and the bombs were in the air and we were all going to die anyway, so shame and rejection and getting things wrong and being afraid simply didn't matter, weren't important any more. Name one thing. What would you do?

He is so tired of being afraid.

He takes the Walkman and slowly climbs the stairs. In his room, the radio signal fades in and out on Tracy Chapman and through the window comes the sound of a splash and a shriek from somewhere beyond the hedges. The T-shirt he's wearing is damp with sweat.

He changes it for a clean one. He puts his other pair of trainers on, the good ones.

He brushes his teeth; tries to tidy his hair.

They're all going to die anyway. Nothing changes that. Quit the program and reload.

When he comes back downstairs, his father is just entering the house. He smiles at Scott.

Hello, he says; and then, perhaps seeing his son more clearly as his eyes adjust, Is everything all right?

Yeah, Dad. It's fine.

Good. That's good. Are you going out?

Yeah. For a while anyway.

All right. Oh, and I meant to say something. Last night's dinner. Caroline and I both thought... Well. It was very considerate. And – I wanted to say – your mother would have been very proud. I think – very proud indeed.

Scott blinks. He says, Really?

Yes. Really.

Scott nods slightly. The words sink in and his body seems to store them somewhere inside; somewhere deep down; not ready, yet, to examine them directly. After a moment he says, Uh, Okay. I'll see you later, Dad.

He closes the front door carefully behind him and walks to Jodie's house.

He holds the Walkman in both hands like a talisman, the cable tangled around its heavy little body.

There is no response from inside the house.

He pictures the bland, cream-coloured rooms, unfolding one after another; all the way up to Jodie's bedroom. Her grey bed. The grey IBM on her desk. Her little row of plastic trophies and prizes from five years in the past. He imagines her in there, furious, wretched, hating him.

I don't care.

He rings the doorbell again: longer.

This time there's movement. He hears something. After a long moment, the front door opens and Scott finds himself staring at a woman he's never seen before. His first thought is that she, too, is bland; cream-coloured. But the moment the thought crosses his mind it's supplanted by another: the image of something rotten, rotted out from within; a stump full of poison.

She says, Yes?

Her eyes are hollow, the pupils like pinpricks.

Scott swallows. Takes a breath. He says, Is Jodie home?

Who are you?

Scott.

She looks at him with naked dislike. Says, after a second, I don't think Jodie wants to see you.

He blinks. He says, I – can I just – can I talk to her? Please?

The woman considers this. Her head tilts slightly. Her expression becomes, just for a moment, dreamy; far-away.

She says, No. I'm sorry.

Scott stands there. He realises – realises with surprise – that he's not going to walk away; not going to do what she wants. Even though she's an adult. Stubbornness rises in him. He doesn't move.

In the end she says, You should go home.

Scott doesn't move.

She says, exasperated, Look. I know all about you. And I don't want you here.

He feels himself flushing. He says, What do you mean?

I know all about you. Jodie's told me about you.

What did she say?

That doesn't matter. She doesn't want to see you. Not now, not ever. Find some other poor girl to – to practise on.

A flash of incredulous anger. He says, sharply, What?

Or better still find yourself a proper girlfriend. And stop this cruelty. Just stop it. Now get off my property.

And she shuts the door, right in his face; shuts it on his expression of bewildered resentment.

. . .

She doesn't know where she is. Trees. Pine needles and sand. Perhaps she is nowhere at all.

The sun is starting to leave the sky now, in fragments.

I should step off the world.

He skirts the perimeter of the Centre but she's nowhere to be found. He handed his card in when he quit, so he can't go in. And in any case, somehow he knows she's not in there.

He has been down to the main road, and through all the little twisting unadopted roads of the Heights; every branch and offshoot. He can't find her.

He starts to see other teens, drifting along casually, in twos and threes. Boys together, girls together. They're in little knots and clusters. There's an air of contained tension – excitement – to them as they pass. One girl is carrying a string of helium balloons which trail behind her, rustling and squeaking in the air.

Scott ignores them. Starts to head home.

Leah is coming up from the junction as he's coming down towards it. She's with another girl, someone he doesn't know. She sees him. Says, Scott?

He feels himself clench for a moment. But then it's gone and resignation drains through him instead. He walks over to Leah and the girl and says, Hi.

Hi yourself, Leah says; and then, to her friend, I'll catch you up, okay?

Sure, the other girl says, with a knowing smirk; and continues towards Susan Lewis's house.

Scott takes a breath; but he can't think where to start.

Leah says, I'm glad I ran into you.

Scott nods slightly. He still doesn't know what to say.

Leah says, Look. About last night. I wanted to say I'm sorry.

Scott looks at her properly for the first time: with surprise. He says, Why?

I got it wrong, didn't I?

He's not sure what she means. He waits.

Leah says, I just... I knew you guys were friends or something. And I wasn't sure if, you know, if you fancied her, or... But then she kind of went off and I thought... And I did ask. I mean, I asked her, if you were going out, but she said no.

You asked if we were going out? Scott says.

Yeah. I didn't want to – you know. But she said...

Scott nods. *She said no.*

You need to fuck off. Please.

I don't want you, I will never want you.

He straightens slightly. He says, Yeah.

So I thought... anyway.

There's a pause.

Scott says, I'm sorry too. I didn't mean to, you know. Piss you off.

She takes a breath and says, I was pretty pissed off. But then we got home and I chilled out. And then I thought about it and... yeah. Like I said. Got it wrong, didn't I?

Scott manages something like a smile. He says, Don't worry. I got it wrong too. Turns out I'm kind of stupid, actually.

Yeah?

Try to sound more surprised.

Leah grins. Her head tilts a little: she's more relaxed now. Scott too. She says, You and me are okay, then?

He says, Yeah. Sure.

She says, Good. Cos I didn't want you to... I'd like if we were still friends.

Me too.

What're you doing this evening?

I don't know. Nothing really. I was going home.

I can still get you in I bet. If you want.

Scott looks vaguely around. The road's empty. The light's going out of the sky. His dad will be in his study. No-one's going to miss him.

Leah says, Come on. It'll be a laugh.

The last of the tension leaves him. He shrugs. Says, Okay. Why not.

Cool, Leah says.

They fall into step together, crunching up the gravel towards Susan's house.

Traffic roars and blares. It's getting dark along the London Road. The cars have their lights on and the lights cut this way and that.

She goes inside.

Charlie's face is surprised, but not hostile. There's no-one else in the shop. Charlie says, Hiya. We're closing, actually. Sorry.

Jodie nods. She wanders between the tables; reaches the

counter. Charlie comes out from behind it, comes to stand in front of Jodie.

Charlie says, What's up?

I did something bad.

Yeah? What did you do?

Jodie shakes her head.

Charlie says, I'm not sure it can be that bad. I mean, you're just a kid. How bad can it be, really?

Her voice is gentle. Almost kind. For a moment Jodie thinks she might start crying.

(Wants to start crying.)

She takes the folded-up flier from her pocket. Scott's drawing of the missiles. She opens it up, working the paper more or less flat. She says, When is it happening? Do you know?

Charlie is looking at her closely. Says, Are you okay? Do you want to sit down?

She finds a stool and Jodie sits; says, more emphatically now, Your friend of a friend who knows stuff. Do they know yet?

Charlie nods. She says, Yeah. It's on. It's tonight actually.

(She has known this, she feels. Isn't it why she's here?)

(Or maybe she just knows it now, in this moment.)

She says, I want to come.

The boy with the Anthrax T-shirt and the leather jacket is holding a cigarette pinched between thumb and finger. There's a washing-up bowl full of ice and beer canted at an angle in the flowerbed by his feet. The boy takes a can out and hands it to Leah; looks at Scott and says, Who's this?

Leah says, This is Scott. He's a friend of mine.

The boy with the Anthrax T-shirt and the leather jacket shrugs and says, Okay then.

Scott says, Hi.

Susan Lewis's birthday party is somewhere behind them now. The transition is swift and easy. They breeze casually through her garden, saying hello to parents, helping themselves to snacks from a table that someone has set out, handing Susan her present – It's from both of us, Leah says – and then just as casually fade back towards the pool house, and round it, and then a ridiculous giggling scramble through the yew hedge, dark with scaly branches scraping at them and Leah's hair getting caught for a moment until Scott helps her free, and they're out into the garden of the house beyond. The boy with the Anthrax T-shirt seems to be some sort of gatekeeper: you have to be known to be allowed further.

But Leah is known.

She opens the can and takes a swig; passes it to Scott. They set off following a winding path of crazy paving, past a little summer-house and a big stand of pampas grass and then onto the lawn; heading towards the house.

17

Charlie's car is a little rattling Allegro with one wing a different colour and the back windows cluttered with stickers. She drives with a loose, carefree recklessness.

Jodie is curled in the passenger seat. She has her hands wedged tight between her legs. She can feel the pulse in her wrists, in her thighs.

You're sure your parents are okay with this? Charlie says.

I'm sure, she says; and then, with sudden inspiration, They think I'm at some party.

Someone has got the stereo turned all the way up, slamming out *Caravan of Love* at a volume that makes Scott wonder if the speakers are going to survive. He sees Aston, the boy whose house this is, trying to barge his way through to the sitting room, shouting for them to turn it down, turn it the fuck *down,* but the hall is clogged with people and he can't get through. Someone – it's Ewan – shoves a drink at him, shouting, Hey, Scotty, join the caravan, man!

And someone else shouting, What the fuck is this *shitty* fucking music? And people laughing.

Scott eases past a tight knot of girls in the doorway. In the sitting room, Aston gets to the stereo, turns the song down. There's a howl of protest; Aston shouting, You're going to get us *busted*, for fuck's sake. Keep it below seven on the dial. Below seven, okay? Jesus fucking *Christ*.

Scott knows some of the people in the room. He sees Kellie, dancing with a group of her friends. He sees Ollie Shaw and Jay Slater hanging around at the foot of the stairs, and changes direction; going instead through the kitchen. There are doors open. He squeezes out onto a patio, rubbing sweat out of his eyes; there's a loose cluster of people out here. Someone's smoking what he thinks is a joint; at least, it smells different to tobacco smoke. But the air's marginally cooler. Behind him the music fires up just as loud as before.

A big, hearty-looking girl is pouring Teachers into the upturned base of a beer can and saying, Don't just sniff at it, okay, you have to snort it right up. Get your nose right into it and snort it right up. You're instantly pissed, I swear to God.

Someone says, That's going to hurt like fuck.

The hearty girl says, Yes of course, but you're instantly pissed. *Instantly*.

Scott wanders past them. He drinks from the plastic cup Ewan gave him; drinks a little at first, and then tips it back, downing all of it.

He has lost track of Leah. They arrive together, but then

she sees someone she knows, and there's a real mob of people downstairs. When he turns round she's gone.

Now the music keeps changing from chart pop to heavy metal, as if there's a battle for control of the stereo going on. He drifts back into the kitchen and swaps his empty plastic cup for a fresh can of beer. There's a girl with brown hair by the fridge; she puts a hand on Scott's shoulder and says, Do I know you?

I don't think so, Scott says. The girl looks pretty drunk.

She says, confidentially, Kellie hates me now. Because I'm going to be a model and she's not.

Yeah? says Scott.

Yeah. She's furious. You don't think I'm shallow, do you?

No, Scott says.

Because models are, aren't they? Because it's all about looks. But not me. They said I have an everyday quality, so – that's not shallow, is it?

No, Scott says. I don't think so. What're you going to be a model for?

Camber Sands Families. It's an advert. You know, for holidays? You're really nice. What's your name?

Scott.

I'm Sandra. Kellie's really, really pissed off with me.

Yeah? Scott says.

I don't think we're friends any more.

That's a shame, Scott says.

No, says the girl. Fuck her, really. She gets everything. She's a fucking cow sometimes.

Right, says Scott. Okay.

So fuck her, right?

Right, Scott says again.

Fuck her. Do you think I'm pretty?

Uh, Scott says; but at that moment the girl sees someone through the kitchen door: she shrieks at the top of her voice – *Cathy!* – and barrels through the people by the breakfast bar; someone's drink slops everywhere and there's a shout, and jeering laughter, and the girl is gone.

Scott opens the beer and stares vaguely around the room.

Everyone else seems to know what they're doing. Everyone else is having fun.

Charlie stops the car in a lay-by ten miles or so outside town, off the dual carriageway. There are four or five other vehicles already here, and a loose group of people gathered behind a tan hatchback where a man is handing out whistles and torches and fluorescent vests and armbands. When Charlie gets out of the car, several of them shout or wave. One girl runs right over and hugs her.

Jodie hangs back, watching.

The people in the lay-by seem to be a mix of types and ages. Quite a lot of them are young, but the man with the tan hatchback is older. Her father's age. There's a small flurry of introductions going on. Some of the people seem rather intense; others are more casual. The general atmosphere in the group feels charged and purposeful. One man is saying, insistently, No, they changed the route. We had confirmation half an hour ago. We're fine here but Gary and Paula and the others need to come to us. That's why we're waiting.

Someone else is saying, The *Clarion's* sending someone this time at least.

What about the *Post*?

No. I told you, he's such a lazy bastard, he won't come to anything after 8pm.

You'd think nuclear war was worth getting off the sofa for.

Yeah, you'd think.

Charlie comes back over to her. Says, almost gently, Hey. Want to come and say hello?

Jodie allows herself to be led over to the group. Everyone knows Charlie and they seem happy to accept Jodie too, though she catches some odd looks from the older people. There are no other kids here.

Someone gives her a plastic cup of coffee from a thermos.

Above them, the hard glitter of stars starts to be patchily veiled. Over towards town, a dull orange glow is faintly visible in the sky where the streetlights are catching the clouds. The weather seems to be changing. There's a low grumble of sound in the distance.

What's that? Jodie says uncertainly.

Thunder, I think, Charlie says. Shit. Should've brought a coat maybe.

They stand around in the lay-by. Then, after a long time, a line of other vehicles comes into view along the road, driving slowly. There are several family cars, a camper van and a truck. The truck pulls off into the lay-by while the other vehicles drive up the road to a point where they can cross the central reservation; they return on the far side, honking their horns cheerfully, and pull up on the verge opposite. A scatter of people emerges and they come trotting across all four lanes of the road to join Charlie's group.

Jodie thinks, *Gary and Paula and the others.*

Everyone is lit strangely, by torch beams and tail-lights.

Charlie is bouncing slightly on her toes, energised, excited. She goes over to the hatchback; says something to the man there. He gives her something from a bag. Charlie comes back and says to Jodie, Here, have a sandwich.

Jodie takes it from her. She says, Thanks.

Her stomach feels clenched shut.

There is a man with a camera: the reporter, or photographer, from the newspaper. He's sitting in the open doorway of one of the cars, smoking a cigarette.

At the further end of the lay-by someone starts singing the chorus of a song Jodie doesn't know, a chanting aggressive-sounding song, and immediately eight or ten others join in. Charlie joins in. She's lit intermittently by torches.

Jodie wonders why Charlie is being kind to her. Why she is allowed to be here. Don't they realise that she is bad for everything, for everyone?

There's the squawk of a CB radio from the truck dashboard, and a man steps briskly over and answers. There's a brief exchange and then the man gets up on the running-board of the truck and shouts, Okay, five minutes, five minutes everyone, they're just past the Northgate junction.

The group is galvanised. The reporter flicks his cigarette away and fiddles with his camera; someone else is setting up a video camcorder on the roof of one of the cars; the singers stop singing, tighten together briefly, then disperse. Charlie comes bounding over to Jodie. She grins and says, You ready?

She knows she is not. She doesn't know what to expect – what is coming – but she knows she is not ready.

She nods and says, Yeah. I'm ready.

Charlie is gone. People are shouting instructions. Someone starts a car engine briefly and there's a short, stupidly loud burst of music, stopping as abruptly as it starts; and a wave of laughter in reaction. They're tense. Jodie too. With them.

Figures are spreading out across the dual carriageway now: torch beams flicker and sweep the tarmac and once in a while stab briefly up into the sky.

A girl squats down at the edge of the lawn to pee. Scott looks hastily away. The girl says, Good luck getting into any of the bathrooms.

Scott says, Yeah?

Yeah, says the girl, I think people are screwing in there. Or puking up or something. Hey, did you see? Lizbeth Jones took her top right off and was dancing in her bra. What a slut. Whoa. That's a whole lot better.

She hoists her jeans and sets off towards the house; then turns and stares hard at Scott, blinking. Says accusingly, You're not Anthony.

No, Scott says. I'm Scott.

I let you watch me *pee*, the girl says.

I wasn't watching you, Scott says.

She considers this; then starts to laugh. He watches her

stumble across the patio towards the music. Far off in the sky, there's a flicker that might be lightning; but no sound comes. At the door she turns and shouts back at him, What are you doing out there in the dark anyway?

And then she's inside and swallowed up by the crowd.

Has anything ever actually happened?

In 1957, the world almost ends. But the accident doesn't seem to give anyone pause for thought: doesn't trigger any kind of scramble to reassess, reappraise.

Instead, later in that same year, the largest ever nuclear weapons testing process in the continental USA begins at the Nevada Test Site. Twenty-seven experimental nuclear detonations are integrated with massive troop movements in order to assess how ground forces will fare, physically and psychologically, in a nuclear theatre of war.

The programme incorporates biological analysis on a previously unconceived scale. More than a thousand live pigs, chosen for their crude physiological similarity to humans, stand in for soldiers and civilians when the bombs are detonated. Some are placed in elevated cages and equipped with a variety of protective coverings. Others are placed behind glass panels in order to gauge the incision wounds inflicted by shattering windows. The tissue damage, radiation exposure, degree of burn coverage and physical trauma inflicted on the animals form vital experimental data, indicating what would happen to people under similar circumstances.

Later, a word comes into circulation to describe the

people of Nevada, Arizona and Utah whose communities fall within the typical fallout zone of these, and subsequent, nuclear bomb tests. They are *downwinders* – those who live downwind.

As part of the same series of detonations, a nuclear explosion codenamed Pascal-A is performed in an underground shaft. It is the first ever underground nuclear explosion. The purpose of Pascal-A is to simulate accidental detonation of a nuclear weapon in the event of, for example, a plane crash. In effect, Pascal-A is an attempt to gauge what might have happened – but did not – following the accidental drop of the 10-megaton warhead outside Kirtland, Albuquerque, two months previously.

There are lookouts further up the road. One of them sends a red flare trailing lazily up into the sky: it hangs there, seemingly unmoving, and for a moment everyone stares; and then there's a concerted rush of fuss and activity through which the rumble of approaching vehicles becomes rapidly audible.

The convoy comes into sight moments later. At the front are big boxy army trucks. The CB radio is squawking again. Someone – Gary – shouts, All right, light them up, folks.

The cars in the lay-bys all switch on their headlamps; and the torch beams all play across the Army vehicles.

Charlie has given her a torch. She points it at the truck and gets a momentary, shocking glimpse of a soldier's face through the side window of the vehicle. His expression is vicious: hateful. Jodie flinches.

And then the rumble of the trucks vanishes, swallowed up by a long, sustained roar of sound, flooding in through her head and up through her feet, the ground shaking: a staggering amount of noise. Into her view come enormously long cargo-carrying machines, their engines throbbing the air. On their load beds she sees the missiles: huge, finned cylindrical bulks, dull and massive. Actual nuclear missiles, thundering past her in the night, close enough almost to touch.

Beside her a man with a camcorder balanced on his shoulder is tracking the missiles as they go and saying in a loud, clear voice, So this is the 501st tactical missile wing of the United States Air Force taking their nukes off on manoeuvres from Greenham Common. We're told this set of exercises will last eight days. All transfers are of course done at night so that the general population remains unaware. We are told that the convoy will pass through the town before turning north...

The noise overwhelms his voice: overwhelms Jodie entirely. They come in an unbroken line, missile after missile, far bigger than she would ever have imagined. Jodie's bowels seem to uncoil and loosen. Her torch beam plays over the dead hulls of the missiles as they pass by – a pitiful finger of yellowish light wandering across their contours. She is appalled at the size of them, and she is appalled too at their silence. Even in the midst of the roaring thunder of the truck engines, the missiles themselves seem to exude silence: to suck sound into their enormous metal bodies.

They are so obviously containers of death.

She feels herself step forward into the road. She feels her

hand reaching out. The rush of air of the next truck buffets her in the face and Charlie is seizing her, dragging her back off the tarmac, screaming *Jesus shit Jodie be careful!*

More flares climb into the sky: and others are lit by the side of the road, burning caustic red and spanning the road with alternate fans of light and shadow as the vehicles pass through. There are intermittent white flashes from the reporter's camera. The lights overhead drift and the shadows twist with them and for a moment there is some sickening echo of No-Man's Land, of the Somme, of a different and pitifully outdated kind of war.

Jodie blinks. Her eyes are crowded now with pallid afterimages. The sky flickers again.

And then the missiles are past. There are more personnel trucks; some of the protestors are jeering at them. But the missiles are gone.

Except not really. She can still feel them.

The last vehicles go past. There is a hollow, hissing stillness for a moment.

Death, destroyer of worlds. She could have reached out and touched it, right there, on the road outside her home.

They are going through town, the man said. Past her house and Scott's house.

Something else is happening. Two vans full of policemen. The doors bang open and grim-faced men in uniform are corralling the protestors, ordering them back towards their cars, telling them to clear the road.

Some won't go. Some are jostling and struggling. The photographer keeps snapping away. One man sits down in the centre of the road with his arms folded and his chin tilted high. The man with the camcorder on his shoulder is trying to film this; but two policemen grab him, and in the scuffle the machine falls and bursts apart on the tarmac in a scatter of small broken pieces.

Jodie hears a woman's voice saying, urgently, Charlie, get the kid out of here, yeah?

Charlie has her by the arm. Come on, she's saying. Let's go. Jodie? Come on.

She lets herself be led to the car. Someone is shouting. Someone else screams suddenly.

Something inside her is breaking apart. She is too small. She is too small and she is not strong enough. How can anyone be strong enough for this. It's breaking now, this is the gap that was there before, that ripped open inside her, only now it's not just a gap it's everything, too big to fathom or contain. Scott is gone and she is alone and she is falling into herself.

Charlie saying Come on. Jodie. Please.

In the car. The car moving. Lights lurch and jolt and steady. She presses her hands between her legs like before but there's no winding this back, it's too late. She squeezes her eyes closed and sees the missiles.

Scott drifts through milling people. Downstairs the music has changed again and now it is deep, bass-heavy, languidly insistent; sexual. Knots of dancers twist in and out of the frame of his vision. A couple in the corner of the room are locked together, snogging as if feeding off each other; the boy's hand is right up the girl's skirt and she's squirming against it rhythmically. He thinks of Leah in his bedroom, her lips slightly parted, her eyes closed.

The air is different. As if someone has wound it up tight.

He finds himself in another room. The curtains are drawn and it's dark. The music is muted here, throbbing, carried through walls and floorboards. A candle is fluttering in the middle of an oval dining table: there's a home-made board, an upturned glass. The people seated around it stare at him: whisper among themselves. Someone says, Do you want to try?

Someone else says, audibly, Shit, what about his *mother?*

Scott shakes his head and goes back out of the room.

The house is unfamiliar. The heavy bass of the music seems to come from everywhere.

Upstairs he moves aimlessly between rooms. Some are locked. He hears, from one, someone crying. From another, a girl's voice making the urgent sounds of sex.

In a room with heavy metal bands on the walls he finds Leah. A small group has congregated here, sitting in a disorderly jumble on the floor, the bed, a couple of beanbags. A fat kid in a striped shirt is at the centre of the group. Leah looks up when Scott appears in the doorway: she exclaims, excitedly, Scott! Come on! And then, to the fat kid, Do Scott. Do Scott.

The fat kid beckons Scott over and stares at him for a moment. He says, That's a tough one. That's really tough. Cos I mean, you'd imagine blond, wouldn't you? But... no, I don't think so.

He presses his fingers to his temples and closes his eyes, frowning.

Come on, someone says, giggling.

Okay. I'm getting something. I'm having to dig deep here, okay? But I'm getting – kind of sandy brown. Kind of speckly sandy brown. McVitie's digestive.

Everyone convulses with laughter.

Scott says, What?

Leah says, almost crying with laughter, Your pubes. Callum can tell the *exact* colour of your *pubes*.

The fat kid says, modestly, It's a gift. I don't like to boast, but – it's a gift.

Someone says, Is he right?

Someone else says, Show us then.

The fat kid is grinning. He says, I'm right, aren't I? I am always right.

Someone says, How do you *do* that?

Leah is saying, Scott. Scott.

He goes over to her. Back in the group a girl is saying, Do me next!

Leah is on the bed. She pulls Scott close and whispers in his ear: Scott. Listen. Look at me.

He looks at her.

She says, Am I the same?

Scott says, The same?

The same. Because I don't feel the same.

He says, How do you feel?

Wobbly. And – divided. Divided into three pieces.

Scott doesn't know what to say.

Leah says, But do I look the same?

Scott nods. He says, Yeah.

Good. That's good. Hey. Was Callum right about your pubes then?

Scott says, He's just looking at people's eyebrows.

Leah says, What?

They're the same.

She pushes him aside. Turns and shouts at the fat kid, sounding outraged, Callum! Are you just looking at people's eyebrows?

The fat kid says, Hey. I thought you were divided into three pieces? What do you know?

Leah says, sounding as though her world is crumbling, I *believed* in you.

There's a group howl of understanding and accusation and amusement. Everyone's shouting at the fat kid, or laughing at him. He holds his hands up in surrender, grinning. And now everyone is looking at everyone else's eyebrows, in on the trick. One girl is saying, loudly, Oh God, now I can't see anything else.

Scott says to Leah, Are you okay?

She nods. She whispers, confidentially, I ate some hash brownies.

Ah, Scott says.

And now I feel wobbly.

Ah, all right then. But you're okay?

I'm absolutely okay.

He starts to move off the bed but Leah says, Scott. Scott.

Yeah?

She pulls him in close and whispers, You're a good friend.

Thanks, Scott says.

Maybe I shouldn't have eaten the brownies. Do you think I shouldn't have?

It's okay. It's fine. Don't worry about it.

He slips out of the room.

Everything is coming apart. Everything is cracking and coming to pieces. The trees. The houses. The tarmac. The sky. Like one of those little sliding-tile puzzles. Each house shifting slightly, trying to make space for the next one; each tree dislocated by a fraction. The gaps in the roadway close and then open. The chain-link fence ripples silently and comes apart and closes. The Heights twitches and stutters and tries to make itself fit into a space that's no longer adequate. The tiles slide and rearrange and slide and Jodie is caught between them, caught in the gaps.

No street lamps on an unadopted road.

No-one sees her. She is invisible. She is the ghost child.

Scott's house is dark and silent; she has to look away. Like someone died.

(Someone did die.)

The house tries to move; to shrink back. But she's desperate. She can hear her heart hammering crazily. She can hear her breath coming in and out, too fast.

The back door is unlocked.

The house tries to jerk sideways away from her. She holds on.

Scott's room is empty. All the rooms are empty. Scott is gone.

She can hear her heart, louder and louder.

She is making a small noise in her throat, like a whimper. It's too loud in the dull air and she tries to stop; but the noise isn't hers to command.

No-one fixes the potholes on an unadopted road. No-one spreads salt in the winter. Everything is patched and filled piecemeal. It's not enough.

The pine trees change places secretly, like gleeful dancers caught out of the corner of the eye.

There is nowhere left to go and everything is breaking open and she is too small, she is not strong enough, there was supposed to be a girl-sized shape cut into the world somewhere but she could never find it and instead the world has crammed itself into her. And there is no room left in her any more to fit the world, she has been cut free and left to drift in the wind.

She is standing by the playground but Scott is gone.

The air is thickening and getting heavier. She can't breathe properly. She can sense the ground trying to wrench itself apart and failing.

She can hear her heart.

Why did you do it?

Why did you say that, why did you do that, what were you thinking?

Why did you hurt that girl?

Why did you hurt yourself?

Why didn't you hurt yourself *better?* Why didn't you do it properly and finish the job?

Too weak to do it right the first time.

Too weak to stop doing it every time since, over and over.

A tattered thing hung together by scars, but even they are coming apart now.

Unadopted means private. Unadopted means unwanted. Unadopted means alone.

She is by the community hall at the top of the Heights. There are pieces of paper on the noticeboard. She can't read what they say; the letters make no sense. Nonsense words. The letters are crawling like ants.

She is standing in the road. Her arms wrap round the shell of her body, tight, tight, trying to still the heartbeat, trying to compress, trying to compact, she is so small already, if she squeezes hard enough she might just snap out of existence, cease to be, except her heart keeps knocking her arms out again, beating her shape back into place, hammering out a receptacle in the shape of a scrawny useless unwanted kid, a kid who fucks up everything she touches, every person she tries to touch, even herself.

She is standing in the road. The stars are not in the right places any more. The stars are crawling like ants and draining out of the sky.

She is too exposed. She will fall through the cracks.

She cannot work out where she went wrong.

Something broke. Something small but important. Small but vital. Something broke and nobody noticed. Was it in her? Or was it in the world?

The ground under her feet is full of tics and twitches. The trees are creaking and their trunks are splitting apart.

The air presses in on her. Her heart punches it away. The air presses in again.

She digs her elbows into her ribcage. Flattens her forearms across her belly. Grips with her fingers. There is a thin line of static drilling through her head like a wire saw; she is threaded on it, unable to pull away.

She is in dark gardens. The bushes and hedges jerk and splinter and move aside to let her through. When they close again there's no trace. There's not even a hole in the air. It's like she never existed.

Patches of darkness shift here and there and she is tugged along by the bright keening sharp-toothed thread that splits her brain. Her feet on grass. Her feet on stone. Her feet on gravel.

Lights well up: big, dim, yellow-toned, blurred blocks of light coming out of the darkness. And sound: a heavy deep-pitched pulse nudging insistently into her, making her want to stagger; but the static behind her eyes holds her upright.

People moving.

A roomful of figures in time with the heavy rhythm of the music.

The static breaks. Evaporates. She puts her hand on the cold metal frame of the patio doors. The thin wire is gone. She is on her own now.

Her heart is louder than the music.

She steps inside the house.

Hardly anyone looks round. Hardly anyone sees her. There are a couple of dull incurious glances and then people go straight back to dancing. The air smells thick with sweat.

• • •

She is Anderson on the planet of the dead, with bone dust and the husks of skulls under her feet.

She sees the future. All their futures.

They will be corporate executives, account managers, directors of business. They will work in data analysis, or banking, or for multinationals. They will be civil servants, or work in PR. A whole generation. They will have middle-class houses. Double garages. Salaries and bonuses. Squash games at the country club.

Will any of them love their children?

(She is too small for this. There is not enough room.)

A boy is shouting something at her or past her: his face leers close then slides by.

She is not Anderson. Anderson is strong enough to contain horrors; she is not. They leak and bleed straight out of her in billows, gusts.

And what about her? What about Scott? Where will they be? What becomes of them?

She can't bear it.

So many people. Everywhere you look there are faces, noise, words. If she were locked in plastic would she still hear them?

She is lost and can't find her way. The keening sound

deep in her throat is back, but the sounds of the party are so loud that she is sure only she can hear it.

She is in a room. Someone has draped a thin green cloth over a table lamp and the room has taken on the quality of being underwater: it is murky and the corners seem not so much far distant as deep and unreachable. It takes Jodie a strange, discontinuous amount of time to move. There is a couple sprawled on the bed, still clothed but slowly writhing. There are clumps and tangles of kids in the shadows and the air is full of drifting smoke and the smells of beer and cheap spirits and sweat. One girl stands alone in a patch of floor as if asleep on her feet: eyes closed, head nodding.

Their parents were like this, in the 60s, they must have been, and look what happened. Look what is left.

Scott is sitting almost in darkness, in a crook of shadow where the bed meets the wall; of all the people in the room he is the only one who looks properly alive. His eyes are still alive. Everyone else has been drawn down below the surface.

She is on her knees beside him and his face is turned to her, a perfect O of astonishment.

Words break out of her. She says, Scott, Scott. Please. Come on. We have to go. Please.

Everything is very slow. Scott doesn't understand. They will be trapped here forever.

She says, We have to go. Please Scott.

She remembers what to say.

She says, Trinity. Trinity. You have to. You promised.

Something changes. Something penetrates, connects. He moves. He struggles up off the floor.

Doesn't ask anything. Doesn't say anything. Jodie seizes his hand, clutching it like a refugee.

They run with their feet slapping on tarmac and gravel. Scott running as fast as he can. His breath tearing. Jodie won't let go of his hand; her grip is painfully tight.

The track up to the heath is pitch black. There don't seem to be any stars. There is the sense of pine trees looming on either side. Scott's feet scrabble and slip on the loose sand. Four minutes is not enough time.

Gorse rips at them. Jodie trips and falls and brings Scott down with her. He hits his head on something. There is a flicker of brilliant light somewhere on the horizon. Another. Scott feels an awful shocked draining sensation. He can hear Jodie whimpering, a thin, constant sound.

They are lost. There is no way to make it in time.

The earth vanishes from under them and they fall. Jodie lets go, crying out. Scott feels the air punched out of him. But it's the gully. He scrambles to his hands and knees and searches for her. Finds her by the sound. They cling to each other. A blinding flash staggers everything: for a fractional moment the gully, the bushes, their appalled faces, the texture of the ground, all of it is starkly revealed and then instantly blotted away by lazily swimming afterimage.

Scott drags Jodie to her feet. They are nearly there.

A huge thunder of sound engulfs them.

18

They are inside the shelter.

They cling shivering to each other in the darkness. All around them is a constant roaring sound. It's everywhere. They cling to each other.

ICBMs tear through the sky. Cities blink and are enfolded. All across the planet great structures of flame lift into the atmosphere and lives are boiled away.

She is trembling. He holds on to her. His hand holds the back of her head.

For a time he thinks he can hear a heartbeat that is not his own. He thinks he can hear her heart beating.

Time passes.

Very slowly the trembling eases.

Everything is black.

Clumsily, in the darkness, they find their way to one of the bedrolls. Scott drags the sleeping bag over both of them. Her knees and elbows keep knocking against him awkwardly. She curls on her side. Scott pulls the sleeping bag over their heads. The roaring from outside is muffled down to nothing. Now there is just the sound of the two of them breathing, two sets of breath, one faster than the other; slipping in and out of mesh every minute or so.

And both slowing, gradually. They huddle under the army surplus sleeping bag in dark musty warmth.

Time slips past, exhaled gradually, one breath at a time.

They become very slowly accustomed to this new dark closeness. Neither of them moves.

After a long, unclear, unmeasurable time, Scott drifts into a sleep broken now and then by fragments of dreams; by a sense of falling; by the unfamiliar breath of someone else against his shoulder.

And he dreams that he wakes suddenly.

Everything is dark.

There is a constant, deafening roaring sound. It's everywhere. It seems to press down and crush him.

The air is thick with dust. He can't breathe. He strains

and tears his way through rubble until something gives way and he feels hot air on his face. The roaring is much louder, buffeting his eardrums, painful, incessant. He is hurt and damaged. He has no idea what has happened. He has no idea what to do.

Scott wakes in darkness so deep that for a moment he thinks he is trapped in the dream. But his arm moves; his hand moves; he scrapes his elbow against concrete as he pushes the soft weight of the sleeping bag aside.

The roaring noise has ceased. Everything is silent.

It is pitch black in the shelter. Even in the middle of the night in his bedroom, some kind of light, however faint, creeps round the curtains from the street lamps in town. Now though he can see nothing at all.

He feels Jodie move slightly against him. She says, Scott?

He says, whispering, Hi.

Are you okay?

I think so, he says. Then, Yeah. Are you?

Yeah.

He is on the verge of saying, What happened?

But of course he knows what happened.

Instead he says, I'm going to try to find the lamp.

He moves slowly, with his hands out. Pitch black, he keeps thinking. He knocks over some tins and packets. He finds the other bedroll. He has his fingertips outstretched, questing, like antennae. He finds a camping lantern on its side in a corner and fiddles the switch on.

Both of them wince and squint until their eyes adjust.

Jodie sits, drawing her knees up and wrapping the sleeping bag around her. Scott sets the lamp down in the middle of the floor.

They look at each other.

Jodie says, We made it.

He nods.

She stares around the small rectangular blank room with a look of wonder on her face. Says again, as if to herself, We made it.

Scott gathers up the scattered tins and packets and starts putting them back where they belong, with the store of food and water. They've filled dozens of plastic bottles and these are stacked in rows against the dividing wall in the middle. The packets and tins and camping stove and everything to do with cooking is there too.

Medical supplies are in the big olive drab backpack, divided among its pockets and compartments. Sundry items are against one of the side walls. The bedrolls are against the back wall, the one buried by the landslide.

Hygiene and waste supplies are in the front room, out of sight for now; it's dark in there. They must have closed the improvised blast door as they came in.

Jodie gets carefully up off the floor and limps slowly around the room. Scott finishes his tidying away. Everything looks strangely well-ordered and neat.

It's silent in the enclosed concrete space. There's no more roaring or rumbling. No sound at all.

She puts her palm flat against one of the walls. It's cool; solid; permanent.

The little camping lantern casts a comforting yellow glow. Every time one of them moves, their shadow leaps to follow on the wall.

Scott says, You're limping.

She looks at him. Frowns. There's a ragged track of dark colour down the side of his face. She goes closer; says, You're bleeding.

Scott looks confused for a moment. He stares at her, up and down. He says, So are you.

He points, and she realises he's right. There's blood on the back of her hand.

They kneel down on the floor facing each other. Scott turns on the second camping lantern and brings both lamps close. Jodie examines his face. There's a livid bruise up on the side of his head, just at the hairline; and blood has run down all the way to his jaw.

Shit, she whispers. Okay.

She gets a pack of gauze and a bottle of water and some antiseptic and sets to work: cleans the broken skin on the bruise, wipes away the blood, puts antiseptic on the wound. Ow, Scott says mildly.

When she's finished, they roll her sleeve up to look at her arm. It seems to be scratches, mainly: torn skin from brambles, or gorse, as they fled across the heath. Scott works carefully down from elbow to wrist, picking out pieces of thorn a couple of times. He washes the scratches, applies the antiseptic.

Did you hurt your leg? he says.

Why?

You were limping.

She moves a little. Yeah, she says. It hurts. It's my knee. I think it's just bashed up a bit.

She touches it experimentally with her fingers. Winces. The knee feels tight, swollen against her jeans. But there's no blood.

I think I just wrenched it, she says. When we fell maybe.

Scott nods. Could be worse, he says.

She says, her voice small, Do you think they hit Sandhurst?

She doesn't look at him. She has her eyes fixed on her feet, drawn up tight in front of her.

Scott thinks for a moment. Then he says, slowly, as if feeling his way, I suppose so. I think so. It felt like it was close.

It did, didn't it?

Yeah. I think it must have been Sandhurst.

Jodie hugs her knees. She's quiet again. When they speak there's a strange hard resonance to the space, the concrete walls setting up odd immediate reflections of sound. When they're quiet the concrete seems to be waiting.

Are we – she starts; then hesitates.

What?

Did we get – burned?

Scott looks at her carefully. He says, No.

And then, after a moment longer, he says, I don't think so.

Okay.

I think... he says slowly. When that second flash... remember?

She nods.

When that one hit, we were in the gully already. Out of the line of sight, I mean. Like the trench Bruce Banner was trying to get to.

Who's Bruce Banner?

The uh, you know. The Hulk, Scott says; and closes his eyes for a moment, wincing.

Scott, she says sharply.

I'm okay. It's just the light, he says.

Jodie turns off one of the lanterns. Is that better? she says.

Yeah. Thanks.

You hit your head pretty hard, she murmurs, gently moving his hair aside with her fingers.

I should take paracetamol I think, Scott says.

She nods: goes to the backpack and finds some. Pours him the water to take it with. Scott downs the two pills gratefully.

Sit back, okay? Jodie says. You don't have to do stuff, you can tell me and I'll do it. What's the next thing?

We need to block the radiation, Scott says. There's potassium iodide.

Jodie finds it. They both look at the bottle.

We have to take it once a day, Scott says.

Okay, she says. How much?

Scott blinks. Uh, I don't know, he says. Doesn't it say?

She squints at the bottle. No, she says.

I think we're supposed to mix it with water, he says uncertainly. But I don't know how much.

Well, Jodie says, If it was supposed to be just a drop or something, it would be in a little bottle with a dropper, right? But it's in a normal bottle.

Maybe a teaspoon or something like that, Scott says.

Yeah, she says. Exactly. Like for cough medicine. Sounds right. We can try that.

Okay.

She fetches two mugs, puts a teaspoon of solution in each, and tops them up with water. They drink slowly. The mixture tastes sour and metallic.

So that helps stop the radiation, she says quietly.

Scott nods.

And we don't have any actual burns. Not, you know. Obvious ones.

He nods again.

So maybe we're okay, she says slowly. Maybe... you know. We were quick enough.

Maybe, Scott says; but he doesn't sound sure.

She looks at him. What? she says.

Radiation's strange, he says. It can take time.

What's going to happen? If we actually did – you know.

Um. Nausea and vomiting are the first symptoms, he says. Do you feel sick?

No. Do you?

A little, he says. But maybe just cos I hit my head.

Jodie's arm is aching. Her knee throbs against the fabric

of her trousers. She says, We should just press on like you said, with the iodine. Wait and see. Once a day?

Yeah. Every twenty-four hours.

Okay. What time is it?

Scott looks at his bare wrist in blank confusion.

I lost my watch, he says. Maybe – at the party? Or on the heath, when we were running...

Jodie shrugs. Okay, she says. It's not a problem. It's okay.

But inside her a voice whispers that it is a problem. They have no way of telling what time it is. If it is night or day. How long has passed while they were both sleeping. How long before they should take the next dose of iodine.

She puts the thought aside; moves awkwardly to lean against the wall next to Scott.

The important thing is we made it, she says again, very softly; almost a whisper.

Just for a moment something tries to slip into the corner of his mind. A little curling tendril of distress. His home. His father.

He squeezes his eyes closed. It's not like he lost anything. Not really. His home has been gone for eight months now. His father has been gone for eight months now.

She looks at him from the corner of her eye. In the woods, near the empty ants' nest, she said *We need a plan;* and Scott made one. Found this place for them. They filled it together but he found it.

He becomes aware of her looking. Glances round at her. Smiles slightly: shyly.

He sleeps for a while, curled on his side; his head resting on the second sleeping bag, which she rolls up for him.

She watches him. The tousle of his hair. His slow breathing.

She's worried about his head. If he has concussion. What are you supposed to do if someone has concussion? She has no idea.

Time goes past, but there's no way to tell how much, except by counting breaths or heartbeats. Eventually she gets up, as quietly as she can so as not to disturb Scott, and starts to examine their supplies more carefully. As well as the essentials, they've both been bringing occasional treats. There are packets of sweets; some chocolate; biscuits; bubble-gum (strawberry flavour in pink packets, watermelon in green); and a pile of comics and annuals that's grown steadily with each supply run.

She has brought a handful of programming magazines. If Scott wants to learn FORTRAN or BASIC, this is his chance.

Not that there are any computers any more, though.

The comics aren't in order. She sits carefully beside them and sorts them methodically by issue number.

When she's finished with the comics, she looks round; and sees Scott has woken up. He's watching her. He smiles.

How are you feeling? she says.

Better, he says. He stretches: sits up properly. Jodie puts

the pile of comics against the wall and comes over to sit next to him.

Do you want some water?

Yeah. Thanks.

They pass one of the bottles back and forth for a moment.

Scott says, So you sorted the comics?

Yeah. All ready. There are a few gaps though.

Scott says, Don't worry, I can tell you what happens.

You know them off by heart?

I know some of them off by heart.

You're a real dweeb, you know that?

Scott says, mimicking her, I've got an IBM. I bet you're jealous.

Jodie sticks two fingers up at him. He's grinning at her and she feels the answering smile on her face.

You look better, she says. You look like you. I was worried there for a moment.

Did I not look like me?

You just looked kind of woozy.

He nods. Says, Well, I feel okay now.

She says, What do you think's happening?

Scott says, What, outside?

Mm.

Scott sits back against the rolled-up sleeping bag. The smile fades and he's silent for a while. His eyes seem fixed on something far away: as if he can see outside the concrete chamber.

He says, Uh... well. Things will be on fire. Things will burn for a long time. The middle of the cities will be just gone, but then there'll be huge areas on fire. And it'll be dark, from the ash. Dust and ash get sucked up, right up into the upper atmosphere, and they don't come down again. They just float there. So, it'll be dark, except for where things are burning.

Jodie is staring at her feet. Then she says, We're safe in here though.

Scott nods.

She says, What about the people?

I don't know. If you were in the blast, you're just gone.

What if you weren't in it? Just near?

Scott shifts uncomfortably. He says, You know Hiroshima? The survivors talked about seeing people get melted like wax. Some of them just melted away, but others – only part of them. Like down one side. Or part of their face. Or one hand because it had been exposed. And I read this thing where they saw stuff running down the street, like wax, but it was really what was left of people.

Jodie mutters, Jesus Christ.

Scott says, almost to himself now, But the blast radius isn't really the thing. The thing's really the radiation afterwards.

She says, The fallout.

Scott nods. He picks at a frayed tear in his jeans. He says, Fallout and nuclear winter. That's what happens now. That's where most of the people die.

Jodie shivers slightly. She says, Not us though.

Yeah. Not us.

. . .

He watches her as they talk. Watches her eyes, in the low glow of the camping lantern. Seeing her sitting cross-legged, steadily organising the comics into order, has reassured him a little. The sick, disjointed, lost look she had before, which frightened him so badly, seems to have faded; gone almost completely.

But he watches in case it returns.

He becomes aware of a dull ache, low in his belly.

Uh, Jodie? he says.

Tell me.

I need to pee.

Right. Yeah. Actually me too.

Okay.

You go first.

Scott takes a torch with him through to the front chamber, ducking through the low doorway. They've set aside empty water bottles in the corner here, in readiness. Next to them is a heavy plastic bucket and a roll of bin-bags and some packs of loo paper. They're going to be in here a long time: they have tried to be practical.

The flat concrete walls seem to amplify sound. Scott's faintly appalled by how much noise it makes, peeing in a bottle: and how long it goes on.

When he comes back, he finds Jodie curled into the corner, fighting back giggles like a little kid.

Fucking *hell*, Oats, she says. What's wrong with you?

I really had to go, okay? he says.

Really? Wouldn't have noticed. It was completely normal. Not at all like the Niagara fucking Falls was happening in there.

You try, he says, grinning despite himself. It's not easy. It's really loud for some reason.

Then you cover your ears. I'm not going if you're listening.

No. No way. You didn't.

I wish I had.

But you didn't. So no.

Cover your *ears*. Do it.

Or what? Scott says. You'll wet yourself? We can just wait. I'm absolutely fine, by the way. Just so comfortable and relaxed now.

I hate you, she says.

I'll cover my ears, he says, still grinning, and hands her the torch.

When she comes back she says, a little shamefaced, Well, okay. You're right. About the, uh. The sound.

I know, Scott says. It's like some weird amplifier in there.

Yeah.

She's silent for a moment. Something seems to be bothering her. He says, What is it?

Okay, look. What about when we need to shit?

Cover our ears.

No. Not good enough, she says.

Scott sees, with delight, that she's blushing. He says, This really bothers you doesn't it?

A bit. It's a bit fucking gross to be honest. If I had my Walkman we could use that, but I lost it.

Scott says, You left it in the kitchen. I tried to bring it round, but... yeah.

Oh, she says, in a small voice.

Silence for a moment.

Jodie says, All right. We sing. Really loudly, okay? Cover your ears and sing until the other person's finished.

Scott looks at her, uncertain. He says, I sing really badly.

What, worse than someone taking a shit? Fuck, man, come on.

Now they're both cracking up. Scott shakes his head: says, Okay, that's a deal.

Thank God. Now let's never speak of this again.

Yeah.

Their first meal is tinned hotdogs and rice. Scott gets the quantities wrong and they end up with way too much rice; and without a watch to time it, it's soggy and overcooked. But the food's hot and filling and they realise how hungry they are. They spoon it up off metal plates, filling the chamber with happy homely clinking noises. Jodie puts the leftover rice aside: there's enough for another meal.

She says, We really are like Topsy and Tim.

I don't know who that is, Scott says.

They're kids in a picture book I had when I was little. Actually there were several books. In one of them they went camping or hiking or something and, I don't know, it kind of stuck. Have you ever been camping?

Scott nods. He scrapes the plate and says, Yeah, once. Kind of. We went to Cornwall. I was really excited, I thought we'd be in a forest in the middle of nowhere or something cool like that. But it was a proper campsite. Me and Ward had one tent, and Ward's parents had another, but there were other families right next door, and a shower block and proper bogs and everything. I thought we'd be in the wilderness but it was more like a housing estate.

Who's Ward?

Kind of a friend. Only they moved back to South Africa.

Oh.

I've never been into, you know, proper wilderness.

Jodie puts her plate down. She says, Neither have I. Only the heath.

The heath's pretty cool though, Scott says.

I suppose everything's going to be proper wilderness now.

Yeah.

They clean the plates carefully using disposable baby wipes. Scott has brought several packs, but they still have to be rationed. They fill the air with the incongruous, childhood smell of talcum powder.

Scott says, I spy with my little eye something beginning with C.

Jodie says, Concrete.

Your turn.

I spy with my little eye something beginning with B.

Bunker.

They're both laughing now.

Morning, afternoon and evening they decide will be defined by meals: in effect, by when they get hungry. It's the most primitive timekeeping, governed by the internal rhythms of their bodies. Night will be when they're tired. Day will be when they wake up.

Jodie scratches a little line on the concrete wall with Scott's knife, to mark the first day. Now they can keep a tally.

They agree to ration the comics, just like food and baby wipes: one in the morning, one in the afternoon, one in the evening. They read them sitting side by side, with the pages spread open: one resting on Scott's knee, one on Jodie's. Scott finds that he can sense where Jodie's eyes are on the page: he realises that she reads much faster than he does. While he's finishing a spread she goes back over the earlier panels. She never says anything – never tells him to hurry up or asks why he's taking so long. She teases him about lots of stuff but not that.

Sitting side by side, their hips touch; Scott's right thigh rests against Jodie's left. Their shoulders touch. Their arms. He is aware of the small, contained heat of her: as though there's a furnace inside her.

She says, We should have brought more books.

There wasn't time.

I know. But still.

There'll still be books out there. I mean, they won't all be burnt up or anything. Some are going to be left.

So is that our priority when we get out? Find books?

Scott says, Well. We can put it on the list.

What's first on the list?

We don't need to worry about this now.

I'm not worrying. I just like to know. How long do we stay in here?

Scott says, Twenty days minimum. That lets the worst of the fallout decay. If we can stay in longer, it's better, if we can stretch the food and water, you know? The longer you wait, the less radiation. But you don't want to end up so weak that you come out after, you know, forty days or whatever, and then fall over from hunger.

Jodie says, Okay. Got it. Twenty days.

So once we're out, the first thing on the list is food and water. We take the backpack and we stock up wherever we can. We're going to be scavenging basically. The thing is, so is anyone else who's survived, so places that are easy to get into – you know, supermarkets and so on – they're going to be empty pretty fast I think. What I'd really like to get is a water purifier. I should've bought one. Or at least tablets, you can get tablets. It's stupid, I was only thinking of what should go in the shelter, not what we'd need afterwards.

Jodie says, You did all right. We'll get one.

And some kind of weapons.

Yeah?

Yeah. I don't think we can assume that there's any law and order any more. I mean, they'll try. They'll have some kind of martial law or whatever for a while. They'll mobilise the army, whatever's left of it I mean. And there's supposed to be a plan to set up aid centres and treatment centres. I think every town council's supposed to have that. But it's going to break down eventually, because aid centres need food, and treatment centres need medicine, and no-one's going to be making those any more. When they run out, they run out. And soldiers are just people. They're going to follow orders for a time but then they're going to realise, this is it.

It's all over. There's no point. So... I think we need to be prepared for that. Be thinking like that from the start, so it doesn't catch us by surprise.

Jodie says, All right. What do we get?

Scott says, I was thinking an air rifle and a crossbow for starters.

Jodie says, What the fuck, Oats. I thought you were going to say flamethrowers or machine guns or some cool shit like that.

Scott grins and says, If we can get a pistol or something, okay. But an air rifle's good for hunting. You can shoot birds, rabbits. Crossbow too. And they're both silent. And with the crossbow you get your ammo back again.

Jodie says, So, okay, air rifle and crossbow for survival. And a pistol each for protection.

Sounds good.

There's a gun shop in Frimley, you know that? They've got shotguns and all sorts.

Yeah. We can break in maybe, like in *Commando*. And the army surplus store has the other stuff. I should've bought an air gun at least. Well. I was a bit low on money.

You did fine. Look at us. We're okay. This was the first step, right? Getting here was the first step and we did it. The rest we'll do one day at a time.

Scott nods.

They're quiet for a while.

He says, Maybe we should turn the lamp out. Save the batteries.

Yeah, okay.

The space goes black. There's no sound from outside. Whatever remains of the world, outside the shelter, is silent.

Scott finds himself unsettled by the darkness and wishing the light was on again; but feels it would seem foolish to say so now. He tells himself to wait.

Jodie says, her voice small in the darkness, Where do we go, afterwards? Do we stay here?

Here like in the Heights? In Camwell?

Yeah.

I don't know. I don't think there's anything here to stay for.

So where do we go?

I hadn't thought that far.

There's a faint scuffling sound in the dark as Jodie changes position. She says, I think we should go to the sea.

Yeah?

Yeah.

Why?

Well... we can fish. Fish won't be poisoned, will they?

Scott says, I don't know. I don't think so. Water blocks radiation, so...

And rivers run to the sea. We can find streams. Fresh water.

Yeah. All right. That's good. We'll go to the sea.

And the sea won't be on fire. It won't be broken and ruined and fucked up. The sea's the sea, always.

There's a long silence in the darkness. Scott begins to wonder if she's fallen asleep. But then she says, quietly, The nuclear winter's because of the dust. All the dust that goes up, that blocks out the sun.

Scott says, Mm.

How long for?

Years I think. Maybe three or four years. It's cos it gets so high in the atmosphere it doesn't come down. It just makes this blanket over the whole planet, and the sun can't get through. Plants are going to die. It's going to get really cold. Animals will starve. And people. So first there's the radiation, and then there's that.

Jodie says, quietly, Maybe it'll be warmer by the sea.

19

She isn't sure whether they doze or not. Time seems to have passed. Later, though, they're both hungry, and Scott switches the lamp back on.

Dinner is the leftover rice heated up with baked beans. Jodie stirs the mixture in a saucepan. The little camping stove hisses quietly.

She says, I saw the missiles.

What? Scott says. In the sky?

No. On the road. I went to the CruiseWatch thing. And I saw the missiles.

Scott blinks. You went to the protest? he says.

Yeah.

How?

Charlie took me.

She stops stirring the pan for a moment and looks at him uncertainly. Scott is frowning, as if struggling to make sense of what she's just said.

She thinks she can see, in his face, something like betrayal.

After a moment he says, What was it like?

It was scary. Really scary. I...

She struggles to find words.

She says, I wish I hadn't gone.

Scott nods slightly. He says, You actually saw them.

Yeah. Really close. I think – I mean, I tried to touch one. But someone pulled me back I think.

I've never actually seen one, Scott says. Pictures, yeah, but for real...

Don't, she says. You don't want to. I wish I hadn't. I really wish I hadn't.

Scott nods again. He seems to have withdrawn into himself slightly.

She says, her voice low, Scott?

Yeah?

I'm sorry.

For what?

For going. Without you.

It's okay, he says.

I know I shouldn't have. And I, uh. I wanted to tell you.

Okay.

Cos it felt like I was keeping a secret. And I don't want to do that. Not from you.

Okay, he says again; but his voice is softer this time.

I really wish I hadn't gone, she says quietly.

She tries the rice and beans mixture with her finger. It's hot. She turns the little stove off and dishes out the food.

They eat with the plates on their laps, leaning against the wall, side by side.

After a while she says, Is it all just going to happen again?

What?

I mean – in a hundred years, two hundred years, when the sky's clear and things are growing, what then? Do we build it all up again? Cars and cities and governments and armies and, I don't know, apartheid and communism and nuclear deterrence and all the same shit? Or do we learn, do you think? Do you think people can learn?

He says, That's not going to happen. We can't do it again. Not ever.

But just saying that isn't enough. We might.

No. I mean we really can't. You're talking about building things back up to the way they were, but we'd be starting from zero. Kind of a blank slate. All the machines, all the technology, cars, computers, oil rigs, power stations, all that, they'll be wrecked. The EMP will have trashed the electronics and everything else will be half rusted away before we get organised enough to start doing anything.

But we could make new ones.

No we couldn't. Technology's like a ladder. You can't just pick up a couple of stones and build yourself a television. How do you make the glass? The wires? Transistors and circuits and all that? You can't start there, you have to start with basic machines. Steam power. Basic manufacturing. You have to climb the ladder, right? Except you can't, cos all the bottom rungs are gone. You need an industrial revolution, and that means coal and oil and iron ore and that was okay the first time cos they were just under the surface, you know, they were easy to get hold of, people could dig that stuff out of the ground with some picks and shovels and a bit of sweat. But we already did that. All that easy stuff near the surface is gone now. All the bottom rungs have been used up. Now if you want coal or oil or copper ore or iron ore it's buried really deep, you have to have specialised machines and electrically-operated lifts even to get down there, and none of that works any more, so... We can't build it up. A planet gets one shot at an industrial revolution and we had ours. So the best we can do, probably, is kind of live off the scraps. I mean, we could smelt bits of iron from old car bodies. Make arrows from broken shop window glass. Scrape gold off circuit boards for jewellery. We'd get to the Iron Age okay I think. But I think we stall there. We don't ever get to make nukes again. Or TVs, or microwaves, or spaceships, or Ferraris, or I don't know, CD players.

Jodie says, I didn't know that.

I read it in a magazine.

They eat in silence for a while.

Jodie says, We fucked everything up.

Not everything. We're still here.

We're pretty fucked up, in case you hadn't noticed.

Scott starts laughing. Yeah, he says. Good point.

Pretty fucking dismal look-out if humanity's best hope is us.

Shut up, he says, grinning. I think we're awesome.

Yeah, but you hit your head pretty hard. That's the brain damage talking.

No. It's not. We're awesome, he says.

He sounds like he means it.

She's quiet for a time; thinking to herself. Then she says, Kind of sad, though. All the things that are gone forever. Like you said. Cars and computers and... I dunno. All that stuff just lost, and no way to get it back.

Scott shrugs slightly. He says, We might not care. Maybe we won't even remember.

What do you mean?

He says, At school we did this poem in English. It was an Anglo-Saxon poem. It's really weird, it's a totally different language, but there was a translation. And it was about the ruins of a Roman city. This Anglo-Saxon poet had walked through the ruins and written a poem about what he saw. People think maybe it was Bath.

Okay.

And this was, I don't know, maybe three hundred years after the Romans left. So he's staring round at columns and temples and villas, all ruined. And he calls it the work of giants. Because his people live in thatched timber huts. They don't have lavatories or fountains or bath-houses or paved roads or lead plumbing, any of the stuff the Romans had. I spose they turned their backs on all that the moment the invaders left. This kind of technology freaks him out completely. Giants must have done it.

Any sufficiently advanced technology is indistinguishable from magic, she murmurs.

Yeah. Exactly. So maybe that's going to be us. A couple of hundred years from now maybe no-one will know what any of this was for. We'll think circuit boards were abstract art, or maps of forgotten places, or something. We'll think cars are the skulls of metal monsters. We'll say cities are the homes of the old gods, but don't go in there, cos the gods are jealous and they'll make you sick.

Jodie nods slightly. Says, Yeah.

Scott says, At least we can't make the same mistakes a second time. We can't do any of it a second time.

They eat the rest of their rice and beans in silence.

They begin the Judge Child story. They both prefer Brian Bolland's meticulous, hyper-real artwork to some of the sketchier versions of Dredd; but Scott says that Bolland doesn't do many strips, precisely because the style takes so long to commit to paper.

I wish I'd brought a sketchbook, he says with real regret. And some pencils.

Yeah. When we run out of these, you could draw us some new ones.

He smiles at that. I can do the pictures, he says. But coming up with the stories is hard.

I'll help, Jodie says. I bet we could do really good stories together if we tried.

Scott looks at her curiously. Her quick, sharp little face looks calmer; almost relaxed. She glances round and meets his eyes. The flicker of a smile.

What? I bet we could.

He says, No. It's not that. I was just thinking – it's okay, isn't it? In here I mean. It's really okay.

Her smile widens. She says, You're so easily pleased, Oats.

. . .

Time slides past leaving no trace. To Scott it feels as though the shelter has somehow lifted free of the rest of the world; is now drifting, uncoupled, moving into some strange unknown unknowable territory.

They lie on their bedrolls, a couple of yards apart, with the camping lantern and the comic they've read on the concrete floor between them. Before long they're both yawning.

Jodie goes to brush her teeth. While she's gone, Scott takes off his shoes and socks and, after a moment's hesitation, his jeans. The concrete floor is cool and dusty under his feet. He folds the clothes.

The first night's huddled closeness; her breath on his shoulder.

Jodie is gone longer than he expects. When she returns she seems preoccupied and self-conscious. She fiddles about with her sleeping bag but doesn't get in. She says, Scott?

Yeah?

Can we move the beds closer?

He stares at her, taken aback. Then says, quickly, Yeah, sure. Of course.

He moves the lantern over to his side and shifts the two bedrolls next to each other. Like that? he says.

Jodie flashes him a quick, nervous look of gratitude. She says, Yeah. It's okay, right? It's just, it's lonely otherwise.

Of course it's okay. I wanted to as well. Cos, uh. It was nice. The first night.

Yeah. Exactly.

Scott goes to brush his teeth. He pees into one of the plastic bottles.

It's not about sex. It's about not being alone. He knows that.

When he comes back, Jodie's in her sleeping bag. She's made them both makeshift pillows from spare clothing. Scott gets into his bag beside her; rests his head on the little bundle of fabric.

Not bad, he says.

Yeah. We forgot pillows.

We forgot a ton of stuff.

It's not the end of the world, she says; and then, hearing her own words, she makes a face. Shit, we can't say that any more.

No, it's okay, Scott says. The end of the world's outside. You can still say it while you're in here.

Okay.

He turns on his side so he can look at her. Now that the bedrolls are next to each other, they're very close. Jodie shuffles round onto her side too. She looks at him for a long time, steadily.

What? he says at last.

Is your head feeling okay?

Yeah, Scott says in surprise. He hasn't thought about his head for a while now. Yeah, it's, uh, it's okay I think.

Good, she says, with quiet satisfaction.

Do you want to turn the light out? he says.

Yeah. Go for it.

He switches off the lantern. For a long time he lies there, hearing the faint sounds of her breathing in the darkness.

They made it. They're here, and they're safe; they've planned well. They have supplies. They have each other.

There's no going back.

His throat feels tight though. He waits; breathes; and the tightness eases and settles and he's okay again.

There's the slightest rustle of movement, as though Jodie has shifted a little in her sleeping bag. He hears her whisper, very softly, Scott? Are you awake?

He whispers, Yes.

She says, so quietly that the words hardly reach him, Why do you like me?

He thinks of how to answer that. *Because of the back of your neck. Because of the scars. Because you're not as unkind as you try to be. Because of your eyes.*

He says, slowly, I don't know. I just do. Not everything has to be because.

He waits for her to say something else; but she doesn't. She seems content with the answer. Time goes past; and the rhythm of her breathing slows and deepens into sleep.

And Scott sleeps too.

20

In Scott's dream they're naked, their bodies pressed tight together, their arms and legs slow and tangled and entwined. The furnace heat of her is against him; and then all around him.

She says, Scott.

Someone is shaking him. His arm.

He fumbles his way into a confused consciousness, in black dark. But there's movement. It's Jodie. She is saying, Scott. Wake up. Scott.

I'm awake, he says blearily. He's aware of her hand gripping his arm, hard. And that he has an erection.

She says, urgently, Scott, I feel sick.

Scott says, What?

I feel sick.

Hang on. Hang on.

He finds the lamp. Jodie lurches out of the bed; through to the other room. There's a pause; then the sound of her retching violently. Scott scrambles out of his bag and pulls on his trousers. He hurries through to where Jodie is hunched over the bucket; he holds her, pulls her close. Says, over and over, It's okay, it's okay, it's okay.

She is sick three more times, with Scott holding her and tending to her and tying up the plastic bags when she's finished. But at some blurred indeterminate time in the middle of the night, Scott begins to feel sick too; and then to vomit; and then both of them are seized with cramps. Diarrhoea follows with appalling swiftness. Neither of them is now in any state to tend to the other, or comfort them, or do much of anything except blunder to and from the lavatory corner.

The air becomes foul, but they pass the point of caring, or even properly noticing.

Scott, doubled up with the twisting pain in his bowels, can hear Jodie sobbing.

At some point the battery in the lamp runs down. The bulb dies to a dim amber thread in the darkness and then winks out entirely.

Time passes.

He tries again to vomit and the spasms just tear at his stomach and throat.

He passes out, or something like it. At one moment he is sitting against the wall, his head pressed against the concrete. The next moment he is sprawled on the floor. Or maybe he has just slept.

Jodie has fallen silent.

The thought takes time to penetrate. She is no longer crying. He can't sense her moving.

He is suddenly properly awake, awake and very afraid.

He croaks, Jodie. Jodie.

He finds his way to her on all fours. Her body is curled tight, knees drawn up to her chin, facing the wall. Scott is terrified. His heart hammers so hard he can't tell if she's breathing or not. He clutches her and waits, desperately, until at last he feels her breath on his hand.

She is breathing raggedly. She is not dead. Scott clings to her: presses himself into her back: gets his arms around her. She is not dead.

Time passes and time passes and time passes.

At some point, floating in the darkness, he hears her whisper, her voice cracked, Scott.

I'm here. I'm right here.

I'm sorry.

It's okay.

I'm sorry for what I said. You know what I said. In the playground. I'm sorry.

It's okay.

I don't want to die. I'm sorry.

It's okay.

. . .

Time passes. There are nightmares. He is falling. He is lost. Jodie is dead. He is dead.

She walks naked out onto the heath. The nuclear blast has erased the bushes and the trees. What's left is a vast, endless plain stretching to a dark horizon. The sky is low and keening and dark. The sand has melted to glass, fused and frozen in every direction; undulating like heavy water. Every time lightning ripples through the clouds, the glass gleams back an echo, dull, green; a smooth endless mirror. The whole heath has scabbed over with it.

Under her bare feet it is smooth and strangely warm, even though the air against her body is frigid. When she looks down, her own pale reflection oils to and fro in the green surface. She is alone on the glass plain. She is the only living creature left in the world.

The glass starts to crack and splinter under her. She gasps in shock as her feet break through the crust into the hollows and cavities below. Curved sickles of glass slice through her soles; slice them ragged; cut right through. Shards and fragments start to lodge in her flesh and grind against the bones of her heels. She whimpers but can't stop walking. Behind her stretches out a trail of footprints thickly sodden with blood. Each step is unbearable but she can't stop. Each step breaks fresh splinters, keen and savage, and her feet are all but gone now, just ruined stumps sliced to tatters; and she still can't stop.

Finally she stumbles; falls. The sharp ground hurls itself at her. The thick glass scab of the heath shatters into knives and spears that punch through her: her desperate outstretched hands, her body, her face. She is pierced through and through. She feels the blood running out in a flood, draining out of her into the thirsty sand below the glass; and the sand soaks it up eagerly. She tries to cry out, but her lungs and belly have been lanced wide and even the breath has spilled out of her and slipped away. She dies without making a sound.

21

Scott hears the scuffle of movement. He senses the shape of her in the darkness. She is moving: sitting up.

He lies still on the floor, dredging up some kind of proper awareness. There is dull pain all through him. His head aches. His throat is raw. But the nausea itself is gone.

Jodie shifts, slowly. She eases away from him. He senses her creep off the bedroll. She is trying not to wake him.

He whispers, Jodie?

He hears her say, Yeah. Hang on.

There are some more scuffling sounds; then a searing white light. Jodie croaks, Ah, fuck.

The light dims or his eyes adjust. She's found a torch. Scott sits up, squinting.

She looks gaunt and exhausted. Her hair is matted with dried sweat: her lips are cracked and swollen.

Scott whispers, You need to – you have to drink water.

She nods wordlessly. Takes one of the bottles and drags it over to him. They lean against each other in the nook of the corner, passing the bottle back and forth. Their hands shake. The water tastes sweet and clean and good. They drain the bottle empty. Scott, moving painfully, gets another. They drink and drink.

After a time Jodie says, What about the, the ration?

Scott shakes his head. Says, No. Drink it. It's okay.

They finish the second bottle. Jodie rests her head back against the wall and closes her eyes. Scott sits staring blankly at nothing.

The water makes a difference. The headache ebbs away a little. They sit, unmoving, side by side, with the torch beam spilling up the far wall.

Eventually Jodie says, in little more than a whisper, We didn't die.

No, Scott says.

I dreamt I did. I dreamt the glass – the glass cut me open.

No, Scott says again. You didn't die. We didn't die.

She's silent for a while. Scott too. His eyes drift vaguely across the texture of the concrete opposite; through the wonky halo of the torch beam.

Eventually Jodie says, Tell me the truth, okay?

Okay.

What happens now?

Scott says, I don't know.

His voice sounds a little louder in his ears. A little less broken.

She says, Bollocks. Tell me.

I don't know what our exposure was. And that's what, you know, that's what decides.

Whether we die or not?

Yeah.

If it was a high dose, is there anything we can do?

No.

Jodie mutters, I'm fucked if I'm going to die now. I want to go to the sea.

Scott feels the strongest surge of emotion. To his shock, tears spring into his eyes. His shoulders start to shake.

Jodie struggles round to look at him. She says, Scott?

His mouth is trembling. He struggles, hard, not to cry; but it's no good. Sobs start to wrench their way out of him. His body lurches with them.

Jodie gets her arms clumsily around him and pulls him close. His head is in the crook of her neck. She holds him as tightly as she can; as tightly as her arms can manage. Cradles him like a child.

At last he stops. No more sobs; just low, ragged breath.

There is a span of quiet subsistence. Recovery. They eat sparingly: cold food, straight from cans. They drink as much as they dare. Scott is concerned that they're both dehydrated. He insists that they drink, and Jodie doesn't argue, even though they both know it will mean trouble later.

They both feel dizzy and spaced out and disconnected.

They lie next to each other.

Sometimes, in the dark, they talk a little. Sometimes they hold hands in silence. They sleep. They wake.

They have lost track of days now. Days have gone the way of hours and minutes. There are no more scratches on the concrete wall. Time is held between the two of them, like a thread in the dark; they feel their way along it together, by touch.

And at some point, out of nowhere in the darkness, he says, I want to stop being afraid.

She says, Afraid of what?

Everything. I'm always afraid. I'm sick of it. I want to stop.

She says, I don't know what the fuck you're talking about. You're the bravest person I know.

As they recover, as the overwhelming, immediate experience of the sickness recedes and something like ordinary strength returns, Jodie becomes more aware that her mouth feels furred and sour. That her clothes are filthy. That her body stinks. They're ordinary concerns. She is well enough at last that they bother her.

She says, Do you think we can use some of the wipes? Maybe half a pack each? Like a bath, sort of. I feel pretty gross. I know we're supposed to save them, but... seriously. I reek.

Scott says, Yeah. Definitely. Me too.

I wasn't going to say.

Thanks.

And clean clothes, she says.

God, yeah. Yes please.

And then we say this is a new morning, fresh start, we ration everything properly from now on. But at least we're clean. Deal?

Deal, he says.

She gathers a pack of wipes, a bin bag, a change of clothes, and one of the lamps. Scott has put new batteries in both of them. In the doorway between the rooms she stops; turns back.

What? Scott says.

You have to promise not to look.

I won't.

Swear it on your balls, Oats. I mean it.

I won't, he says gently. Really. I wouldn't do that.

She believes him.

In the front room she strips everything off and throws her old clothes away. She works her way down her body with the wipes, from face to shins, using them one at a time and rubbing hard. She goes over armpits and crotch and bum several times. She tries to reach the small of her back, making awkward jabs at it with her arm twisted up from below. Even with the concrete wall between them she feels frighteningly exposed; raw; laid bare; even though, really, she trusts him with her life.

The clean clothes go on and with them relief and safety and a return of confidence.

Then she brushes her teeth until they feel silky against her tongue. She brushes her tongue, and the roof of her mouth, making herself gag; and rinses her mouth; and when she's done she feels new, newly minted, a fresh-struck talcum-smelling version of herself.

She goes back through almost laughing now and says, Your turn. It's really worth it by the way. Seriously.

While Scott is gone, she tidies the room. Everything is a mess but she works steadily. She rearranges the bedrolls and smooths down the sleeping bags. She sings under her breath as she works. She clears away rubbish and tidies the scattered provisions and supplies that they've kicked over in the darkness.

On the floor beside the backpack she finds a small colourful cardboard packet. She picks it up: stares at it. It's a pack of Durex.

Her chest feels suddenly tight; squeezed; but she breathes, and breathes again; and the little rush of panic fades. Instead she finds herself with a surreal impulse to laugh: to give in to giggles.

The truth is she's thought about this. Ever since they saw the magazine pages on the heath, and she found herself wondering about Scott's body.

The idea of sex used to be unimaginable. Not just the terrifying exposed vulnerability of the nakedness, of being seen, but the far more horrific thought of *someone else inside you.* Her mind used to reel back from it: would just recoil.

But these past few weeks, the strangest thing has happened. She's found herself – very cautiously, very tentatively – turning round and round the thought that if it were Scott, then it wouldn't be *someone else.*

It would be Scott.

Even inside her, it would be Scott.

And. As it turns out. Apparently, given the condoms. He has thought about this too.

Thinking about it is still scary. But not in the same way. Not for the same reasons. It is like reaching the edge of a cliff and seeing over for a second and your stomach dropping.

He's so practical. He's thought ahead. Gone to the shops and everything.

The giggles are trying to come back now.

Why do you like me?

I don't know. I just do.

She finds herself believing it, properly, for the first time; trusting it all the way.

She puts the condoms carefully into a side pocket of the backpack, and closes the flap over them; and after a second, goes back to tidying.

Her stamina is painfully low and by the time he comes back she feels exhausted; but the room is neat and his face lights with a smile. He says, Wow.

Yeah.

Not bad.

Jodie settles herself on her bedroll. She won't let him see how much it's cost her. She says, Make us some breakfast if you like.

Is it breakfast or lunch?

Let's say it's breakfast. I want to start again. This is a new day, remember?

Okay, he says.

She watches him looking along the tins and packets. His look of concentration. His dirty blond hair in a tangle.

Neither of them has thought to bring a comb or a brush. But his face is clean and, it seems to her, quietly at peace.

She says, idly, We can read a Dredd afterwards. Or two. We're owed, aren't we? We must have missed some. How long were we out of it?

I don't know. Three or four days maybe.

We could have three in a row, then.

Scott nods. He turns to her with a tin in one hand and a packet in the other. How about meatballs and noodles? he says.

For breakfast?

I was thinking it's kind of like bacon and eggs.

How exactly is meatballs and noodles like bacon and eggs?

He shakes his head. Yeah, he says. I just really want bacon and eggs. Okay, forget that. What do you fancy? There's spaghetti hoops.

No, she says. Do it. You made me want it now.

She watches as he boils water; makes the noodles; heats the tin of meatballs. When he hands her the plate she wolfs it down. She's starving.

It's good, right? Scott says. I mean it shouldn't be but it really is.

Most important meal of the day, Jodie says with her mouth full. I wish we had butter. Butter on noodles is the best.

Yeah, I wish we had ketchup.

You'd put *ketchup* on this? You're a sick man, Oats.

Don't you like ketchup?

Of course I do. Just not on fucking *meatballs,* you freak.

Scott's laughing quietly. Jodie puts her empty plate on the floor beside her and sighs with contentment. Scott stretches widely: luxuriously.

Do you want pudding? he says.

What do we have?

Fruit cocktail. Custard creams.

You know, we made some really suburban food choices, she says, shaking her head. Give me a custard cream, okay?

They sit side by side eating the biscuits in companionable silence. When she's finished, she brushes the crumbs off her lap onto the concrete. Scott leans his head back against the wall.

That is so much better, he says.

Jodie's quiet for a long time. At last she says, If I tell you something, you have to promise not to laugh, okay?

Okay, he says easily.

It's just... I know it sounds stupid. But I think this is the happiest I've ever been.

The moment she's said it she wishes the words back again. Scott turns to look at her. Jodie can feel the heat rising in her face: she looks away. Coughs.

I told you it was stupid, she mutters.

No, Scott says. It's not. Me too.

They sit without talking for a long time, as strength seeps back into them. Jodie relishes the feeling of clean skin and clean clothing. The feeling of having just eaten: her belly full and warm. The bunker feels safe again: almost cosy, with the gentle light from the camping lantern.

Scott brings three comics over from the pile, and puts them next to his pillow. Jodie curls on her side to watch him.

This is like bedtime stories, she murmurs.

We just had breakfast.

I don't care. I never had bedtime stories. I have to make up for lost time.

He darts a quick, curious look at her.

I mean I had *books,* she says after a moment. I had lots of books.

No-one read them to you?

At school they did sometimes.

Your mum didn't read you stories?

Jodie doesn't answer. Scott turns on his side, too; on his elbow; so they're facing each other. His eyes, in the lamplight, seem strangely deep: like tunnels. She looks at him, unblinking, for a long time.

Finally she says, Did your mum used to read to you?

Yeah.

Tell me how it was. I mean... if it's okay. If you don't mind saying. Cos...

No, it's okay. I don't mind, Scott says.

But he doesn't speak. Jodie waits. Scott is no longer looking at her; his eyes are fixed on the floor between them.

She shuffles a little closer to him; finds his hand with hers; gently laces her fingers into his. Scott blinks.

He says, quietly, When I was little my bedroom wasn't in the attic. That used to be a storage room basically. My bedroom was at the end, right at the end. Past the bathroom. It's a little room. It's just little. And it was, uh, there was this blue and white wallpaper. And a white wooden box for my toys. And a chest of drawers. And my bed.

Jodie nods.

So when I'd done my teeth and got into my pyjamas she'd read me a story. Or make one up sometimes. She used to make stories up, just out of her head.

What kind? Jodie says.

Just... adventures. Travels to far-away places, things like that. The pyramids, or ancient Rome, or the Grand Canyon. But they'd always end the same way. They'd always end with me coming home, and going to bed. So no matter how far away or what the adventure had been, that was always – you know. Like safety. It was always safe at the end.

Jodie closes her eyes. She nods.

And when I was learning the piano she used to sit next to me on the stool. I'd play and she'd say, Careful. Or, Now's the tricky part. Or, you know. That was really good Scotty.

She can hear in his voice how his throat has tightened. She waits.

Scott says, And we'd make things together sometimes. At the table in the kitchen. I'd draw things. Or we'd cut up paper. Sometimes my dad would join in. We'd be in there, all of us. Sometimes we'd cut out paper people and put them in a kind of collage landscape that she made, with hills and trees and a river. My dad was hopeless. It was really funny. He'd try to make people and they'd come out awful. My mum kept saying, We've got enough trees, Jeremy, we don't need any more. And he was saying, It's not a tree, it's a person, can't you see? And my mum – she was laughing so much, me too, we were laughing till we cried.

He pauses. Thinks for a moment. Says, It was actually pretty cool of him to do that. He didn't have to. We always laughed at him, I mean, every time. But he still joined in. He didn't mind.

There's silence for a while. Jodie feels the warmth of his arm against her arm. The soft pressure of his fingers.

Scott says, Now all he does is work. Not really though. He pretends to work. He's made up this imaginary thing he's doing. This story we both pretend is real. And he just lives in it.

She nods, ever so slightly. The despair, the emptiness, in his voice cuts right into her.

And I don't know why. I mean, why can't he – what's he even *thinking?* I just – I don't understand. I just really don't understand. It's like he's not even sad. He isn't even sad she died.

That's not true, Jodie murmurs. Really. It's not true.

She opens her eyes. Scott is looking at her. He seems very small somehow; very much like a child. He says, Do you think so?

I know so. I heard him talking. That night with the dinner. He was talking to Leah's mum.

Caroline? Scott says.

Yeah.

You heard them?

She nods. I went downstairs, she says slowly. I didn't mean to – I mean, I wasn't trying to spy on anyone. I was just kind of fucked up. Anyway, I, uh. I heard them.

What did he say?

Jodie thinks for a moment. Remembering.

She says, He said he wished he was a better father. That he wasn't getting anything right and he knew it. But he didn't know how to do better.

Scott stares at her. Says, He said that?

Yeah. I was right outside the window. I know that's not cool. Sorry.

What else?

They were just talking about her. It was all about you and her. How he misses her. How he loves you. I don't remember what he said exactly, but it was in his voice. Really strongly. All the time. You could feel it. I could feel it.

Scott stares at her.

After a while he says, Thanks.

You're welcome, she says softly.

He says, Jodie?

Something in his voice. She feels herself go very, very still.

The kiss is bewildering. It makes no sense. That it should feel like this makes no sense. When Scott finally breaks awkwardly away she whispers, No. Do it again.

He traces the contours of her face with his fingers; her hair; the nape of her neck; shyly, almost with wonder.

She's never felt like she was the source of wonder to anyone before.

This is the edge of the cliff and her heart is hammering and she thinks, *Just keep walking.*

She says, Can we, uh –

Scott draws back slightly.

She can feel the blood in her face. She says, Can we turn the light off?

He says, surprised, Yeah. If you like.

Only, maybe you should put a rubber on first. Cos – in the dark. I don't know. Are they fiddly?

Scott looks utterly blank for a moment; then says, a little at random, Um, you have to – yeah, they kind of...

So maybe do it now? I moved them. Sorry. Hang on.

She finds the cardboard pack and hands it to him. They both stare at the condoms for a moment. Scott is blushing furiously. Jodie has a sudden almost overwhelming urge to laugh: but she doesn't.

He says, almost a whisper, Are you sure?

She nods quickly. Then, with a sharp pang of uncertainty, You do want to, right?

Yeah, he says. Yeah. It's just – everyone says it hurts the first time. For girls I mean.

I know, she says. I heard that.

I don't want to hurt you.

She looks at his face: at the doubt, the concern there. The last shreds of apprehension slip away. She squeezes his hand. She says, I hurt myself all the time, remember? It's okay if it's you.

Afterwards, in the unbroken expanse of darkness, they lie curled against each other; tangled together. The sounds of their breathing slip in and out of mesh again, ragged and amazed.

She feels his fingers trace across the inside of her wrist. She feels him touch the tiny raised scars there, where her pulse leaps.

Her hand moves and closes over his and holds his fingers against her heartbeat.

The darkness seems to fit itself around her; around the two of them. Like it's carved out a little space, here in the bunker, just the right size and shape for her and Scott.

His head is resting just beside hers. She can feel the heat of his breath on her forehead.

The way his body felt – the way their bodies felt together – keeps flashing through her.

His hand is resting loosely on the jut of her hip. On her skin. One of his knees nestles between hers. And nothing inside her is panicking or clenching or loose with fear; nothing is coming apart or breaking. It doesn't seem possible, but it's true.

Scott's hand moves up the side of her body, from her hip to her waist to her shoulder; he strokes the side of her neck, and then her face. Then it's gone. He says, quietly, I'm going to turn the light on, okay?

Okay, she says. She sits up; draws her sleeping bag tight around her. A moment later, the light comes on, and they both blink until their eyes adjust.

Scott is sitting up too. His own sleeping bag is loosely tangled around his waist. One leg is free. His hair is tousled and he looks comfortable and happy and a little self-conscious, all at once. Jodie feels a rush of affection.

How do you feel? she says.

Good, he says. Really good. I – really good.

He looks almost bashful. She can't help grinning.

How about you? he says. Was it okay? I mean – you know.

It did hurt a bit, she says. But only for a while. And after that... I don't know. It was the weirdest thing. I didn't know you could be that close to someone and it could still feel – you know. Safe.

I know, Scott says.

I'm really glad we did it, she says.

So am I. Really glad.

How long have you wanted to?

Scott shrugs. Ages, he says.

Wow. Really?

Yeah, really, Scott says; and, after a moment, Can we do it again?

Fucking hell, Oats, let's catch our breath a bit, okay? she says, sounding appalled.

Scott starts cracking up. I didn't mean straight away, he says.

I mean – feed me a biscuit and let me read a comic first, man.

I didn't mean *now,* Scott says again, shaking his head. I just meant... sometime. In the future.

Yeah, shut up. I know what you meant. Yeah we can do it again. Jesus. Sex maniac.

They sit there looking at each other. Scott doesn't seem

to be able to stop smiling and Jodie's finding this more and more funny.

This is so weird, she says, shaking her head.

What is?

You. Happy Scotty is just weird.

Sorry, Scott says. I'll try to stop being happy.

Hey. Was it embarrassing buying the rubbers? Or were you cool about it?

Scott shakes his head. It was *so* embarrassing, he says. Really. I wasn't at all cool. I mean I tried. I was getting bandages and plasters for the first-aid kit and I put in deodorant and toothpaste too, you know, to bulk it out and then I just dropped them in at the end really casually like, Oh yeah, might as well get some of these too, actually.

She pictures it, and starts to giggle. That's very smooth, she says. *Very* smooth.

I know.

I bet they've never seen anyone do that before.

Shut up. It was awful. The woman at the till looked like one of my teachers. I thought she was going to say, Put those back at once.

You must've wanted them really badly.

Well, yeah, Scott says. Couldn't you tell?

Yeah, I could tell, she says.

Scott laughs softly. He looks at the floor; runs his fingers through his hair a few times, trying to untangle it; getting nowhere. She watches him. There's quiet delight in her. The light from the camping lantern catches his ribs; the lean muscles of his arms. She remembers him mowing the lawn that first day, in the sunlight; lost and unaware. The desperation that came over her. Remembers thinking *fuck you.*

And now she's sitting here with him and there is something inside her chest, pressing outward, opening her. She can almost feel her ribs creak. It's calm and patient and it feels enormous; far bigger than her; astonishingly big.

She has no word for what this is.

She realises how tightly her hands are clutching the edges of the sleeping bag in front of her; and suddenly it seems like the stupidest thing in the world, to be still hiding away from this boy who was just inside her, who she trusts unquestioningly: trusts with her life.

Scott seems to feel her watching him. He looks up, a little quizzically. Says, What?

She makes her hands let go of the zipped edges, and shrugs the sleeping bag aside so he can see her.

Her arms twitch once, a kind of vestigial instinct to cover herself, to squeeze herself in small and out of sight; but she makes them stay at her sides and she makes herself sit still and she makes herself breathe and wait.

She is scrawny and unformed and cut and scarred and helpless: and he can see all of it now. She waits for him to be dismayed. For him to pull back.

Instead, a look of shy admiration creeps across Scott's face.

He is staring at her openly. She can feel his eyes track across her. They hesitate, uncertain for a moment, on the scars on her thighs. Then move to between her legs. And her belly. Her chest. Her face. She feels it as clearly as if he were touching her, as if fingertips were being run up her skin.

Jodie feels herself exhale.

She says, I just thought... it seemed kind of stupid, not to... you know, since we, uh...

Scott nods. He says, Yeah.

He does it too: puts his sleeping bag aside. Jodie stares. Adding how his body looks in the lamplight to how his body has felt in darkness. No longer imagined. Naked and unguarded; exposed. Real. Defenceless. Strong.

22

They finish the Judge Child quest with real regret: it's one of the best stories so far. Scott puts the comics back carefully at the bottom of the pile. Later on they become hungry and Jodie volunteers to cook. She discovers two tins of All Day Breakfast with beans, egg, sausages, bacon, all built right in.

I can't believe you didn't find these, she says. Fucking meatballs and noodles and all the time we had *this*.

I forgot I bought them, Scott says lazily. Where were they anyway?

Behind the backpack.

That's why, then.

He watches her as she moves about the little chamber. She has put clothes on: jeans and a T-shirt, almost instinctively. But she hasn't covered her arms like she used to. She lets him see the scars there.

When they've eaten, and carefully wiped the plates

clean, they curl together on the bedrolls and turn out the light and have sex again, for much longer this time.

Afterwards they just lie together without speaking; a sleepy companionable silence that stretches on and on. Then Scott feels blindly for his T-shirt; finds it; and puts it over the lantern before turning the switch. A little bit of light glows through the thin cotton, but subdued, like twilight. It makes the chamber shadowy and mysterious.

That's nice, Jodie says quietly. I like that. Hey. I think we're getting better at sex.

Me too.

How long do you think it takes to get really good at something? I mean, with the piano, how often do you have to practise?

Every day, Scott says. At least an hour.

Wow. Okay. Should've bought more rubbers, man.

Scott laughs. He touches her hair, just behind her temple; moving his fingertips there. He says, You're beautiful.

She flinches. Draws away from him slightly. She says, Don't do that.

Don't do what? Scott says.

Say stuff like that.

Why not?

She shakes her head like she's trying to get rid of something. Says, I just – you're the only person I trust, okay? And I really like that I can trust you. That's a new thing for me. It's so much more important than some stupid compliment.

Scott's silent: frowning at her.

I know I'm not pretty, she says. I don't care. And you

don't care either, if you're... you know. If we're fucking and everything. So it's fine. It's good. Just – don't say stuff that's not true.

Scott feels a strange, low anger for a moment. He says, carefully, I didn't say you were pretty.

Silence comes over them. Scott rolls onto his back, staring at the low ceiling. There are deep wells of shadow at the corners of the room where the light doesn't reach. The concrete looks like photos he's seen of the surface of the moon.

It blurs and shifts slightly. He can feel tears pricking his eyes and he blinks them away.

Jodie says, Come on.

Scott doesn't move.

She says, What? What's wrong? Jesus.

Say something you like about me.

There's a scuffle of movement beside him. What? she says.

I want you to tell me something that you actually like about me. One thing.

She shifts uneasily. Says, Look, I'm sorry, okay?

Okay. But tell me something.

She's quiet. Scott waits. The anger starts to drain away, little by little. Above him the ceiling is no longer veiled. But what creeps in instead is an ache, deep inside his chest.

Jodie says, I, uh. I like the comics.

No, Scott says flatly. Something about *me*.

Silence. He wonders if perhaps this is it: if she has no reply at all.

Finally she says, in a small voice, I like that you can do

things. Make things. Like the dinner party. And this. It's – you make me feel safe. If we survive it's going to be because of you.

She's quiet for a bit. Then she says, When I said the comics, I didn't mean the comics. I meant that you gave them to me. I could've laughed at you. I *was* laughing at you. And you, uh. You did it anyway. That's what I meant before, when I said about being – being brave. Anyway it's not one thing. It's everything. So.

Scott draws in a breath; exhales. The ache has gone now. He says, Okay.

There's silence again; for a long time. Then Jodie says, very quietly, You need to know that I hurt people.

What does that mean? Scott says.

I just do. I hurt people. I'm going to hurt you. If we – you know. If we stay together.

Who told you you hurt people?

No-one told me. It's just what happens.

I think that's bollocks, he says. You're not going to hurt me.

I went into your bedroom, she says; and she sounds almost desperate. I went in when you weren't there. I saw the drawing you did of me in the bath. I went through your stuff.

Scott turns to look at her. In the dim light her eyes are bright and earnest. He says, Why don't you want me to like you?

I do want you to. I do.

You keep trying to make me stop liking you. Like in the playground. And I'm not going to.

You need to know. You deserve to know what kind of – of person I am.

I know what kind of person you are.

But there's more, she says hopelessly.

What if I don't care?

She sniffs; wipes her nose with the back of her hand. She says, You should care.

But what if I don't? What if you tell me all the shitty things about you and I still – like you, and think you're beautiful, and want to have sex with you? What're you going to do then? Beat me up or something? You're too small.

She sniffs again. Looks down. She seems to be thinking to herself, working something through.

At last she says, very quietly, I could stab you with scissors.

Scott snorts out a laugh. Jodie has a wonky, lopsided smile on her face. It comes and goes.

She says, I just – I don't understand you at all.

Yeah. I know.

But I always understand things. Everything except you. You fucking freak me out.

Scott shrugs. His hand goes to her hair again; this time she doesn't pull away. He teases a strand of it between his fingers and says, Did you really break into my house?

You left the door open, she whispers.

I'm going to do more pictures of you and I'm going to hide them in weird places and see if they move, he says, almost as if to himself. That way I'll know if you've been in there.

She draws her legs up a little; shuffles very slightly closer to him. She says, I'll do it. You know I will. The moment you're out the door.

Cool, Scott says.

Later on, Scott pours them both some water mixed with sachets of vitamin powder. It's sickly but they drink it. Once they're done, he counts the remaining water bottles carefully; then counts them again. A narrow, worried look steals into his face.

How much have we got? Jodie says.

Not enough.

Do we need to ration it?

He nods. Yeah, he says. We drank too much.

We had to or we'd have died, she says simply; and Scott doesn't disagree.

He works out a plan to stretch the remaining water. The problem, they realise, is that they have no idea – not really – how long they've been in the shelter. The safety margin Scott set, of twenty days, is stark in both their minds; but they have lost track of how many days have passed. And, of course, they have no real idea of how long those days – portioned out only with sleep, and hunger, and now desire – have lasted.

While he arranges the bottles and notes down amounts, Jodie moves the medical supplies from the side wall into one of the corners; and then drags their bedrolls across into their place. Scott looks round.

What are you doing?

Changing things, she says. I get bored easily. Come and look.

He comes over and sits beside her. Wow, he says. This is totally different.

Shut up. It is different. Now the doorway's over there.

I'm not sure I can handle this, Scott says.

Jodie draws her knees up and pulls the sleeping bag over them. She says, So when the water's gone we have to go outside.

Scott hesitates. He seems about to say something. Then he changes his mind; shuffles into place beside her. He pulls his own sleeping bag around him.

Yeah, he says. That's right.

Tell me what it'll be like, she says; and lets herself lean slightly against Scott's shoulder. He looks at her for a moment; dips his head to the side so his cheek rests against her hair.

Well, he says slowly. The heath will have burned I think.

Okay. So there's ash everywhere.

Yeah. And it'll be dark.

Because of the dust, she says. In the atmosphere. Nuclear winter.

Yeah. Everything's going to be dark.

She lets herself lean into the crook of Scott's neck. Her knees tilt against his knees; she can feel the warmth from him. She whispers, We need to be careful.

I know, Scott says. We will be.

Tell me, she says.

. . .

A dream within a dream. Scott tells it, to start with: the story unwinding slowly as Jodie listens. Every so often she asks questions, or fills in details; until, after a while, it becomes a shared thing, something they're handing gently back and forth, their low voices making it real, until it gradually comes to fill the space between them.

They leave the shelter.

The heath outside is a blackened waste. The sand hasn't melted to glass, like in Jodie's nightmare; but it is thick with ash, a vast undulating expanse of dead ground from which the charred stubs of trees stick like broken fingers. The sky is grey and heavy and feels like it's pressing down close on them. There's no sun. The clouds seem to dredge up a permanent twilight, though in the far distance they see lurid patches of colour: cities burning.

Their footsteps kick up puffs of fine sooty dust as they walk towards town. It's hard to get their bearings with the familiar landscape of the heath burned away; but eventually they find their way to the stark concrete expanse of the Flats, and see the shells of houses beyond.

They're shivering hard. The clothes they took into the shelter were T-shirts, thin jeans; clothes for a summer that's long since been snuffed out.

They skirt the Heights. Neither of them wants to see what remains there. No going home. No looking back. If they're to live, they have to start anew.

They head for the London Road, going carefully and quietly and keeping a constant lookout. But they see no other survivors. They see bodies though: in cars, tangled across both lanes; on the pavement; huddled in doorways. They steel themselves. There's no avoiding it: you can't look away because wherever you turn, there are more.

They're torn between wanting to see evidence of life, and being afraid of what they might find. Of being preyed on. They move with the caution of paranoia.

The town centre has been gutted by fire. A lot of buildings have burned to the ground; others are still standing but hollowed out. Scott thinks the fire has been the result of secondary causes: gas leaks or something similar. This hasn't been a blast target, or they would never have survived to get to the shelter. They pick their way along the periphery of the shopping centre. The place is cold and empty; full of charred rubble and tangled debris. There's no electricity. The only sounds are the crunching of their footsteps and the thin shriek of wind between the buildings.

To Scott's huge relief, the army surplus store is still standing. The windows have been blown in and the floor inside is gritty with broken glass but the fire hasn't reached this far. There are corpses, near the back of the shop; several people have died here. They do their best not to look.

Scott says, Clothes first.

They scavenge what they need. Heavy, hard-wearing winter gear in dull drab colours. They strip off their flimsy summer clothes and leave them on the floor of the shop. Lying there discarded, they seem to belong to a past that's already fading from imagination, from understanding.

Maybe we won't even remember.

Layers of new clothing go on, smelling mustily of smoke

and canvas: singlets, long-sleeved shirts, sweaters, thick camouflage jackets. Tough grey-green trousers made of some dense fabric, cinched with canvas belts. They ditch their trainers for walking boots. As Jodie laces hers up she realises that she's no longer shivering; that the deep, biting cold is at last being held at bay.

She straightens and glances over at Scott. The unfamiliar clothing has changed him: he seems older. She sees, for the first time, how he will look when he's a man.

She says, quietly, Not bad.

You too, he says, with a slow smile.

The shop has military MRE meal packs in big cardboard boxes. Some seem already to have been broken into and scavenged, but some are intact. Scott finds them both backpacks: a smaller size for Jodie, a bigger, bulkier one for himself, and they load food into them.

Although the electromagnetic pulse from the nukes seems to have stalled all the cars and wrecked a lot of electrical systems, Jodie finds a battery-powered radio that still works; but it picks up nothing but atmospheric howling and static from one end of the dial to the other. Still, she puts it in her backpack; just in case.

They find tablets for purifying water, and metal canteens; and together, shying away from the bodies, they pick their way into the back of the shop and find a lavatory. There's no running water, but the cistern hasn't been flushed; they fill the canteens, add the tablets.

Scott takes an air rifle and a box of pellets, for when the food packs run out; two sleeping bags that they can zip together; and a lightweight bivvy tent.

It's only sposed to be for one person, he says. But I think we'll fit if we don't mind being a bit scrunched up.

I don't mind being scrunched, she says. Give me the tent, though. You're never getting all of that in your backpack.

While Scott loads the supplies, Jodie takes a compass, matches, fire steel and flint, two torches, batteries for the torches and the radio, and a handful of Ordnance Survey Landranger maps that cover the route from Surrey down towards the coast.

When they're done, the backpacks are full. They settle them on their shoulders and leave.

On the periphery of town they discover the remains of a makeshift military encampment. There are big, marquee-sized tents of khaki canvas, and trestle tables, and hastily-erected wire fences. Some sort of a marshalling station or emergency medical post. But it's as deserted as the town itself. A large, shallow pit has begun to be dug at one end, but not completed. A thick sickly stench billows from the adjacent tent; the canvas is flapping back and forth in the wind. They glimpse a low mound of corpses.

Data points, Jodie mutters.

Scott nods.

They trudge along the road towards Frimley. Soon the sky darkens towards night and the air becomes painfully cold. They find a patch of scrub land near an industrial estate and pitch the tent there, creeping inside out of the low howl of the wind.

They sleep nestled close against each other.

Dawn is a baleful strip of colour across the horizon. They

continue on towards Frimley. There, at the gun shop, they break in; find pistols and boxes of bullets.

Jodie says, No flamethrowers. Fuck.

These will do, Scott says. It's just in case.

She has expected the gun to make her feel safer. But when he hands it to her, its dense cold mass in her hand feels like an echo, small but real, of the enormous dense cold mass of the missiles. She finds herself shaking. She puts the gun down on the shop counter and says, carefully, No. I can't. I don't want it.

Scott seems to understand. He looks uncertainly at his own pistol; and, after a moment's reluctance, he leaves it behind also.

That night, camped in the foyer of an office building, they make a fire from broken furniture and in the glow of its warmth Jodie spreads the maps out on the floor. Between them, they chart a route that heads more or less south-west; looping and curving to avoid the cities that will now be lethally-radioactive blast sites.

The next day they start early on their journey to the sea.

They keep deliberately away from population centres most of the time. There's not just the radiation: there's also the likelihood of disease, from the corpses. But at intervals they still make circumspect, wary incursions into small towns, to restock food and water.

Scott always looks for books. They allow themselves to carry one each. Jodie always checks the radio. There are never any voices.

The first animal they see is a fox. It crosses the road near them at dusk one day. Scott slowly unslings the air-rifle from his shoulder but then can't bring himself to shoot. They stay stock still as the fox noses around the abandoned cars and drifts of litter and then trots off into the gathering gloom. They watch the animal out of sight. Jodie finds she has tears in her eyes.

The temperature plummets further and further each night. They sleep huddled together for warmth. There are no stars.

They continue south-west. Days pass and a fine, grainy snow starts to fall intermittently. They cross Salisbury Plain. When they first glimpse Stonehenge, lifting out of the twilight, the rocks dark against the thin snow, it stops them both in their tracks, dumbfounded. They stare, blinking the snow out of their eyes. The standing stones root the landscape in another age. They could be five thousand years in the past; or the future.

When the nuclear winter eventually passes – when seasons return – when things start to grow again – the stone circle will still be here. Will still tell when to plant and harvest. When the solstice will arrive. There are no computers any more, but this will endure.

They reach the coast somewhere west of Dorchester. There are houses here, undamaged. They could walk into any one they like, take it over. But neither of them wants to. The houses, the cars, the roads, the cities, the various technologies of the past few hundred years, have started to feel now like testaments to the war: to humanity's relentlessness. Great hives of greed and industry and pointless tribalism, gutted and irradiated by man-made bombs. Neither of them wants to be reminded.

We need something, though, Scott says.

Then let's start again, Jodie says.

In a low scoop of land beside the sea they find a spring of fresh water tumbling out of the ground. It feeds a stream that winds down to the beach. They decide to build their shelter beside it.

The shelter is a rough approximation of an iron-age roundhouse. They make it from scavenged timber and corrugated metal, clad with sods of earth. Scott draws up plans and tests them until he's satisfied that it will hold; will be good enough. They dig it a little way into the ground as protection from the elements. When it's finished there's a fire in the centre and a hole in the roof to let the smoke out. It takes time but they work on it steadily. They have all the time in the world.

There is life in the sea but, as with the fox, they find themselves reluctant to kill anything. They decide to live as best they can on the remnants of the old world: canned and dried food should stay them for years before they will need to resort to fishing. And they can grow things, when the sun returns.

Scott's air-rifle rusts slowly and they don't bother to clean it. They will beat their swords into ploughshares.

Everything is twilight. The sea is dark, restless, grey and green. But it's still the sea. Every morning, Jodie wakes early, wraps herself in a blanket, and goes down to the shore. She sits for an hour or more alone, listening to the slow wash of the waves; waits patiently for the darkness to lift.

23

She wakes softly: cocooned in black. The bunker is entirely silent. She lies without moving.

The strange huge pressure is still inside her: calm and patient. She can feel it keeping pace with her heartbeat, pulsing slowly. She still has no name for it; all she knows is that it's new to her, entirely new, and that it has come from Scott. She wonders now if it is perhaps strength: if Scott has made her strong.

She allows herself to become aware of sensations, moving through her.

Her belly feels hollow and hungry again: a simple, animal feeling; almost pleasant.

There's a dull soreness between her legs. She remembers what that's from and feels a flush of delight and quiet astonishment.

One hand has gone to sleep where she's been lying on it.

She moves slightly. She's starting to become aware that something's not right. She can't tell what it is.

The little concrete room is perfectly still.

She says, very quietly, Scott?

She puts her hand out, onto his bedroll. It's empty.

She sits up. Listens intently. She would know the sound of his breath anywhere now. But the shelter is entirely silent.

He walks in his sleep.

And she lets her breath out, slowly, slowly.

He walks in his sleep. It's over.

It's not his fault.

For a small while she allows herself to stay sitting in the darkness they've shared. She wonders if she might cry; but in the end, she doesn't.

Then she switches the lantern on and gets dressed.

Scott's jeans and trainers are still beside his bedroll. Jodie gets up, and goes through to the other room; and along the little passage to where the makeshift door has been slid aside; and out of the shelter.

It's dawn. The sun is just coming up. The air outside the shelter is motionless and cool and faintly scented with sand and heather and lichen. Birds are singing in the birch trees. Somehow, throughout everything, her body has clung to its circadian rhythm: she has woken with the sun.

She stares in wonder at the smooth blue sky; the bright yellow gorse flowers.

Then, after a moment, she pads around the corner of the

bunker and eases her way very gently along the little path through the bushes.

The gully has been swept clean. Heavy rain must have fallen at some point.

She remembers the flashes in the sky when they were running. The thundering sound, on and on.

A broad fan of pale dusty sand has been washed out of the gully and has dried fine and smooth among the mallows, like moon dust. In the early dawn light it's the colour of paper. The colour of a healed scar.

Scott's bare feet have left crisp, clear footprints.

She stands there for a long time.

She wonders what comes next. For them. For the world.

She thinks of the roundhouse by the sea; the two small figures on the beach; everything starting again, but different, no way back, no way to be the same.

It has happened now and she is no longer afraid.

Whatever comes.

Anyway.

The morning air moves very slightly, stirring the bushes, light and cool against her face.

She walks, following his footsteps. Her trainers puncture the thin crust of the sand just like Scott's feet have done: precise, satisfying. The ground is firm and strong.

She sees him towards the top of the gully, near the ridge line, standing there thin and pale, a chalk drawing of a boy in T-shirt and boxer shorts.

If he's asleep she mustn't wake him. That's important.

But he's not asleep. When she comes close he turns, and sees her.

She manages a lopsided smile and says, Hey Oats.

Hey, Scott says quietly.

In one hand he's holding something. A piece of paper.

She goes up to him. Presses gently against him.

Scott says, I'm sorry.

No. It's okay. It was going to happen eventually, right?

He doesn't answer.

Jodie stares around the heath. It's all still there. Everything's still there. Nothing has been burned away.

How long have you been out here? she says.

I dunno. A while. It was dark when I woke up.

Jodie can hear insects looping to and fro through the gorse.

She says, What've you got there?

He holds the paper out to show her. She takes it from him. It's a photocopied flier: wrinkled, like it's been out in the dew and then dried. On it are their faces. Jodie's picture from two years ago: a school photo. Scott's more recent. Maybe last summer. There's the number for a police hotline, and a message asking for any information, anything at all, about the missing children.

Jodie reads it through. Reads it again. Then just stares at it blankly for a long time.

Finally her gaze lifts back to the heath. Where did you find it? she says.

Just here on the ground, Scott says. It must've blown... look.

He points. Another flier, caught in a bush some distance away; hanging there like a little paper ghost.

Fuck, Jodie whispers.

Scott puts his arm around her.

Silence. His arm around her narrow shoulders. She fits into the hollow of his body as if made for this space. On the horizon, the jagged tops of the pine trees are dark against the brightening sky.

Scott says, very quietly, almost a whisper, My dad will have been scared.

She nods. After a moment she says, If he was scared it means he loves you.

Scott swallows. He says, Are you going to be in trouble?

She exhales. Says, I think we both know the answer to that.

What will they do?

I don't know. It doesn't matter. I don't think there's really anything else they can do to me.

You can blame me, Scott says.

Oh, I'm definitely blaming you, Jodie says. Scott made me do it.

They look into each other's faces. There is that same shy wonder. He pushes the hair back from her forehead.

He says, You're so fucking cool.

Jodie can't help smiling. She says, Shit, man, I know.

They walk slowly together up to the top of the gully, to where the land crests. There, to one side, is the same flat patch of scrub grass where they sat to eat bread and cheese and to look at the piece of nuclear glass from the Trinity test site. They sit there again, side by side. Scott smooths the piece of paper with their faces slowly between his hands.

I like this, he says. I think we look okay together.

Jodie nods. She scuffs her feet in the dust. The air. The

gritty ground. The coarse dry grass against one thigh. Her body and all its small, barely-perceived sensations. Touching against her side, this boy. Somewhere beyond them, waiting, the world.

This is where most of the people die.

Not us, though.

The sun is warm on their faces. After a while she stands: stretches. Scott gets up too. He looks calm. Ready.

She says, lightly, So. What do you want to do now?

Acknowledgements

My thanks to everyone who has helped with the journey of this book – particularly to Val Hoskins for tireless support and good cheer; to my family for all their encouragement; most of all to Chon, first reader and best friend.

About the Author

Guy Burt was born in the UK and now lives in Spain. He is a novelist and BAFTA-winning screenwriter. *The Glass Field* is his fourth novel.

www.guyburt.com

www.ingramcontent.com/pod-product-compliance
Ingram Content Group UK Ltd.
Pitfield, Milton Keynes, MK11 3LW, UK
UKHW040621060326
468683UK00009B/728/J

9 781919 440309